HIGH PRAISE FOR THE NOVELS OF

Susan Johnson

"Flat-out fabulous, sexy [novels] so textured they sometimes compare . . . to the phenomenal Judith Ivory."
—*All About Romance*

French Kiss

"A fine, heated erotic romantic suspense with [an] emphasis on the erotica."
—*Midwest Book Review*

Hot Spot

"A red-hot read . . . The writing is crisp and fast-paced . . . her characters are all one of a kind and make us laugh."
—*Romance Reviews Today*

"Johnson writes one hot story . . . quite a bit of humor, spicing up this fast read."
—*Romantic Times*

Hot Legs

"Versatile author Ms. Johnson adds a new element to her terrific writing as *Hot Legs* shows. Her mix of pop and sizzle blends expertly with a zany plot and charismatic characters. I enjoyed every minute."
—*Rendezvous*

"A perfect ten . . . Susan Johnson's writing is exceptional, and I plan not to miss any more of her releases."
—*Romance Reviews Today*

"Funny, romantic, steamy, sexy! A great read!"
—*The Best Reviews*

Hot Pink

"The sassy, bold heroine of this fast-moving book . . . will appeal to fans who like their tales geared more toward women of the twenty-first century who go after what they want and aren't afraid to get it. I loved it from beginning to end."
—*Rendezvous*

continued . . .

Wine, Tarts, & Sex

SUSAN JOHNSON

BERKLEY SENSATION, NEW YORK

THE BERKLEY PUBLISHING GROUP
Published by the Penguin Group
Penguin Group (USA) Inc.
375 Hudson Street, New York, New York 10014, USA
Penguin Group (Canada), 90 Eglinton Avenue East, Suite 700, Toronto, Ontario M4P 2Y3, Canada
(a division of Pearson Penguin Canada Inc.)
Penguin Books Ltd., 80 Strand, London WC2R 0RL, England
Penguin Group Ireland, 25 St. Stephen's Green, Dublin 2, Ireland (a division of Penguin Books Ltd.)
Penguin Group (Australia), 250 Camberwell Road, Camberwell, Victoria 3124, Australia
(a division of Pearson Australia Group Pty. Ltd.)
Penguin Books India Pvt. Ltd., 11 Community Centre, Panchsheel Park, New Delhi—110 017, India
Penguin Group (NZ), 67 Apollo Drive, Rosedale, North Shore 0745, Auckland, New Zealand
(a division of Pearson New Zealand Ltd.)
Penguin Books (South Africa) (Pty.) Ltd., 24 Sturdee Avenue, Rosebank, Johannesburg 2196,
South Africa

Penguin Books Ltd., Registered Offices: 80 Strand, London WC2R 0RL, England

This is a work of fiction. Names, characters, places, and incidents either are the product of the author's imagination or are used fictitiously, and any resemblance to actual persons, living or dead, business establishments, events, or locales is entirely coincidental. The publisher does not have any control over and does not assume any responsibility for author or third-party websites or their content.

Copyright © 2007 by Susan Johnson
Cover design by Monica Benalcazar
Cover illustration by Voth/Barrall
Book design by Kristin del Rosario

PRINTING HISTORY
Berkley Sensation trade paperback edition / July 2007

Library of Congress Cataloging-in-Publication Data

Johnson, Susan, date.
    Wine, tarts, & sex / by Susan Johnson.—Berkley Sensation trade pbk. ed.
        p.   cm.
    ISBN 978-0-425-21540-1
1. Cooks—Fiction.   2. Restaurateurs—Fiction.   3. Women vintners—Fiction.   4. Minneapolis
(Minn.)—Fiction.   I. Title.   II. Title: Wine, tarts, and sex.

PS3560.O386458W56 2007
813'.54—dc22
                                                                                    2006102183

PRINTED IN THE UNITED STATES OF AMERICA

10 9 8 7 6 5 4 3 2 1

Wine, Tarts, & Sex

One

"I'm not sure I'm interested in Minnesota wines. My menu's going to be slightly different from yours," Jake Chambers added politely, when he was really thinking, *Minnesota wines . . . no way.* "Just how much flack will I get from the local wine growers' association if I don't buy their wines? Are we talking boycotts, picketing, letters to the editor—what?"

Chaz Burnett grinned. "This is Minnesota, man, not an activist state like California." The former owner of the restaurant Jake had recently purchased shrugged. "I just like to support the local growers. If you don't see these regional wines on your menu, don't sweat it. Restaurants change hands; shit happens."

Jake understood there were ramifications to former customers when taking over a restaurant and making radical changes. But then again, his road to success had been paved with radical change. "I'd like to be amenable. It's just that my wine list is—"

"I know—world-class." Jake had restaurants in San Francisco and L.A. that always made everyone's top-ten lists. "Hey, I understand your reluctance to offer less distinctive wines, but"—Chaz jabbed a finger at Jake—"FYI, some of our local stuff is pretty damned good. Judd Jacobson's for one, and darling Livvi's, too."

"Darling Livvi?" There had been something in Chaz's tone that required further explanation.

"Man, I'd buy her wine even if it wasn't a class act—because *she* sure as hell is. She's one smokin' hot babe with a bod and face that actually used to grace the covers of magazines. But her Frontenac reds are really first-rate. I suggest you try them."

"What about her? Married, single, available?" The habitual man-to-man queries when talk of cover models entered the conversation.

"Single. And I don't have personal experience, but rumor has it, she's not above enjoying herself if the mood moves her. Picky, but available, if you meet her criteria."

If he hadn't been interested before, Chaz's last sentence had gotten his attention; that phrase, *if you meet her criteria*, was intriguing. Not that he had Neanderthal impulses when it came to women. In fact, he never much cared who was in charge so long as the payoff was beneficial all around. But he hadn't reached his current level of success without acquiring well-honed principles of constraint, nor had he come out to Minnesota to play. Quickly dismissing his sexual thoughts, he returned to the business at hand. "So then, we're all set here?" Jake nodded at the two large duffel bags near the door. "I understand you've been packed for a week." He'd met all the staff that morning.

"Packed and ready to launch. Thanks, by the way, for buy-ing my furniture and stuff sight unseen. It would have been a pain to have to clear out my upstairs space. The cleaning staff put everything to rights this morning: fresh sheets, towels, that sort of thing. And you can always rent it out if you don't like it."

"Nah—I'm good. I prefer being close to the action until every-thing is up and running anyway. After that"—Jake shrugged—"who knows."

"You're not actually thinking of settling here permanently, are you?"

"Probably not." More like million-to-one odds: no. But it never paid to give too much away in the ephemeral world of fine dining. A chef's presence could make a big difference in the success of a restaurant.

"Personally, they're gonna have to bury me on Saint Barts," Chaz declared. "I've been wanting a place there so long I'm never leaving. In fact, the way this deal all came down, let me tell you, man, it made me believe in miracles—like this was all some big cosmic enchilada. Offenbach's *Topaz* had just come on the market. I was lusting after it big time, trying to figure out how to swing a deal, and then out of the blue you called and said you wanted to buy my restaurant."

Jake grinned. "Definitely a psychic phenomenon." And the fact that he wanted a restaurant with a prime location on the Mississippi River.

"No shit. I finally must be living right," Chaz said with a grin. He put out his hand. "Since I have a two o'clock flight to paradise, I'd better hit the road. Good luck, man."

Jake took Chaz's hand in a firm grip. "Same here."

"Check out my new place next season," Chaz offered. "The views are a helluva lot nicer than the ones here. Not that I'm knocking river views."

"Hey, each to his own," Jake said with a smile. "And don't be surprised if I show up in Saint Barts."

"You always have a place to stay, amigo." Chaz turned to go. "Not to mention prime room service," he said over his shoulder as he walked away.

A minute later, the front door shut on Chaz Burnett, and Jake surveyed his new restaurant space with that feeling of anticipation and impatience he always experienced when taking on a new venture. He'd given the staff a month's vacation so he had time to start renovating the bar and redoing the menu. With luck, the River Joint would be open for business in six to eight weeks.

And this time, he wasn't interested in pleasing the food critics or decorators or even a certain segment of the population that followed, lemminglike, each new entry onto the restaurant scene. This place was for himself alone. No pretensions, no sleek decor. He wanted it to be comfortable and laid back, a neighborhood joint that just happened to have world-class food and wines.

He'd earned the right to indulge himself in this labor of love. The fact that he used to spend summers near here with his aunt was only a nostalgic bonus to his new creative endeavor.

Everyone in his organization had tried to talk him out of buying in the Midwest. The profits wouldn't compare to those in major metropolitan centers, they'd argued. But he'd lost interest in profits alone a long time ago—or he'd been fortunate enough to be allowed that luxury.

People only eat bland food in the Midwest, he'd been cautioned. And even if he wanted to introduce more eclectic cooking, the ingredients couldn't be found locally, his colleagues had warned.

"Not true and wrong," he'd replied. "Besides, I need some downtime." Which was perhaps the more cogent reason for his flight to what his West Coast cohorts perceived as the outland of the world. He'd been working too hard and playing too hard. "I'll check back with you in six months," he'd added, knowing he was leaving competent managers in charge of his restaurants. "Consider this my long-delayed sabbatical."

At thirty-five, he'd been in the business in one form or another for twenty years, and while wildly successful in every sense of the word, he found he wanted more or something else or something different.

Not that he knew what the hell *something different* meant.

But he'd given himself six months to find out.

Two

Olivia Bell, known as Liv for obvious reasons—or at least obvious reasons to anyone who had been plagued with the teasing designation Olive Oil in grade school—lifted her booted feet up on the railing of her front porch and leaned back in her chair.

It was hotter than hell today, especially with the sun at high noon. She was dripping with sweat under her jeans and T-shirt, her fingernails were dirty as usual—no matter she'd scrubbed them after working in her vineyard—her pale hair was a riot of curls with the humidity at near record highs, and even unkempt and sweaty, she was happy, content, and really grossly self-satisfied. Sitting on the porch of her old farmhouse, surveying her vineyard that bordered a bubbling creek running through

her land, she felt as though she'd found that much-lauded promised land. Or at least her own little piece of heaven, she decided,
opting for a modicum of modesty in her assessment.

Lifting the glass of wine resting on the arm of her chair,
she studied the deep ruby tones sparkling in the sun before
bringing the glass to her nose and inhaling the scent. Perfect:
lush; ripe; a brooding, classy beauty. Taking a sip, she held it
in her mouth, savoring the voluptuous flavors and long, sweet
finish.

Times like this made all the years of hard-ass toil as a model
worth it.

More than worth it.

Six years ago she'd saved up enough to buy this farm in
the rolling hills of the Saint Croix Valley. Even though most of
her modeling friends thought she was crazy, they'd given her a
memorable two-day party send-off after the spring shows in Milan, and she'd retired to the life of a farmer. Last fall, her first
credible vintage from mature grapes had come on the market to
universal acclaim—at least in her little part of the world.

Which was good enough for her.

She didn't have grandiose aspirations.

After years of traveling the globe from one fashion shoot to
another, after seeing just about all there was to see in terms of
sights, both people- and planet-wise, she was more than happy—
in the words of Faust—to till her own garden.

She'd probably made more money than she deserved for simply smiling into camera lenses. But then she didn't set the rates.
And thanks to a seemingly insatiable demand for young blonde
models with good cheekbones, she was now able to enjoy the

rewards of her labor and make some damned fine wine in the process.

But in terms of seeing that her small business continued to prosper, as soon as she finished her glass of wine, she'd better shower, dress, and drive into town to make her usual Monday deliveries to her restaurant customers.

Three

Chaz's restaurant was the last on Liv's list, and by the time she pulled up to the back door, it was after six. The door was ajar as usual, but the reggae rhythms Chaz liked to have blaring from the loudspeakers were gone, and instead the muted sound of piano music could be heard.

The restaurant was always closed on Mondays; maybe Chaz was auditioning some new entertainment.

Lifting a case of wine from the back of her pickup truck, Liv moved toward the kitchen door. Shoving it open, she walked in, set the case on the stainless steel counter, and left to get a second case. A few moments later, finished with her delivery, she glanced around the kitchen, wondering where Chaz and Louie were. Chaz's bookkeeper, Louie, who had no life unless comic book conventions counted, was always at his desk in the back of the kitchen crunching numbers.

Everything was strange enough that rather than barge into the dining room where the music was coming from, she opted for discretion. Chaz might be hitting on some female piano player. He hit on every good-looking woman who came into range. "Hey, Chaz!" she called out, figuring she'd let him know she was here, and he could respond or not. "Delivery!"

The piano music abruptly stopped.

Whatever he was doing apparently allowed for interruptions. Moving toward Louie's desk to drop off her invoice, she placed it in his in-box.

"The delivery people dress better around here."

Spinning around at the low, husky tone, she saw a tall, dark, more than ordinarily beautiful man instead of blond, boyish Chaz standing in the doorway to the dining room. "Where's Chaz and Louie?" she asked, ignoring his comment as well as the approval in his quick, raking glance. She was used to men looking at her like that.

Jake glanced at his watch. "About now, I'd say Chaz is in the Miami airport waiting for his flight to Saint Barts; Louie's on vacation."

Liv gave him a questioning look. "And you are?" Although she was pretty sure she already knew, a second glance having confirmed her suspicions.

"Jake Chambers. The new owner." Taking in the printing on the side of the cases—Liv Bell Wines—he quickly reconsidered his stance on Minnesota wines and smiled. "You must be darling Livvi." And she certainly was, from her golden curls to her slender tanned feet—the face and body in between definitely magazine-cover material.

"Chaz calls everyone darling. Don't read too much into it."

"Wouldn't think of it." He was more than ready to ignore that warning tone in her voice, seeing how he was suddenly re-examining his plans to lead a monastic life during his downtime. The blonde in his kitchen looked damned fine in that red flower print summer dress, green strappy heels, and not much else, if her pert nipples straining the fabric of her dress were any indication. "Do you need help carrying in anything?"

He suddenly found himself thinking plans were made to be broken—a purely libidinous but irresistible impulse. Enjoying some *downtime with benefits* might not be so bad.

"No, thanks. I've heard of you," Liv added, her gaze deliberate, not sure whether he was hitting on her.

He smiled faintly. "It must not have been good."

"You're not from around here, that's all." His thick black hair had been pulled back carelessly in a short, untidy ponytail, accenting his stark cheekbones and dark, exotic eyes. And whether she found his fame or his beauty disturbing was unclear.

"Do I need vetting?"

His smile this time was incredibly sensual, as though he knew very well he didn't need vetting. Nor did anyone who looked like him, she thought. Even casually dressed, or maybe *because* he was casually dressed in sandals, jeans, and a white T-shirt with the logo of his L.A. restaurant in small letters on the left side of his muscled chest, he exuded a kind of accessibility, as though he wasn't a famous megachef or breathtakingly handsome, as though he was an ordinary man.

When he wasn't.

But her voice was composed when she answered; she'd met more than her share of notable, handsome men. "No, of course not," she said. "Forgive me if I gave that impression."

Her restraint was palpable. "Not a problem." He smiled. "Tell me about your wines. Chaz says they're excellent." Something beyond his male predatory instincts made him want to put her at ease.

He didn't know why it mattered that he see her smile.

He knew less why he was making the effort.

Maybe he was overtired and not thinking straight after leaving L.A. at five that morning. Or maybe he was in a good mood about his new restaurant and wanted company. Bottom line though—libido or not—there wasn't a man alive who wouldn't be interested in meeting darling Livvi's criteria—picky or not.

She was one gorgeous woman and not in a beautiful blonde from Hollywood or Vegas way. She exuded a fresh wholesomeness, like say—she worked in a sunny vineyard. Her skin glowed, her eyes were a clear aquamarine, her pale hair was bleached by the sun, and that hint of cleavage just barely visible above the scooped neck of her dress was—let's face it—damned enticing.

"Care to give me a taste?" Understanding her startled look required further explanation on his part, he gestured at the case of wine on the counter.

Had he known her startled look had to do with something else entirely—something warm and tingly revving up in her pleasure centers, something wholly sexual—he would have been gratified.

It must have been too long between men, Liv thought, trying to remember when last she'd had sex, when she'd last felt that delicious jolt of desire.

Shit. Not that long ago.

So much for abstinence as an excuse.

But regardless, it *felt* like it must have been too long, she decided as a lustful heat shimmered through her body and settled between her legs as her body opened in welcome. Like wow—she'd never felt the urge to jump a guy on first sight before.

Although, perhaps her sudden, bolt-from-the-blue carnal cravings were predicated by the samurai comic books she adored or her penchant for Japanese films. That Jake Chambers's Eurasian looks were nothing short of awesome could not be ignored. Or maybe there was some real basis for the pheromone theory, and she could blame a sudden blast of biological stimuli for her unusual response. Or it could be her inexplicable horniness was based on some weird familiarity. She'd actually met Jake once years ago in L.A. "Sure—we can taste my wines if you like," she said, making sure she made it clear *what exactly* they were tasting. "And I don't know if you remember, but we met before," she added, hoping banal conversation would help mitigate her outlandish rush of desire. "We were introduced at your restaurant in L.A. It was years ago—I forget exactly when—but it was around the time of the Academy Awards." Perfect. Cool, detached—or at least her voice was. Her body continued on its own willful path.

"No way we met," Jake said. "I would have remembered."

"I was with someone *and* with a large group."

That explained it, at least. He didn't zero in on other men's women.

Do not throw yourself at him, she nervously warned herself. *Be sensible. Fucking customers on the more-or-less first meeting isn't a good idea.* With that prudent maxim in mind, she decided

wine-tasting wouldn't be in her best interests. Alcohol, her sordid cravings, and Jake Chambers up close and personal weren't a
good combo. "Maybe we could take a rain check on the wine
tasting," she said, resisting temptation. "I actually have friends
waiting for me at Taglio's. I probably should go." Tapping her
wristwatch, as though to temper her Freudian slip of the tongue
in using the word *probably*, she smiled politely. "Good luck with
your new venture."

The venture he had in mind had nothing to do with restaurants. "Why don't you give your friends a call," he said, his smile
as polite as hers. "Tell them you'll be a little late."

She sucked in her breath. Obviously, she'd been in the con-
vent too long when she was interpreting bland statements like
that as sexually explicit invitations. He was probably just talking
about wine tasting.

"Stay a while," he murmured, holding her gaze for a provocative moment, her little sucked-in breath having kicked his libido
into overdrive. "Fill me in on the local scene or"—his voice
lowered—"say . . . your vineyard . . . or whatever."

Okaaay—*that* wasn't about wine tasting or, for that matter,
about actual conversation. It was pretty much about sex.

So now what?

It wasn't as though she was completely averse to impulsive
sexual encounters. And it wasn't as though Jake Chambers was a
complete stranger. Although she didn't know how much that
mattered in her current lecherous mood.

So—cool reason or rash impulse? What would it be?

"I'd better not," she said, telling herself that self-denial was a
virtue. "But thanks for the invitation." Then, turning, she
walked away while she still could.

Four

As the kitchen door shut behind her, Jake offered up a small prayer of thanks to whatever Zen spirits had saved him from his own stupidity. A couple of hours from now he would have been wondering how the hell to get some woman he didn't know out of his bed.

Remember dude, you're the guy who is going to live a hermit's life for awhile.

After years in the celebrity glare that included the usual celebrity groupies, he was on a self-imposed rest cure, looking for that *something different* in his life. And let's face it, a woman like Liv Bell, ex-model and vineyard owner in a state that had snow on the ground five months of the year, did not exactly qualify. She would have been more of the same—just another beautiful blonde. And sometimes too much of a good thing was too much of a good thing.

So get a grip.

Don't let your libido call the shots.

Stick to business.

Which, now that his brain was back in charge, meant getting the River Joint off the ground. Glancing at the two cases of wine on the counter, he debated how best to get rid of them.

Did homeless shelters take wine donations?

Turning the key in her truck ignition, Liv found the sound of the engine coming to life audible evidence that she could persevere in the face of temptation. Putting her truck in gear, she drove away from a very close call. Whether it had been mature judgment or saved-by-the-skin-of-her-teeth impulse, she was damned glad she'd walked away. Jake Chambers was exactly the kind of man she'd seen once too often in her career as a model. Rich, good-looking, successful, fawned over by one and all—and, unfortunately, convinced they deserved the kudos.

In other words, an egomaniac.

Definitely not her cup of tea.

Not that she knew what manner of man that might be.

But she'd know when he came along.

And in the meantime, her life was about as good as it got.

Twenty minutes later she was parking behind an uptown restaurant and looking forward to meeting her friends.

The three women had known each other since grade school, and whenever their schedules allowed, they met for lunch or dinner. Shelly was divorced, no children, Zoe was married with children; Shelly was a futures trader; Zoe had been a public defender before marrying and having kids.

"You're late," they said in unison as Liv reached their table.

Liv grinned. "I almost didn't show up. Had my better judgment not kicked in, I wouldn't have. *The* Jake Chambers is in town. He bought a restaurant on the river where I deliver wines. And he hit on me."

"Everyone hits on you," Shelly said with a grin. "But hey— we would have understood if you'd bailed. He's definitely studly."

Zoe held up her hand. "Maybe not. I saw in the *National Enquirer* that his last girlfriend left him for a woman."

"You can't believe anything in the *National Enquirer*," Shelly said. "Facts, babe, not gossip; that's the bottom line."

"I don't know. It was that movie star, what's her name, the real quirky one with the blonde frizzy hair." Zoe lifted her brows. "Everything is not as it seems in Hollywood."

Shelly frowned. "Don't start on the Tom Cruise thing again, pul-ease. I like his movies. Who cares about the rumors?"

"Well, rumors aside on this one," Liv said, signaling the waiter for a drink. "If Jake Chambers can't please a woman in bed, I'd be real surprised. He practically oozes sex appeal."

"So why did you show up here?" Shelly asked, brows raised. "Seriously, it's not as though you've found your one and only yet."

"Unlike you, darling, I haven't been looking." Shelly had been dating with the same take-no-prisoners determination she gave to the futures market.

"That's your problem. You actually think Mr. Wonderful is going to walk through your door someday and sweep you off your feet. Ha!"

"Hey, it worked for Cinderella. And Anna Karenina—although

stupid Tolstoy had to do one of those nineteenth-century male chauvinist morality tale endings. Idiot. But whatever—I'm not in a rush. I'm happy. I haven't had to split up my holdings with an ex"—she dipped her head—"no offense, but I've heard that can be real pricey," she said with a grin. "And remember, I've dated so much I've reached the picky stage."

"Picky or not, Jake Chambers would top anyone's list. You should have given him a shot."

"Nah. The Jake Chamberses of the world don't fit in my game plan. Maybe an organic farmer would appeal, or better yet another vintner. Or if I don't find that perfect man, I'm good. I have two aunts who never married, and they're happy as clams. No stress, no grief—I figure they'll live till they're a hundred and ten."

"I don't know . . . Jake Chambers's kind of stress might be worth a try. Think of him like a box of truffles—just a sinfully delicious treat. And when the last truffle is gone, it's gone. Then it's back to health food and the responsibilities of life."

"If you're so hot for him, Shelly, you go out with him. I'm sure he's available."

"Shelly's lusting after Jim Balfour," Zoe said with a wink. "He's won her admiration for his studly way with the futures market. He pulled in a million in commissions last week, and apparently that's Shelly's aphrodisiac of choice."

Shelly made a face. "Very funny. Not that money isn't a turn-on, but Jim's cute, too."

Zoe grinned. "How cute exactly?"

Here's where the ladies reverted to form, dissecting what most appealed to them in the male species. Liv sat back with her French martini the waiter had just delivered and listened with half an ear to the conversation. Her concentration kept slipping away to those male qualities in Jake Chambers that were still rattling her cage. There was something about him: a brute virility, a ruggedness not often seen in the world of the rich and famous, the challenging look of a man who hadn't been housebroken and might never be. *Jeez, snap out of it,* she silently chided herself. Since when was she interested in whipping a man into shape?

Since never, that's when.

And bottom line, if Jake Chambers didn't want to be housebroken, he wasn't going to be, no way no how.

Don't even think about it.

He was a customer. No more. No less.

Zoe was talking about her oldest daughter, who could play the piano with considerable skill at age six. Liv concentrated her attention on the merits of a Montessori education that were being extolled and ordered another drink.

Five

 In the course of the next week, both Jake and Liv were busy enough to relegate heated memories to the discard bin.

But on Monday when Liv was making her usual deliveries, she found herself experiencing a heightened disquiet on a couple levels as she turned into the alley behind Chaz's restaurant.

First, sales weren't her strong suit, and whenever she had to pitch her wines, she was nervous. While Jake Chambers hadn't refused the bottles Chaz had ordered last week, she wasn't sure he would remain a customer. There were lots of wines out there and even more wine merchants. He didn't have to buy hers.

Secondly, she had to admit, his image had popped into her thoughts once or twice in the course of the week. He had killer sex appeal, there was no denying it. So it would be a matter of keeping her cool and remembering this was a business call. And also remembering that men like Jake Chambers weren't on her wish list.

When she walked through the door into the kitchen, she saw him in the back, seated at Louie's desk, a phone to his ear.

He swung around at the sound of the door opening, lifted one hand, fingers splayed, indicating five minutes, and then pointed at a table and chairs near the doorway into the dining room.

Fucking a she looks good, he thought, wondering if she always made her deliveries in sexy dresses and spiky heels. But hey, it was a great sales tool. It was working for him; after a dutiful week of celibacy, it was *really* working. Cutting his conversation short, he told his supplier he'd get back to him.

"Sorry," he said, walking toward Liv a moment later. He jerked his thumb back toward the desk. "I've been on the phone or the computer nonstop ordering shit. I repeat," he said with a smile, sitting down on the other side of the small table, "delivery people look a helluva lot better out here."

She smiled. "Thanks. I'm meeting friends for drinks. How are things going? Are you making progress?"

"Yes and no," he said, leaning back in his chair. "Things never go smoothly on all counts. I'm used to it."

Trying to ignore the impressive width of his shoulders on display in his lounging pose, she nodded toward the two cases of her wine stacked under the counter. "I thought I'd stop by and check, but I'm guessing you're not interested in any more of my wine."

Oh, Christ—he hadn't moved them very far. "I've just been too busy to get back to you. Actually, I am interested." In her, not her wines, particularly in that sunflower-yellow dress with those little ties on her shoulders that looked like they'd open real easily. "Why don't I double Chaz's order." How could it hurt to have sex with another good-looking blonde? In this case, a blonde with big, lush breasts that he could reach out and touch if he was real stupid, he thought, flexing his fingers against the uncool impulse.

"You don't have to be nice just to be nice." He obviously was, but for reasons that didn't bear close scrutiny, she found herself willing to overlook his diplomatic reply.

"No, really, it was an oversight. I've been busy as hell." He smiled. "Has anyone ever told you that you're a lame-ass salesman?"

"I know. Fortunately, I don't have to actually make a living doing this." She pushed her chair back, realizing she'd better leave before those hard muscles under his T-shirt got to her any more than they already had.

"Why don't I try your wines as long as you're here," he quickly suggested, his weeklong celibacy steamrolling over saner counsel. "You could give me some background on your operation."

She glanced at her watch, lied to herself that this was strictly business, and said, "Sure, why not. I have time."

The word *time* hung in the air for a flashing moment while two minds sent up word balloons rife with possibility and/or knotty complications.

But man of action that he was or impelled by a libido that decided it would have no more of this ignominious abstinence, Jake quickly came to his feet and held out his hand. "Let's sit in the dining room. The view is better."

His hand was large and strong, Liv thought when she shouldn't. When, if this was just about a wine order, she wouldn't have even noticed. As she rose and placed her fingers on his palm, as his hand closed over hers, even had she been concentrating with a laser-sharp focus on business, the seismic tremors that shook her would have been enough to blow any mission statement to kingdom come.

Freaked out, she snatched her hand away. "I'll get the wine," she said, enunciating with special care to mitigate her breathiness. "Why don't you find some glasses and a corkscrew." Seriously, she didn't want to be aware of his closeness, his formidable size, his heated gaze. For sure, she didn't want to yield to her tumultuous desires. Not with a man like Jake, who could compete in the Guinness book of one-night stands. Not that she was necessarily against casual sex. She was just against casual sex with Jake Chambers, celebrity.

Quickly pulling out a bottle of her red and one of white from the cartons, she deliberately preceded him into the dining room. Setting the bottles on a table near the windows, she sat down and gave herself a good talking to.

"You're right, the view is great," she said in a normal tone of voice as he approached a few moments later. She was feeling better, more in control. She wasn't fifteen. She could manage him.

"I've had my eye on this place for awhile. I'm glad the timing was right for Chaz." Setting four glasses down, he opened the red wine first with a deftness that bespoke considerable experience. Pouring them each a glass, he sat down across from her and lifted his glass in salute. "To Liv Bell Wines."

"I confess to a certain prejudice. I hope you like it."

After a smell, a swirl, a taste, he said, polite as hell, "It's excellent. My compliments. Tell me about your vineyard." If she talked, he didn't have to, particularly when it came to discussing her wine. While it was passable—not that he had expected more from the cold Midwest—he wouldn't have been able to offer praise with any conviction.

She told him a little of how she'd decided to get into the business, a brief, edited account short on the passions that motivated her. She talked about her various grape varieties, her small winery, several of the people who had influenced her decision to start a vineyard. He was surprised to discover she had a chemistry degree—so much for the blonde bimbo designation—and more surprised to hear that she'd worked in several of the really fine boutique vineyards in France. Too fucking bad she had chosen Minnesota to practice her craft.

"I know Michel Chapoutier and Olivier Bernard, too. Nice places to learn your trade."

"And the weather is better than here."

So she knew and still had gone astray. Not that he said a word. "Let's try the white," he said instead.

"It's made from one of our locally hybridized grapes. It's a blend of an ice wine and a table wine and not bad, if I do say so myself."

After tasting it, he offered his compliments and asked her some more questions about her vineyard.

In turn she asked him about what had prompted him to become a chef, their conversation a variation on the what-sign-are-you getting-acquainted discussions. His account was even more abbreviated than hers; Cornell, the Culinary Institute, and apprenticeships in some of the better restaurants on the planet.

"You've seen a lot of the world."

"I expect you have, too."

"More than enough, thank you. I'm in my Faustian stage now, and I'm pretty damned content."

"I guess I'm on that same search myself." He lifted his glass. "To fulfillment."

She lifted her glass and smiled. "Amen."

She was interested, he could tell. He was a master at recognizing willingness in a female. Not that she was flirtatious as was normally the case with him. But Liv Bell didn't have to press; not when she looked like she did. He expected she was more familiar with sitting back and waiting.

It turned out he was wrong.

Abruptly rising from her chair a few moments later, she said in a voice that was either crisp or taut or some equivocal register in between, "Thanks for the conversation. But my friends are waiting. I'd better go."

"Don't go."

She opened her mouth to say, *Why*, but didn't.

"Forgive my bluntness," he said, responding to the flush on her cheeks, coming to his feet with deliberate slowness in order not to frighten her off. "It's just that you've been on my mind." To her flaring gaze, he added, "Honestly," not realizing the truth of his statement until he spoke.

"I'd rather not be on your mind." She half-lifted her hand. "No offense, but I've deliberately left that glitzy world behind."

"Me, too."

Her gaze narrowed as though assessing his authenticity.

He smiled. "Word of honor."

He looked so artless for a moment, she couldn't help but smile. "Yeah, right."

"No shit. I have. Or I'm trying. You reach that stage—" He shrugged.

"When you've seen and heard it all."

"Exactly. In fact, I was going to work on being a monk for a while." He smiled. "But then you came along."

"I wouldn't want to lure you from the path of righteousness." Even as she spoke, she was struggling with the vice versa part of that equation.

"Please, lure away. You intrigue the hell out of me."

He was way too sexy and too beautiful, and she seriously hesitated for a moment. "Thanks, but no thanks," she finally said, tamping down her willful carnal urges. "I just don't see an upside. And my friends are waiting," she added, perhaps to bolster her self-control more than for any other reason. "I'll deliver your order next week." Swinging around on her spiky heels, she walked away.

"I'll make you dinner afterward."

The soft, lush intonation drifted after her. She knew what *afterward* meant. She knew what *before* afterward entailed. She should keep walking. She should go through that door, get in her truck, and drive away. "What would you make?" she asked, turning back.

"Anything you want." His smile was benevolent. "Anything at all."

Oh my God! She could feel his sexy promise of *anything* pulse through her vagina, whisper over her nipples, drift across the heated surface of her skin, spike through her brain. "I'm really tempted," she said on a small, caught breath. "I've never had a personal chef," she murmured, or any of the other pleasures her brain was suddenly conjuring up just looking at God's gift to women standing no more than six feet away.

"There's always a first time for everything," he said softly.

He obviously wasn't talking about food. Nor was she actually thinking about food.

"If it helps," he added, moving toward her slowly, as though understanding her indecision required a certain degree of finesse, "I'm probably more tempted than you. I *was* planning on going to bed early and watching TV." He lifted his shoulder slightly in a small renunciatory gesture as he reached her. "You changed my mind. I think it's—" He caught himself before he said something outrageously stupid like *the glow of your sun-kissed skin*. Instead, he lightly touched her bottom lip with the pad of his index finger. "You know you're beautiful. You hear it all the time, I expect. But you are."

She started to say, *Thank you*, but his mouth suddenly covered hers and swallowed up her words, his kiss hard, invasive.

And a helluva lot more feverish than he would have liked.

He abruptly jerked away. "Christ—I'm going to scare you off. Sorry." Drawing in a deep breath, he flashed a boyish grin. "Maybe we should have another glass of wine and give me time to cool down."

"Let's not." Blatantly aware of his tantalizingly *huge* erection that had been very recently pressed against her stomach, her libido way past jazzed, she said in a tone of voice that could only be categorized as decisive, "I'm not really in the mood for more wine right now." Reaching out, she ran her fingers over his rock-hard penis stretching the denim of his jeans. "And he doesn't look like he is, either."

As his erection swelled larger, he murmured, "So I don't have to worry about scaring you off."

She gazed up at him from under her lashes. "Not unless this gets too big for me to handle."

The implication in her statement set off a chain reaction of salacious possibilities; it took him a millisecond to restrain his baser instincts. "Why don't I keep it under control, then."

"You can do that?"

He wanted to say, *Maybe, if you stop doing what you're doing*, but he wasn't abstemious by nature, so he lied and said, "Sure I can." No way was he going to equivocate at this point. Particularly when they were both in the same frame of mind. Mustering up what he hoped was a casual tone, when he was, in fact, seriously cautioning himself to restraint, he gestured toward the kitchen. "Care to go upstairs?"

She smiled. "Definitely." Turning away, she moved toward the kitchen.

Darling Livvi doesn't play games. Nice, he thought as he followed her.

"I can't stay long," Liv said as he caught up with her. "I really do have friends waiting."

He didn't often hear the equivalent of *Wham, bam, thank you, ma'am* in reverse. In fact, he never had. Whether inspired by vanity or selfishness, he pulled his cell phone from his jeans pocket and held it out. "Give your friends a call. No sense in rushing." Although he didn't know if he could give her any guarantees about the first time. He was fucking primed.

"I'll give them a heads-up at least," she said, taking the phone from him. "Although you don't have to make me any food, if that's what you're thinking."

"I wasn't thinking about food."

She smiled. "Two minds with but a single thought. It must be karma."

"Damn right," he said, grinning back, although his karma was pretty much self-motivated and action-oriented. "Tell your friends you'll meet them later." Much later—but he was polite enough not to say so.

Stopping at the base of the stairs, Liv punched in a number and, leaning against the doorjamb, she smiled at Jake while she waited for someone to answer.

"Something came up," Liv said a moment later. "No, it's not a man. Why would you say that?" She grimaced faintly. "I left my phone in my truck, okay? And for your information, that's not true. It's business. Yeah, yeah, cute. Look—I'll be there before you anyway. You're usually late. Yes, absolutely—it's business. I swear." And she flipped the phone shut while her friend was still talking.

"Sounds like you were getting some static."

"Shelly always thinks everything's about a man. It may be for her—she's been dating a lot since her divorce—but it's not for me." Liv flashed Jake a rueful smile. "Present company excepted. You turn me on. What can I say?"

"Lucky me." Apparently darling Livvi's criteria tonight was just basic cock. Not that he took issue.

"Lucky us, I hope," she murmured with a sidelong glance.

He grinned. "Are you going to be demanding?"

"Does it matter?"

"Fuck no."

"I didn't think it would."

"What does that mean?"

"It means your reputation precedes you." She smiled. "I know friends of friends of friends. Women always talk." Like he was hung and knew how to use it. As for the *National Enquirer* story, she highly doubted it after feeling the size of his dick.

"I'm at a disadvantage. I haven't heard anything about you."

"There's nothing to hear. I lead a simple life."

"You haven't always."

"Yes, I have."

"Even in the L.A. scene?"

"Even then. I'm careful in my friendships."

"Like now?"

"*Usually*—I'm careful in my friendships." That at least was true. "I must have been working too hard. And suddenly, you were here reminding me to take some time to play." Lies, lies, lies; she hadn't planned on touching Jake Chambers with a ten-foot pole.

"I can't think of anyone I'd rather play with," he said with a grin. "After you." He nodded at the stairs. "I'm living mostly out of my suitcase; forgive the mess."

She almost said: *The mood I'm in, it doesn't matter.* But, opting for something less revealing, she said instead, "Not a problem."

Six

Following her up the stairs, Jake took note of the flash of crimson soles on her spiky heels—Louboutin's trademark. "Sexy shoes," he said.

"They're my fuck-me shoes."

"That's what I was thinking."

She swiveled around enough to give him a grin. "I could say it's just an expression, but under the circumstances, you might not buy it."

"Sure I would." He knew how to be polite.

"Let's just say it's part of the karma. I don't feel like explaining." What could she have said, anyway? *I don't often do things like this.* Like he was going to believe *that.*

"Karma—whatever . . ." He didn't need an explanation or a road map to anywhere. Darling Livvi was one hot number, from her fuck-me shoes to her no-nonsense take on sex, and whether it was karma or good old luck, he was going with it, no questions asked.

Was there a note of equivocation in his *whatever*? Stopping on the step above him, Liv turned around. "Are you sure about this?"

"Unless you're going to tell me you're a man," he said with a grin, "I'm sure."

She smiled. "I thought I might have been too direct."

"No way. Everything's good. Lead on."

Male certainty, she thought, resuming her ascent. Not that she was surprised. Nor would she have had even a moment of equivocation if any of this was even *remotely normal*.

Au contraire.

Her hots for Jake Chambers was unusual. She'd never been instantly turned on by a man—and she'd seen more than her share of handsome men on her world travels.

Although trying to figure out why this was happening wasn't in the cards right now. Her carnal impulses were in charge.

And whether cause or effect was driving her, the goal was the same.

"Holy shit." Arrested at the top of the stairs, she stared at a very large four-poster bed, its provenance India, if the voluptuous female nudes that figured as bedposts were any indication. The piece of furniture was set center stage in a large room that otherwise appeared to be a living room. "Some of Chaz's usual subtlety, I see." She shot a glance at Jake, who had come up beside her.

"You got that right," Jake said, drily. "Is it too much? We could go somewhere else." He liked that she hadn't seen it before, her surprise obvious. That it mattered that she hadn't seen it before, he chose not to consider.

She glanced at her watch, thinking, could she wait if they went somewhere else? Easy answer: no. Then her friends were waiting, too, so time was a factor.

"Are you on a tight schedule?"

"No," she lied. "Sorry." Although why was she even worrying about Shelly et al. at a time like this? Her mother's courtesy-to-others mantra drilled into her in childhood was to blame.

"So—do you wanna go somewhere else?"

Back in the real, more selfish world, her gaze flicked down to his crotch, then up again. "I vote to stay here." She smiled. "How's that?"

He would have been happy fucking her on the dining room table downstairs, but ever courteous, he said, "I second the vote. Come on." He took her hand. "Let's see if this *Kama Sutra* bed has any good vibes."

The magenta satin duvet cover and pillow shams had the same over-the-top bawdiness as the bed, the fabric not only embroidered in gold but befringed and betasseled with reckless abandon.

"I feel as though I should charge you," Liv teased as they reached the bed. "Is this from a bordello, or is it some decorator's idea of camp?"

"Let's hope it's camp. Although in my current lustful mood, I want you to know, money's no object."

"Cute." She smiled. "Not that I wouldn't be willing to open my checkbook at the moment if I had to." She glanced at his erection. "For that."

They were both experienced enough and past gorgeous

enough to know that neither of them had ever had to pay for anything when it came to sex. They didn't belabor the point.

"Sit down." He kicked off his sandals. "Let me help you with your shoes—and don't look at me like that. I don't have a fetish. I'm just being polite."

"In that case"—Liv smiled as she sat on the shockingly pink satin—"I'd be delighted."

"Louboutin has the sexiest shoes on the market." Kneeling at her feet, unbuckling one black ankle strap, he glanced up and winked. "Merely an objective observation. I won't ask to lick your toes."

She laughed. "I'm relieved. As for Louboutin, the man knows women. I have a closet full of his shoes; they make me feel good." *Like the touch of your hands*, Liv thought, her senses on full alert, superheightened, as if she'd inhaled an aphrodisiac, and the love potion was kicking in big time.

Any talk of feeling good definitely struck a chord, although Jake's feel-good senses had nothing to do with shoes or Christian Louboutin's expertise in interpreting female psyches. He didn't even believe in karma, although an experience like this could make him a convert. It wasn't every day a sexy woman like Liv Bell walked into his kitchen. He'd give fate a nod on this one.

And maybe an obeisance or two as well.

Or ten or twenty, he decided, deeply appreciative of the scene unfolding before his eyes.

Once sans shoes, Liv had tumbled back onto the bed and was in the process of stripping off her lacy panties, her silken thighs and blonde pussy a damned inspiring sight.

Quick to take his cue, he pulled his T-shirt over his head and dropped it.

A second later, green silk panties joined his T-shirt on the floor.

He unsnapped his jeans.

She looked up, her dress half off. "This is sooo bizarre," she murmured, the sound of the snap having buzzed her back from her jazzed-up, take-me-I'm-yours trance.

"Don't knock it. Karma's karma."

"You think?"

He shrugged. "Absolutely." No way was he stopping. Not with her dress down around her waist and her lush boobs scorching his retinas.

"Okay," she said, as though maybe she'd needed permission. Then he slid his jeans down his hips and legs, stepped out of them, and any hesitation she might have had instantly vanished. She wanted what was under his boxers with or without karma or reason or practicality. Someday, she'd question her obsession. But. Not. Right. Now.

Back on track, she slid her dress downward, slipped her legs out, and tossed the bright yellow silk aside. Kicking the duvet down to the foot of the bed, she figured she'd worry about whatever there was to worry about later—like tomorrow or never. "Yesss, normal sheets," she exclaimed. "Chaz has not gone completely Bollywood." Falling back in a languorous pose that was second nature to her after ten thousand photo shoots, she lay on Chaz's six-hundred-count lavender cotton sheets and said with a smile, "As you may have noticed, I'm in a slam-bang mood."

He grinned. "Are you on speed, or something better?"

"I wish I had that excuse. I'm straight and sober, and have no idea why I'm suddenly so impatient. Maybe it's your eyes; they're gorgeous. Although your splendid hard-on can't be discounted, either," she added, her gaze flicking to his crotch. "Oh, yeah, definitely a factor . . ."

"Speaking of factors," he murmured, his dark gaze focused on her pussy, prominently on display as she lay with one leg slightly bent at the knee and tipped to one side. A tantalizing glimpse of her pink labia commanded his attention, her soft, plump flesh glistening wet, as in *ready for action*.

"Do you need help undressing?"

His gaze came up, and he grinned. "Can't wait?"

"No. Don't ask me why. I haven't a clue."

"Give me a second to find a condom," he said with a smile, quickly stripping off his blue boxers, "and I'll be right with you. Knowing Chaz, I'm guessing there's some around." Jerking open the drawer on the bedside table, he lifted out a string of foil packets. "Score."

"Thank God. I was about to panic." His engorged, waist-high erection was making her even hotter. With a suffocated groan, she cautioned herself to patience while every feverish nerve in her body screamed its dissent.

In the act of tearing open a foil packet, he paused at the sound of her muffled groan and glanced over. "You *are* on a real short fuse, aren't you, babe?"

"Sorta," she whispered. "I apologize."

"Hey, don't apologize. I'm counting my blessings."

She watched him roll the latex down his stiff prick with swift precision, her cunt pulsing and throbbing in anticipation, all her senses primed and aching to feel that huge dick slide inside her.

The condom in place, he leaned over the bed, setting his hands on either side of her shoulders, and dropped between her legs in a supple flow of muscled strength. "Time to get this show on the road?" His voice was soft, his smile close.

"If you don't mind." There it was; courtesy even in extremity.

"Do I look like I mind?"

She smiled. "You have my eternal thanks, believe me."

He almost said, *Who would have nailed you if I hadn't asked?* But seconds away from sinking his dick into her cunt, he whispered, "My pleasure, babe."

He didn't even have to use his hands.

She shifted her hips slightly, adjusting her wet-with-longing cleft over the head of his penis . . . until she was right on target.

He pressed forward, entered her, and gave it up to whatever was making him feel this good.

Everything proceeded in perfect harmony—faultless to a fault, as Robert Browning would say—the quintessential fit of slick cunt and hard cock, of time and circumstance, of uncompli-cated desire.

She gasped softly as her G-spot nerve endings made contact with his hard, rigid penis.

He heard her gasp but neither paused nor stopped, single-mindedly intent on sinking hilt-deep into her silky warmth. Slowly forcing his way in, he felt her flesh gradually yield to his size and length, and when he eventually reached bottom, he grunted in satisfaction.

That low, guttural sound triggered every primal nerve in her body; all the complexities of civilization vanished, and she became incarnate female to virile maleness. Not necessarily a completely tractable female with her twenty-first-century mind-set, but definitely and certifiably receptive.

Even as she took note of her peculiar reaction, her body shamelessly contrived to further advance the act of mating, flooding her vaginal tissue to allow better access, making her more available, easier to fuck.

Acknowledging the added lubrication, Jake shifted his tempo marginally, moving with less caution now, sliding in and out more forcefully, no longer concerned with curbing his forward motion in order not to hurt her.

She responded, accommodating his rhythm, her hands clutching his shoulders, her feet braced on Chaz's lavender sheets to better meet the power of his downstrokes. Each time he was completely submerged, she'd arch upward to experience that exquisite, fierce ecstasy, holding her breath as the flame-hot rapture flooded her senses. As he'd withdraw, she'd whimper, reluctant to relinquish the intoxicating pleasure, pleading. "Stay, stay, stay . . ."

He never did—knowing better, intent on the ultimate sensation—and after a millisecond suspended at the extremity of his withdrawal, he'd plunge in once again and smile faintly at her gasp of pleasure.

Her orgasm wasn't long in coming.

Not that he'd thought it would be in her self-described slam-bang mood.

She quietly climaxed on one of his downstrokes, dying away on a sigh and a wave of molten bliss.

He was surprised at her constraint, having expected something more violent and vocal from a woman who approached sex with such dispatch. As he rested in her, waiting for her last ripple to fade away, she lay motionless and silent.

Christ, had he hurt her?

Or had she freaked out?

Was she some head case? Not an impossibility in the idiosyncratic world of modeling.

Although, primed as he was for his own climax, he decided further speculation could wait. Time enough to worry *after* he came.

Moving into a smooth, practiced rhythm, he'd no more than settled into a lazy rock 'n' roll undulation than Liv picked up the dance, her hips swinging in time to his, matching each deft flux and flow with gratifying precision. Her little breathy pleasure sounds started up again, too, warming his throat and curiously insinuating themselves into his psyche that had been, to date, immune to such tender sensibilities.

Fucking had always been just about fucking.

Why his psychic receptors were absorbing her soft, frenzied utterances with such clarity was weird, although not altogether bad, he had to admit, bombarded as he was by a full array of seriously prodigal sensation. In fact, it was pretty much the opposite.

"I am *so* turned on," Liv panted on a particularly deep plunging downthrust. "I'm going to *simply expire . . .*"

"Wait a second. We'll expire together." Okay, so his psyche wasn't completely weirded out. He could still deal with the practicalities.

It took maybe another five seconds—give or take—and once she started to scream, he half-smiled. *That's more like it*, he thought and proceeded to let himself go and come . . . and come . . . and come . . . in some all-time ejaculatory record.

They were both panting big time when it was over.

"Fucking a," he whispered, braced on his elbows, his chest heaving.

"Fucking a," she whispered back, eyes closed and gasping for air.

That they were both experiencing an epiphany of sorts failed to register in either of their brains. Not unusual under the circumstances with them both mildly unstrung. Their incomprehension aside, the eccentric brain synapses were nevertheless stored away, the file drawer shut and labeled for future reference.

The maxim, *Ignorance is bliss*, was appropriate to the occasion.

In terms of immediate reality, Jake came to his senses first, probably through force of habit. He wasn't a practitioner of touchy-feely after-sex conversation—a common enough trait in males. Easing away, he sat on the edge of the bed, stripped off the condom, disposed of it and, turning back, was about to say something polite in the way of farewell.

But surveying Liv's voluptuous, sprawled pose, her skin flushed rosy pink from some screaming-ass sex with *him*, he reconsidered, or maybe his libido did. "You don't have to leave just yet, do you?" he heard himself ask, the voice obviously his, although the remark was so shocking, he looked around hoping someone else might have spoken.

"I'll stay for a while." Her gaze shifted to his rising erection. "Let me know when he gets tired or you do. Since I seem to be megahorny tonight"—she made a little grimace—"I'm not capable of sound decision making."

"Maybe it's this bed." Jake gestured at one of the florid nude bedposts. "I'm pretty much in overdrive myself. Although, I did promise you dinner, so"—he shrugged—"it's your call."

"Right now I'm thinking ten more orgasms, not dinner."

He grinned. "Only ten?"

"I didn't mean to sound so greedy. Whatever you want, of course. You decide."

"The way I'm feeling, I figure we'll fuck till I collapse."

"No wonder all the ladies like you."

He probably shouldn't say that all the other ladies never made him feel like he'd taken a fistful of X when he hadn't. "Uh-uh, it's you, babe." No sense in playing games, he thought for the first time in his life.

It was an evening of revelations.

Or with luck, it would be.

He had plans.

Not that Liv didn't have a few of her own, her feelings as outré as Jake's.

Seven

But Jake played the gentleman first.

"Let me find some towels," he said.

"From the looks of this brothel bed," Liv murmured, stretching lazily, "I'd say look in the bedside table."

It took him a moment for his brain to assimilate what she'd said, because he was busy thinking she looked like some lush Titian nude when she arched her back like that. Or was it Rubens? Not that it mattered when her boobs were lifted into perfect cushiony roundness like that. And they were real—a novelty for ones that big. Dragging himself back to earth, he said, "You're probably right. This place screams Mustang Ranch."

"Have you been there?"

"Uh-uh." Leaning over, he opened the door on the bedside table. "I know people who have. It seems a waste of time to me.

There you go, babe," he added, grabbing two towels, sitting up, and handing her one. "You called that one right."

"Chaz isn't a romantic."

"No shit. He has a complete drugstore in there. Mouthwash, Altoids, a gross of condoms, and whadda you know—gold-plated handcuffs." Reaching down, he pulled them out and swung them in her direction.

"If you don't behave, I might have to use them."

He gave her a look. "Over my dead body."

"So you're not into bondage."

"Not much."

"Ever?"

"Is this a quiz?"

She opened her arms wide and smiled. "I'm done. No more questions. You may direct the entertainment."

His brows rose. "I wouldn't have type-cast you as submissive."

"With a dick like yours, I'd be stupid not to be. I'm sure whatever you decide to do will feel mighty fine on my pleasure scale."

"So I may indulge myself."

"Us, sweetie," she said with a smile, figuring she was way past any opportunity to play the shrinking violet.

"Right." He liked that she didn't play games, a rarity in his world. Throwing the handcuffs back into the bedside table, he quickly wiped himself off and came to his feet. "Do you need anything? I need a drink of water." Smoothing back his hair with both hands, he readjusted the binder holding his ponytail in place. "How about you?"

"Me, too—water."

"There's plenty of liquor or wine around here—champagne, if you like."

"I'd mostly like you."

He grinned. "Yes, ma'am." Had she known that her words had a familiar ring, requests like that frequent years ago when he was in culinary school and waiting tables on the side in upscale restaurants? It had been pretty much a fucking smorgasbord in those days. Between work, school, and keeping the ladies happy, sleep had been scarce.

He had a good feeling that getting to know darling Liv might be déjà vu all over again. "Rest up," he said with a grin. "I'll be right back."

But he wasn't.

Liv could hear him rummaging through Chaz's kitchen cupboards, drawers opening and shutting, cabinet doors ditto, the sound of a refrigerator door closing with that soft thud of a vacuum seal.

"Need help?" she called out, her voice drifting over the glass block walls separating the living/bedroom area from the kitchen in the loft space.

"The kind of help you can give me doesn't require you moving. Take it easy, reflect on the state of the world—or not, considering the current chaos. Better yet, count the condoms we have left. I was thinking we should try to use them up."

Liv smiled. "You do know how to sweet-talk a lady."

"How about some tapas? Does that put you in the mood, too?"

How did he know? she thought, jumping out of bed. Standing in the open doorway to the kitchen two seconds later, she decided not only was her personal chef more gorgeous than one could ever imagine — his awesome cock alone capable of making one starry-eyed — but here he was making her tapas, her all-time favorite food. "When I heard the word *tapas*, I thought I must have been dreaming. You're going to feed me tapas?"

He shot her a grin. "That's what I do, babe. Feed people. Besides, I'm hungry. I forgot to eat today."

"Just for the record, I hate people who say they forgot to eat. I would *never* forget to eat."

He wasn't about to argue with her. "Whatever you're doing seems to be working." His gaze raked her from head to toe in a quick appraisal. "You're every man's fantasy."

"Back at you. You're definitely centerfold material." She smiled. "As is your spectacular friend," she added with a tip of her head to the pertinent object.

"As long as you're happy, we're happy. Do you want a robe? There might be one around here, although I thought we'd eat in bed."

Jeez, he was a humble man, even with his looks and celebrity. How unusual was that? She knew men who looked like him who had egos from hell. "Bed sounds good. For whatever," she murmured teasingly.

He looked up from cutting chorizo sausage in a blur of motion and offered her a flashing grin. "Food first and then whatever. And I'm definitely open to suggestions."

Ever since she'd arrived in the doorway, he'd been swiftly slicing and dicing while keeping an eye on two pans on the stove. Flipping in ingredients from time to time, he'd toss them with an effortless flick of his wrist before resuming his cutting. His movements were sure, smooth as silk, his unruffled calm Zen-like. Clearly, his expertise extended beyond the bedroom.

Leaning over to pull out a bottle of champagne from an

under-counter wine cooler, he opened it with a deft twist and set it next to two glasses. "Lucky for us, Chaz left his kitchen fully supplied. I'm guessing he entertained up here."

"He did. Chaz didn't like to be alone. He always had people around."

"From the looks of his stock of condoms, I'd say women in particular."

"He was known for his beautiful waitpeople."

She'd kept her statement gender neutral, so out of curiosity, he asked, "Was he a switch-hitter?"

She shrugged. "Don't know. I just met him after I started my winery. He's a local boy, though. Or was."

"Very much *was*, according to him. Apparently, Saint Barts is his nirvana. He said he's going to be buried there."

"What about you?"

"About what?"

"Do you have any burial plans?"

He laughed. "Not in the near future, I hope. Do you ask that question often?"

"Not really. Coming from the West Coast, I just thought you might have some avant-garde notions . . . you know . . . like green burials."

"Haven't thought about it. You?" Was she into crystals and shit? Not that it was going to curb his enthusiasm in any way. As soon as he ate something, he was going to take care of his hard-on.

"My only plans are to live to a hundred." She grinned. "So I've got time. What are you making?" She moved closer to the stove.

"Chorizo and chickpeas, some cubed potatoes with a few

spices, and a hot green olive vinaigrette." He pointed at one pan. "And this"—he jabbed his knife at the other pan—"is Gambas al Ajillo, Spanish shrimp. It should have garlic, but in the interests of not offending you, I left it out, but there's some bay leaf, chili pepper, olive oil, and shrimp, of course, served with that crusty bread over there." He nodded at an earthenware platter. "Pour yourself a glass of champagne and get two forks from that drawer"—he jabbed his thumb sideways—"while I get this food on some plates." Opening the door on one of three waist-high ovens, he drew out a sheet pan of toasted tortillas and proceeded to break them into pieces. Setting a bowl of freshly made, chunky tomatillo salsa on a platter, he surrounded the bowl with the hot tortilla chips, briskly shoved it aside and, lifting the steaming pan of shrimp from the burner, piled the contents on another plate in a perfect mound. The chorizo dish was assembled as quickly. "After you," he said with a smile, tucking the champagne bottle under one arm, arranging two platters on the same arm, picking up the tomatillo plate and two cloth napkins with his other hand. "I make a great steak-frites, too, if you feel like it later."

"Are you kidding? I won't be able to move after all this food."

"Then feel free to lie there and think of England."

"No joke. I might take you up on that."

"You won't hear any complaints from me."

"You're way too accommodating. You must have to kick women out afterward. Between your great cooking and fabulous dick, I doubt anyone wants to leave."

Avoiding a reply to the kicking-women-out remark, which hit damn close to home, he said, "Actually, I don't often cook . . . at times like this." He politely chose the bland phrase. "I was just hungry." He wasn't about to admit to either her or himself that having her stay might have figured in his decision to cook.

"Then I lucked out."

"I'd promised you a meal, although this is just starters. Feel free to hold me to my offer." For some reason she was making him operate way the hell out in left field. Not that he was about to parse his feelings at the moment; he had more interesting options. Such as eat, then fuck until he couldn't get it up anymore.

He arranged the platters between them on the bed, handed her a napkin, drank down the glass of champagne she'd given him in one long draft, set the glass aside, and then, dropping into a propped-on-one-elbow sprawl, waved his hand at the food. "Please . . . be my guest."

Seated opposite him, her legs crossed in an effortless yoga pose, she lifted her glass of champagne in his direction. "This is way nice."

"Yeah . . . I agree."

Their eyes met, and they both felt the freaking magic.

Absurd, he thought.

Only in movies, she thought.

"The food's getting cold," he said. The last person in the world to subscribe to voodoo emotion, he picked up a shrimp and took a bite.

Quickly draining her glass of champagne in an effort to dismiss the radical feeling with a dose of alcohol, she laid the empty glass on the bed, picked up her fork, and speared a piece of sausage.

They ate in silence for a brief time, both busy rationalizing away that moment when their eyes had met—words like *aberrant* and *crackpot* common to their thoughts.

Liv spoke first. She was less comfortable with silence. "This is absolutely delicious." She waved her fork over the food. "It's perfect. Thank you."

"You're welcome." He smiled. "I've been eating out since I came, but fortunately, Chaz's freezer and larder were full."

"Having a personal chef is *very* nice."

"You within reach is nice. Even if you're doing a number on my head. But, whatever . . . I'm not complaining."

"I'm feeling a little wacky, too. And it's not as though this is virgin territory for me"—she lifted her hand to the room at large—"you know . . . sex."

"No shit. Are you tired, too? I was up all night ordering stuff." He shrugged. "That's my excuse."

"I slept for eight hours. I have no excuse." She nodded at his erection. "Other than the bewitching power of that."

"Then I'd better keep up my strength," he said, reaching for another shrimp. "These are supposed to be aphrodisiacs, right?"

"So that's why I'm wetter than wet." She wasn't about to tell him the truth—that she'd been riding a lustful wave from the first time she saw him.

He held out the shrimp. "So what d'you say? As long as we're on a roll?"

"I guess," she said, trying to sound blasé when there wasn't a chance in hell she could have actually refused him anything.

"Open up, babe." A *genuinely* blasé tone.

I am already, she thought. But she opted for discretion, since lusting women probably weren't a news flash for Jake Chambers.

Easing upward, he slipped the shrimp into her mouth. "Now bite."

His softly enunciated command shuddered through her vagina

with an electrifying jolt. He was sure of himself, confident, familiar with women doing what he wanted. She shouldn't have responded to such arrogance, but a hot rush of liquid longing flooded her cunt, and as though she were without will of her own, all she could think of was, *Please, please, fuck me NOW, NOW, NOW!*

Maybe he could read minds. His gaze narrowed slightly. "How about five minutes from now?" he said before falling back into a sprawl.

"Thanks." She didn't pretend not to understand; although it took effort to offer an urbane smile when she was really much, much too eager. "I blame the shrimp for my horniness."

He smiled back. "Whatever works. Give me a few minutes, though. I need nourishment. I wouldn't want to disappoint you."

As if, she thought, surveying his spectacular cock, undiminished and tempting. "Take your time."

He looked up, a forkful of chorizo poised halfway to his mouth. "Really?"

"I was being polite."

He grinned. "Gotcha. Four minutes and counting then," he said, all chivalrous gallantry.

A short time later, after consuming a good portion of chorizo and shrimp, he set about clearing the dishes from the bed. Clearly experienced at stacking dishes, he picked up the perfectly balanced pile of plates and, twisting around, set them on the floor in the most gorgeous display of sinuous, tawny-colored muscle she'd ever had the good fortune to see. "You must work out," she murmured, as he pulled himself back up in a supple surge of rock-hard abs.

"I do a little kendo." He tossed the napkins and empty champagne bottle on the floor. "Fourteen hours a day throwing pots and pans around the kitchen also helps keep you in shape. Are we done talking?"

"Whatever you say, boss."

His brows flickered. "You mean I didn't have to eat that fast?"

She smiled. "I appreciate it, of course."

"I thought you might. And with dessert waiting, I had plenty of incentive to hurry." Seizing her ankles, he flipped her onto her back and in answer to her wide-eyed look, said with a lazy smile, "Any special instructions?" Without waiting for an answer, he ran his palms up her legs, eased her thighs apart and, silently thanking Chaz for his oversized bed, adjusted himself comfortably between Liv's legs. Glancing up to meet her heated gaze, he quirked one brow. "No orders? Last chance."

"Just a minute," Liv murmured on a suffocated breath, her vagina pulsing so hard the desperate ache slid all the way up her spine and spiked into her brain, his idea of dessert, his outrageous desirability and magnetic appeal making her unstrung and ravenous when she was *never* ravenous. "I'm not sure I like . . . being . . . out of control," she gasped.

"Sure you do."

"Screw you," she breathed, pissed at his casual assurance. She should have listened to her voice of reason downstairs and kept walking when she had the chance. Now she wasn't so sure she could.

"Hey. I'm barely holding it together, too," he gruffly retorted. But rather than explain, he put his hand over her mouth—the male answer to baffling doubts. Abruptly dipping his head, he opened her dewy cleft with his fingertips and ran his tongue up her slick tissue with delicacy and finesse, with perfect

GPS know-how in terms of nerve locations. He could have been thoughtfully arranging a fantasy dessert to best effect, so exacting was the placement of his tongue and fingers. As though he knew to perfection how to turn her on—or maybe the scores of women before her had been a universal sisterhood when it came to getting off this way.

In due course, when her labia—major and minor—had been excited to a frenzied nicety, he turned his attention to her clit, and if being out of control had once been an issue, it no longer was.

Complete and absolute sensation took precedence.

Carte blanche, as it were, on the road to ecstasy.

For the next blissful interval only Liv's breathy moans and orgasmic cries punctuated the silence of the loft. Jake deftly brought her to climax once, then twice, and lifting his head slightly, he paused, waiting for some cue about a possible third time.

Stabbing her fingers through his thick hair, she jerked his head back.

Definitely a cue. He got back down to business.

And Liv gave herself up to raw, over-the-edge, soul-stirring rapture that insinuated itself into every sensitive, greedy nook and cranny, every rapt nerve and throbbing bit of flesh previously unaccustomed to such neon-lit carnal splendor.

Not that she was currently in the right frame of mind to consider that past discrepancy.

For his part, Jake found Liv's total abandon appealing. That she was completely genuine in a world given increasingly to spin and pretense held a distinctly down-home charm. Or perhaps it was disarming only in contrast to his glitterati world where poseurs were the norm.

Not that any of his philosophical reflections were relevant up against his increasing randiness. And just as soon as darling Livvi came again, he was going to replace his tongue with his cock and blast off.

"Oh God, oh God, oh God—oh God," she panted.

Perfect timing, he thought, gently sucking her clit as her third orgasm ripped through her vagina. She was definitely on some kind of hair trigger. Not that he was complaining when it would soon be his turn. Although he knew better than to stop what he was doing until her last little sigh died away. Even then, he gave her time to return to the real world before easing back and resting on his elbows.

"You're way too good," she breathed, glancing down at him from under her lashes. "I'm writing off Shelly tonight."

He liked that she didn't ask. He particularly liked that her plans matched his. He'd written off Shelly a long time ago. "I was hoping you'd stay," he said with a smile, "seeing how it's my turn now."

"Definitely. After that last glorious orgasm, I owe you. Any special instructions?" she waggishly inquired.

"In my current purist frame of mind," he murmured, coming up on his knees and reaching for a condom, "all I want is the feel of your hot cunt closing around my cock. Say a couple hundred times."

She gave him a sunny smile. "I'm really, *really* glad I stopped by."

He glanced up as he ripped open a foil packet, a smile slowly forming on his finely modeled mouth. "Believe me, I couldn't have asked for a better wine merchant." He unrolled the condom over his throbbing cock, snapped it in place, and, placing the flat of his hands on either side of her arms, smoothly dropped between her widespread legs.

It was a seriously unforgettable sensation, he decided a moment later, as he glided inside her soft, slick warmth, her cunt's tightness conforming to his hard-on with a highly provocative, all-absorbing reluctance. His toes curled, a thin film of sweat appeared on his forehead, and only with sheer will did he resist his body's inclination to enter her at ramming speed. But by the end, he was champing at the bit, more impatient than usual, more frenzied, and when he finally bottomed out, only then did he notice her tautness. "Christ," he muttered, instantly pulling back. "I didn't mean to hurt you."

"You didn't." A soft almost inaudible sound.

He met her gaze, his brows rising faintly in query.

Her nostrils flared, and it took her a moment to find her breath. "I don't actually believe in karma, but the earth moved back there."

"No shit," he grunted. "And I don't believe in much of anything."

A smile lifted the corners of her mouth. "So . . . can you do it again?"

"Like this?" He glided back in.

Her eyes drifted shut, she raised her hips into his downthrust, accentuating the stunning pressure. "Exactly like that," she breathed, sliding her hands around his neck. "Don't ever stop . . ."

He knew what she meant; he had no intention of stopping. Nor would he have, if the phone on the bedside table hadn't begun ringing at such jarring decibel levels it hurt his ears. Swearing, he glanced at the phone. But too far gone at the moment to consider answering it, he concentrated instead on the onset of Liv's next orgasm, ultimately joining her in another mind-blowing climax so awesome it momentarily drowned out the ringing of the phone.

They lay collapsed afterward, replete.

He unconsciously shifted on his elbows, not crushing the woman under him hardwired into his brain.

"It stopped," Liv murmured.

"What?" He was still drifting in that never-never land of sweet gratification.

"The phone."

"Good."

They both ignored the red voice mail light that had started blinking. They both had better things on their minds.

Later though, when Jake was once again capable of coherent thought and speech, he debated listening to the message. But it was getting late. Whoever called could wait until morning.

If the phone hadn't rung again moments later and yet a third and fourth time shortly after that, he might have persevered in his decision. But he'd been in restaurant crisis management too long to ignore the fourth call.

"Do you mind?" It was politesse only; he was already rolling into a seated position on the edge of the bed and stripping off his condom. A second later, he punched into the voice mail and listened to the increasingly frantic messages before glancing at Liv. "I have to respond to these," he gruffly noted. "My manager in L.A. is negotiating for some hard-to-get wines. Devain's vine-yard only produces a few cases a year." He smoothed his palms over his hair and blew out a breath. "I don't want to lose them."

"You don't want to lose wines like that," Liv murmured, stretching lazily, knowing Devain as well as any wine connoisseur. "No problem. I'll wait."

His dark brows came together in a frown. "This could take a while. He's a prick to deal with."

Coming up on her elbows, she looked at him squarely. "Are you brushing me off?" She was never brushed off, which may have accounted for her mildly pugnacious tone. Or maybe the idea of relinquishing the pleasure he offered displeased her more.

"God, no," he said, leaning over and dropping a conciliatory kiss on her cheek. "Stay a week." Anyone knowing Jake would have been shocked by his statement. "In fact," he added, immune to previous lifestyle habits when right after this phone call, getting off again was number one on his list, "I'll be right back with something to amuse you while I talk this over with Eduardo."

"I'm not in the mood to read," Liv drolly noted.

He winked. "You won't be reading, babe." Coming to his feet, he jabbed a finger at her. "Now, stay put."

"Yes, sir, whatever you say, sir," she teasingly replied.

He grinned. "I can see we're gonna get along just fine."

They were already getting along finer than she'd ever gotten along with anyone, but his ego probably didn't need further stroking.

She watched him walk away: tall and tanned—swarthy by nature, she suspected—muscled like a stevedore, handsome as sin . . . with a cock to die for and a real proficiency at using it. She'd be crazy not to wait.

And before she had time to do more than thank her lucky stars for having stopped by, Jake returned from the kitchen balancing a large, peeled zucchini upright on his palm. It had been carved into a realistic facsimile of an erect penis with smoothly rounded glans, sculpted veins and the slight arc of full-blown arousal.

"Here's something to keep you interested until I'm off the phone. I wouldn't want you to be unhappy while you're waiting."

"It doesn't look like I will be. You're so very talented," Liv purred, her body already opening in anticipation.

"Ice swans or dildos, it's all in a day's work," he said with a grin. "But more importantly," he added, sitting down on the edge of the bed, "let's see if I figured the size right. I was guessing you'd like the economy size." Leaning over, he eased her legs apart with one hand and slipped the smooth head past her labia, slowly forcing the large dildo deep inside her.

The coolness, the exquisite pressure instantly triggered her already overwrought nerves. She shivered as a shimmering rush of arousal washed over her. No longer questioning her inexplicable longing, she basked in the feverish glow instead, giving Jake high marks for estimating the perfect, optimal size. The zucchini was big, but not too big or almost . . . almost . . . too big in the most exquisite possible way.

When he finally whispered, "There. It's all the way in," and nudged it just a little deeper with his palm, she shut her eyes against the wild, explosive delirium convulsing her senses.

"I'm not usually like this," she panted a moment later, as if she needed to apologize for her lack of restraint. But with an enormous dildo cramming her full, with her every sexual receptor singing the "Hallelujah Chorus" at frenzied pitch, she decided it didn't really matter about restraint or the lack thereof.

"Hey, everything's good," Jake whispered. "Go for it."

How sweet he was—not selfish, chivalrous even, thinking of her pleasure, apparently understanding the finer points of truth and beauty as related to unbridled desire as well.

And since when had she felt the need to apologize for her sexual urges?

Never.

So there.

Having rationalized away her novel unease having to do with really blissfully countless orgasms that she had to admit were unusual even in her worldly take on life, she stopped quibbling or thinking at all and gave herself up to the extraordinary, super-acute pleasure occasioned by Jake's sculptural talents.

She screamed more than usual when she came the next time.

Perhaps he wouldn't make his call just yet, Jake decided. Perhaps he'd first talk to her about making less noise. Diplomatically, of course.

On the other hand, it wasn't as though Eduardo would really give a damn.

Christ, what was he thinking?

Withdrawing the dildo marginally, he shoved it back in and smiled faintly at her gratified sigh. "Enjoy yourself, darling. I'll make this quick," he murmured, settling once again into a gentle, adroit rhythm of arousal as he reached for the phone.

Negotiating via a conference call with Eduardo and Devain to save time, Jake kept the conversation as brief as possible. He wasn't in the mood to quibble over price, which speeded up the process considerably, not to mention Jake's French was serviceable enough to soothe over Devain's notorious irritability.

A price was agreed on in mere minutes, the rare wines locked in for Jake's restaurants. As Jake made his adieus, Christophe Devain, owner of one of the best vineyards in the world, said, "Jake, *mon ami*, my regards to your lady. Such lovely little moans. I envy you your evening's pleasure."

Jake didn't offer demur. He only said, "*Merci*," understanding how fortunate he was to have darling Livvi in his bed.

Immediately Jake set down the phone, he forgot what—only hours before—would have been a coup of prime import. Rare Bordeaux vintages were dismissed from his thoughts, as was Eduardo's earlier hysteria. Reaching for one of Chaz's convenient supply of condoms, he shifted his attention to more pressing activities.

A moment later, the zucchini dildo was tossed aside, Jake settled between Liv's legs, and the two individuals on the Bollywood bed returned to their quest for the perfect orgasm.

Eight

The next morning Jake walked Liv out to her truck. "Christ, the sun's barely up," he muttered, squinting at the pink glow in the east.

"My work crew comes in early. I try to be there in case anyone has any questions. Or wants to bitch. You didn't have to get up." She grinned. "I could have sent you a dozen roses and a thank-you note."

He grinned back. "Make it red roses. You *did* work me pretty hard."

"I should apologize"—her brows flickered—"although I think I did a bunch of times already."

She always had—right before she asked for it again. "Hey, babe, I'm only teasing. The pleasure was all mine." He opened the driver's door for her.

She climbed in, Jake shut the door and, rolling down her window, Liv said with a smile, "Thanks again. I had a really good time." No one in Minnesota ever got in their car after a visit and just drove away. The Minnesota good-bye was lingering and often involved several extra cups of coffee—although in this case sex had been substituted for coffee.

"Come keep me company again—anytime." Jake's reluctance to have her leave had nothing to do with Minnesota good-byes. He was still horny.

"I might take you up on that."

"Please do. I'm at loose ends for a while. I'll feed you, too." For a man who preferred one-night stands, he surprised even himself with the invitation.

"It's busy this time of year for me. I'll give you a call before I come over."

"Don't bother. Come anytime." Every word he spoke was such a clear departure from normal, he was thinking he must be losing it. And how much he could contribute to fatigue was unclear.

The first few bars of Natasha Bedingfield's "Unwritten" echoed in the morning air.

"Shit, that's my phone," Liv muttered, rummaging through the mess on her truck seat to unearth it. Plucking it from under a denim jacket, she glanced at the caller ID. "I better take this," she murmured. "A friend from the past."

"Go for it. I'm not in a hurry." Screw it. He liked her *and* the sex. No way he was going to analyze this to death. "Stay for breakfast," he offered.

"I wish," she said, flipping open her phone. "But my crew . . ." she whispered. "Hi, Janie," she said in a normal tone. "What a nice surpri—hey, slow down, slow down. Oh, Jeez—sorry; I left my phone in my truck. You're *where*? Okay, gotcha. Hey . . . don't cry. You'll be fine here. No one in New York ever even *thinks* about Minneapolis. I'll come and get you. It'll take me about twenty minutes. Don't move."

Flipping the phone shut, she turned to Jake. "Crisis in paradise as you may have surmised. Like the soap operas my friend from New York used to star in. Apparently, Janie went to the gym yesterday and came back to find the locks on the apartment had been changed. Neither the doormen nor servants would let her in, no matter how big a scene she made—and knowing Janie I expect it was a doozy. Luckily, she'd taken her little boy with her for his swim lesson or she wouldn't have had access to him. Gypsy fate there. Anyway," Liv added, "they're at the airport Hilton. She's been trying to get in touch with me since last night. Moral of the story—never marry a Mr. Big who's already divorced three wives."

"You wouldn't be talking about Janie Tabor?"

"You know Janie?"

"I did a long time ago. She was trying to break into movies like every other woman who came out to la-la land from small-town USA. Mind if I come along?"

Liv hesitated. "I'd better ask Janie. She's pretty uptight right now."

"I'll wait."

He said it so calmly she figured he knew what Janie's answer would be. And sure enough, when she called and asked, Janie screamed, "Jake's *there*? Put him on the phone!"

After a lengthy conversation that made Liv beaucoup curious about their past as well as making her just a little pissed for some stupid, unknown reason, Jake said good-bye and handed Liv her phone. "Let me grab my wallet and lock up. I'll be right back. Want me to drive?"

"I'll drive." What she really wanted to say was, *Tell me everything*, because what she'd heard of their conversation sounded just like the soap operas Janie used to star in before her marriage to one of the richest men in New York. Not that Liv hadn't tried to talk Janie out of marrying a man who was into serial marriages. *Short* serial marriages. But at the time, Janie had been tired of acting and tired of dating. She'd also been nervous about her biological clock, along with pop-psychology issues like where she was going with her life. She'd been twenty-nine and had spoken longingly about wanting a baby of her own in the same sappy phrases as one of the flaky characters she'd played on the soap operas.

Not a good reason to get married, Liv had thought.

Particularly not a reason to marry someone like Leo Rolf, who already had five children by three former wives.

But then Liv had always been a romantic, unlike Janie, who was looking for someone rich to take care of her and give her a baby. Liv was still holding out for that *great true love that passeth all understanding*. Or something along those lines.

The passenger door suddenly slammed shut, jarring her from her mindless reverie. Returning to reality, she gave Jake one of her practiced, camera-ready smiles. "All set?"

"Yep. Ready to hit the road."

For a man who had been complaining about the early hour just minutes ago, he was suddenly raring to go. Not that she should care or even give it another thought. Just because she'd spent one night having fabulous sex with Jake Chambers didn't give her the right to question his motives.

The sex had been prime, but that was it. End of story.

Particularly with a man like Jake Chambers, who'd spent years enjoying all the pleasures of life without so much as finding himself engaged, let alone married. Leo Rolf should take lessons.

"Traffic should be light this time of day," Liv said, firing up her truck. "Tell me how you know Janie?" Crap. Where did that come from? Hadn't she just cautioned herself against overt curiosity?

"We lived together in L.A. for a while. She needed a place to stay, and I had plenty of room."

His tone was casual. But men were always more nonchalant about living arrangements. Like the time she thought she might actually be falling for Serge in Paris, and she'd found out the apartment she shared with him was his wife's. Perhaps that memory added a little edge to her voice. "Living together like roommates you mean?"

He stopped humming under his breath and gave her a quizzical look. "Yeah. For a while."

"Oh, crap." She could feel the blush stealing up her cheeks. "It's really none of my business. I shouldn't have asked. Please . . . go back to your humming."

"Look, I probably don't have to explain Janie to you. She's nicer than hell; I like her. But let's face it, she looks out for numero uno first. My story is hers in reverse. I came home one day and she was gone. She'd left with a New York director who'd promised her a part on Broadway."

"I'm sorry." Leaving midtown, Liv turned onto the freeway ramp. "If it's any consolation, she's done that more than once."

"Don't get me wrong. I didn't die of a broken heart. I was just surprised. A note would have been nice. But we had our good times, and I wish her well."

"How long did you live together?"

"About a year."

She almost said, *Holy shit, that must be a record for you.* Jake Chambers could pretty much have his pick of women—and did. "That must have been a long time ago," she said instead.

"It was—like a couple lifetimes ago. You know, I'm hungry again. Let's eat breakfast somewhere after we pick up Janie."

Was he politely changing the subject, or was he really hungry? Was he going to ask Janie to stay with him again? Was last night's world-class sex all she was going to get of Jake Chambers now that Janie was in town? If she knew him better, she could ask him all of the above.

Shit, the morning after really *could* be awkward. Munch's painting of the young woman seated on the edge of the bed, while replete with nineteenth-century moral overtones, did portray a kind of universal uncertainty typical of those occasions.

On the other hand, she wasn't exactly the bashful type.

"Is Janie going to stay with you?" So sue her; she wanted to know.

He gave her another of those quizzical looks. "Not unless you don't want her at your place."

"She's fine with me. I just thought I'd ask."

He smiled. "I wasn't planning on picking up where Janie and I left off, if that's what you were thinking."

"I wasn't, okay?"

He looked amused. "No problem, then. By the way, I meant what I said. Come and see me anytime."

It was scary how his casual invitation could make her entire body begin to rev up again. It was even more scary that a happy, blissful glow seemed to inundate her psyche. She'd never felt either of those sweep-you-off-your-feet sensations before Jake Chambers and his magnetic force field had entered her life.

Apparently, the phrase, *warm your heart*, wasn't just BS.

"How long have you known Janie?" Jake reached for the power switch on the radio. "What's a good local station?"

"The second button. Top forty. I met her in New York." Liv glanced his way. "She'd just come out from L.A. But Tommy Farrell didn't get her that Broadway part."

"So I heard." Sitting back, he jabbed a finger at the radio. "Great song."

"Yeah. It always puts me in a good mood."

"So you were living in New York? With a modeling career, though, I suppose you would."

"I had an apartment there at the time. Janie stayed with me for a while after Tommy dumped her. She needed a shoulder to cry on."

"She's good at crying."

"It wasn't so bad. I had my whiny moments, too. And we did a lot of clubbing in those days. She's fun to party with."

"Do you miss the bright lights?"

"Uh-uh. I came here to escape the bright lights—camera lights included. I was raised not far from here. My comfort level is far, far away from big cities."

"You must have lived in them a long time though? Modeling careers start young, don't they?"

"Usually. But I didn't get in the game until my senior year in college. Someone entered me in some contest, and two weeks later I was walking the runways in Milan. I started late, and I stopped just as soon as my bank account made me financially independent.

But what inspired you to relocate to the boondocks? I was born here. I have an excuse."

He grinned. "Midlife crisis."

"It's a little early for that, isn't it?" She eased left onto the Crosstown freeway ramp. "What are you—thirty-one, thirty-two?"

"Thirty-five. I started asking myself why the hell I was working so hard."

"And you thought you'd find the answer here? Did you throw a dart at a map?"

"Close. I knew about Chaz's place, and then my aunt has a lake home in Wisconsin. She told me to check it out and see how it's looking. No one's been there for years." He smiled. "Except yard people and a handy man or two."

"Where in Wisconsin?"

"A place called Deer Lake."

She shot him a look. "You're kidding."

"You know where it is?"

"About ten miles from my farm."

"So we'll be neighbors. Come over and borrow a cup of sugar anytime," he said with a grin.

"Tempting. Although you won't be living there, will you?"

"If you're close by, maybe I'll change my mind."

"You should package that charm, darling."

"Feel free to bring *your* fine package over to my place. I'm available twenty-four-seven." Christ, maybe he really was having an early midlife crisis. He couldn't recall ever offering a woman carte blanche entrée to his life before.

"You're sorry you said that, aren't you?" She took a right.

He laughed. "Does it show?"

"Oh, yeah. Look, last night was great. But no sense making too much of it. How's that?" Did she sound mature or what?

He smiled. "A relief. Although, I gotta tell you, you're screwin' with my head, darlin'."

"Not for long. Once we pick up Janie and Matt, the focus will shift to the soap opera star in our midst. Prepare yourself for tears."

"Will do."

"Although she may have matured now that she's a mother."

"You're joking, right?"

Liv shrugged. "I was being polite." Janie hadn't sounded very mature on the phone with her sobbing and screaming.

"Okay, so we'll brace ourselves. The kid's probably used to her hysteria by now anyway. How old is he?"

"Threeish. He has four given names—Matthew Tabor Carter Nicholas—so he could be just a tad spoiled."

"Like his mother."

"So we're on the same page."

"In so many ways, babe," he said with a wicked grin.

In an effort to still her wildly beating heart, she said, businesslike and cool, "I'd better call my working partner before we get to the Hilton. I'll let Chris know that I'm going to be home later than I thought." Keep everything in perspective, she warned herself. He was talking about sex. It wasn't about beating hearts.

"So, does Chris live on your farm?" Jake asked as she flipped her phone shut after a brief conversation with her vintner. Why it mattered, he chose not to examine.

"Sort of."

"What does that mean?" Realizing his voice had sharpened, he quickly said, "Sorry—I was outta line to ask."

"Actually, Chris and his wife live across the road on a small property I own. She's still in law school, so they're living frugally. The house is small; it was originally a log cabin that was enlarged."

After hearing the word *wife*, Jake's good humor resurfaced, and the smile he turned on Liv could have melted stone. "It's nice you have backup."

"I don't like to impose on Chris too much, though. He has his hands full with the wine making."

So if she stayed over, she wouldn't necessarily have to drive home at the crack of dawn, Jake thought. "I understand," he politely replied. But he found himself contemplating a lazy morning in bed with her. "Then again," he softly added, "if you were to give Chris a heads-up, you might be able to stay for breakfast next time. I make a pretty good apple-cinnamon French toast."

"Maybe I could," she said with feigned calm. No way was she going to appear overeager with Jake's old flame, Janie, waiting for him at the Hilton.

"Perfect," he said, like it was a done deal.

Nine

It took a few moments for Liv to calm herself after his invitation to stay for breakfast, delivered as it was in that low, sexy tone. Not to mention his done-deal certainty that conjured up in her mind delicious images that had nothing to do with food. But calm herself she did, because sex was sex. It wasn't the Taj Mahal in moonlight. Particularly with a perennial bachelor like Jake.

It helped that one of her favorite songs came on the radio, diverting her attention from her body's much too eager-beaver desires. Thank God for Terri Clark reminding her of what bad-ass men could do to your peace of mind. By the time she turned into the Hilton Hotel drive, she was more or less in control of her emotions.

Fortunately. Because the second Liv pulled up to the front door, Janie came flying through the double doors with little Matt in tow. She was red-eyed from crying, waving frantically. But however stressed, she'd managed to put herself together in a colorful Narciso Rodriguez slacks outfit that was screamingly out of place at an airport Hilton.

"The drama queen," Jake murmured, reaching for the door handle. "Take a deep breath."

"Gotcha."

As they exited the truck, Janie cried out in a voice that would have carried to the last balcony at La Scala, "Jake! Liv! You've *saved* my *life!*"

The few other guests getting cabs for early flights swiveled around to stare, Janie's ringing words delivered with soap opera histrionics.

Running toward them on jeweled sandals, Janie mustered up a quivering smile that would have been labeled as one of quiet desperation in drama class. "You don't know how *absolutely grateful* I am to have you *both* come and get me! How *perfect!*"

As she reached them, she hugged them both with the fervor of someone rescued from a desert island, while her son stared up at Liv and Jake with the caution children afforded strangers.

Taking note of Matt's uncertainty, Liv bent down and murmured, "Hi, I'm Liv. I'm a friend of your mother's. What's *your* name?"

"Sweetheart, say hello to Liv!" Janie prompted. "He's only three, don't expect much," she added in a murmur. "His nanny can barely speak English. Leo wanted Matt to learn French."

And sure enough, little Matt said, *"Bonjour,"* with a toddler lisp.

Squatting down so he wasn't intimidating, Jake smiled. *"Bonjour, mon ami,"* he said and was rewarded with a wide smile.

Matt nodded and smiled as Jake continued speaking in French, and before long he allowed Jake to pick him up. Turning to his mother, Matt lisped, "We're doing to det toys."

"That sounds like fun." Running her hand down Jake's arm, Janie softly purred, "You always were such a darling."

"My brother has a boy about Matt's age," Jake said, ignoring Janie's seductive purr. "I know Toys "R" Us is a hit for any kid."

"Is that so. I'm sure Matt will enjoy the experience." Janie was more au courant on couture design than toy stores, but in her wronged-woman frame of mind, her husband became the arch villain apropos toys as well. "Leo insisted on nothing but educational toys. He was such a control freak about everything, including Matt." She exhaled a little plaintive sigh. "I can't tell you how much I appreciate you being here for me." She offered them a small, wounded smile. "I don't know what I would have done without you coming to my rescue."

"Hey, what are friends for?" Liv said kindly. And Janie's drama aside, Liv knew she'd do the same for her.

"Why don't we get out of here?" Jake suggested. "And let these people get on with their lives." He nodded toward the silent crowd that had assembled to watch the drama.

Janie immediately posed for imaginary cameras. "My goodness. Where did everyone come from?" If there was a spotlight, Janie liked to be center stage.

"They're probably catching early flights." No way was he going to mention the scene she'd made, when making scenes was one of her favorite activities. "Do you have luggage?"

"Over there." She pointed at a bellman standing beside a cart

piled high with green Hermes luggage. "Leo hadn't discontin-
ued my charge cards yet, so I did a little shopping before we left
New York. Thank heaven you have a big truck, Liv. Really, it
must be fate, although my astrologer said as much this morning
when I called her. She said today would be a very good day
for me. And sure enough, I have my two dearest friends with
me," Janie added in a little breathy voice. "Actually, you never
did say how you two happened to be together"—her suddenly
narrowed gaze flicked from one to the other—"so *early* in the
morning?"

"Business," Liv quickly replied. "I was delivering my wines to
Jake's restaurant."

Jake shot Liv a look but didn't blow her story. "Liv gets up
early, and I didn't sleep last night. It worked out well."

Janie's perfect brows arched upward. "You're a long way
from L.A."

"I'm opening a new restaurant here. An experiment of sorts."
There was no point in going into the circumstances that had
brought him to Minneapolis. "Are we set to go?" Without waiting for an answer, Jake moved toward the truck with Matt.

After setting Matt in the backseat of Liv's crew cab and buck-
ling him in, Jake helped the bellman load the luggage, and
before long they were on their way to Toys "R" Us, Janie and Liv
in front, Jake squeezed into the backseat with Matt.

When Jake and Matt returned to the truck after shopping,
Matt was all smiles, Jake was carrying three large bags, and all
was right in one little three-year-old's world.

Meanwhile, Janie had filled in Liv on the travails of married
life, particularly about how the needs of a rich, temperamental,
egocentric husband always had to take precedence.

The recital made Liv appreciate the blessings and virtues of her single life.

The Bakery on Grand where two young chefs offered one of the better breakfast menus in town was their second stop. Jake ate as though he hadn't eaten in days, Liv not far behind in terms of putting away food. Matt was content with pancakes in the shapes of bunnies and hot chocolate. Janie picked at her frittata and drank espresso. Maintaining a size two figure did not allow overindulgence.

After breakfast, Liv dropped off Jake at his restaurant.

"Let me know if you need any help," he said, standing at Liv's open window.

Janie leaned forward so she could offer him a sultry smile. "What kind of help, darling?" she murmured in her best femme fatale voice.

"Not that kind, Janie. You're married."

"Since when did you get scruples?"

Jake nodded at Matt. "Bring Matt down sometime, and we'll play video games."

Her brows drew together in a faint frown. "If you're worried about Matt's psyche, I've already talked to my lawyer about the divorce. He said if Leo isn't obstinate, I'll be free in a couple months."

Jake smiled politely. "Good for you. Thanks for driving, Liv. I'll give you a call with my next order." He had a feeling he'd be buying more Minnesota wines than he'd planned.

"Okeydokey. Have a good day." Putting the truck into gear, Liv drove away quickly before something was said that might make Janie suspicious. Not that Liv felt she had to hide anything;

it was just simpler not having to explain last night. Not that there was anything to explain. They'd had sex, and that was that. It wasn't a federal case.

Fortunately for Liv's mild unease, Janie was focused on herself, as usual. She kept up a running commentary on Leo's numerous faults as they drove through downtown, although she was careful to speak in a muted tone. And since Janie was in the mood to vent, not listen to advice, Liv was required only to nod from time to time or murmur a consoling phrase.

By the time they'd reached the suburbs, Matt had fallen asleep. After tucking her jacket under his head for a pillow, Janie sat back down and really began giving up the dirt on her philandering husband.

Wow, Liv thought, after the twentieth exposé of Leo's marital misconduct. Not that she wasn't aware of how the rich and famous lived their lives. Rules weren't made for men like Leo Rolf; they were pretty much self-centered pricks. From the sounds of it, he'd grown tired of his fourth wife and was in the market for number five. Not that Janie had known how serious he was about it until it was too late. "You had a few good years anyway," Liv offered sympathetically. "And you have a darling little boy. You always wanted a child. Look on the bright side, sweetie; you'll end up with enough money so you won't have to work again if you don't want to. That can't be all bad." What could she say? Certainly not the truth. Like, *I never would have married the shit in the first place—money or no money.*

"I know. I keep telling myself that." Exhaling softly, Janie added, "There is a little something I haven't mentioned."

Here it comes, Liv thought. Somewhere in the back of her

mind, she'd figured as much. She hadn't heard from Janie for years. "How little?" she asked, not that she didn't already know the word *little* was a major euphemism.

"It depends on whether he finds us or not."

"He—meaning Leo?"

Janie nodded. "I called you because I'd heard you'd gone back home, and I knew you lived in some small town out in the middle of nowhere. I need to hide out until all the divorce details can be worked out."

"Hide out?"

"Leo's going to want custody of Matt."

"You don't have a prenup?"

"Hel-lo."

"Yeah, I figured you did."

"Not that it matters. Leo's threatened to fight for custody, prenup or not. He did that with his second wife and won full custody of their daughter. Lisa not only lost her daughter but was left practically penniless after she paid her lawyers."

"You talked to her?"

"I ran into her at a charity fund-raiser, and she made a point of warning me. She's married again."

"Someone with money, I presume, if she was at a charity fund-raiser."

"Of course."

Janie's reply was couched in the don't-be-stupid tone of a woman who hadn't married for love. *Silly me,* Liv thought. "What makes you think Leo won't find you at my place?"

"Matt and I have false passports. Our housekeeper despises Leo, and she has a friend who has a friend—you know, that sort of thing. It was simple. I called her the instant I found out that Leo had locked me out, and she gave me the address of this person in Queens. Naturally, she couldn't let me into the apartment, or she'd lose her job, but she packed up my jewelry and sent it out with the houseboy. Anyway, we used the passports to buy our tickets, so we're completely incognito."

Liv was thinking she was getting into a whole lot of trouble with talk of false passports and vengeful husbands. Not to mention, she'd seen Leo Rolf throw his weight around once at a dinner party in New York. It had not been a pretty sight.

"You talked to your lawyer about this, and he's on board?"

"Well . . . sort of."

"Sort of how?"

"I told him I was going home to stay with my mother."

"The mother you haven't spoken to in years?"

"I thought it sounded sensible. I gave him your number, though, in case he has to get in touch with me."

Great. It wasn't that she wouldn't help, but she could already see all the machinations in play that were so Janie. Her perceptions weren't always in line with reality. In fact, rarely. "Let's hope your lawyer can handle Leo if he decides to play hardball."

"Brad is one of the best"—Janie smiled—"and he's really sweet, too. He said not to worry about a thing. He's in the ring for me. Did I say he just got divorced?"

"No. Is that good?"

"Possibly. I'm not ruling out anything. He's handsome and much younger than Leo. I don't plan on marrying an older man again."

Not unless he's really rich, Liv silently reflected. But she wasn't going to be judgmental just because they had divergent views on life. They'd been friends a long time. "Well, let's hope that Leo doesn't figure out where you are, and everything will be copesetic."

"Minnesota is outside Leo's radar. It would never cross his mind that I'd come here."

"No doubt. Most of our visitors come to fish or hunt."

"Eeewww. Well, for sure that's not Leo. He doesn't even eat fish. You know, I feel very clever having thought of such an out-of-the-way locale," Janie smugly noted. "What *do* you do all day in a place like this?"

"I have a small vineyard, so I work."

Janie's brows lifted high. "Really. You actually, like, dig in the dirt and whatever in your vineyard?"

Liv smiled. "Actually, yes. I like it."

"That explains why you were talking about delivering wines to Jake. He's gorgeous as ever, isn't he? There are times," Janie murmured, "when I wonder if I made a mistake walking out on him. Is he hooked up with anyone here?"

"He just arrived last week. I don't know about his women." It wasn't a lie; she didn't have a clue.

"He's going to be enormous fun to have around. Jake is always up for anything. Nor do I believe for a minute," Janie said with a soft snort, "that a woman's marital status is a deterrent for him. In Hollywood, the land of revolving-door marriages, he was up to his neck with offers from all kinds of women. He was probably just being polite because he doesn't know you very well."

Actually, in some ways he did know her well. Not that Liv was about to parse words when they *were* more or less strangers. Although, certainly, those circumstances could change, she thought, smiling.

"What are you smiling about?"

"I like this song," she lied. The radio had been playing softly in the background.

"Me, too. Leo had that band play at my birthday party last year. The lead singer is sooo hot. Leo almost went ballistic when I flirted with Richie."

It appeared there might be more than one side to this divorce story, Liv decided. She'd seen Janie in action more than once when she zeroed in on some guy. And men like Leo who purchased trophy wives didn't like to play second string to some sexy, young, hired-help rock star.

There were rules in the cash-for-beauty game.

And the person with the money held all the cards.

Not that she had to involve herself in Leo's problems.

She had plenty of her own now that Janie was moving in.

Ten

"Get—me—Roman!" Leo punctuated each word with a fist to his polished desktop. "That fucking bitch Janie is *gone*!" he bellowed, glaring at his assistant who had come running at the screaming summons from his boss. "That cunt Betsy McCall—all sugar-sweet and malicious—just called to tell me she'd seen Janie at the airport yesterday. Janie had the fucking *balls* to take Matt out of New York! Don't just *stand* there! Fucking *do* something!"

Ben began backing toward the door. "I'll get right on it, sir," he said with the blank look he'd learned to cultivate at times like this when Leo was going off the deep end.

Since he'd been given the orders to have the locks on the apartment changed, Janie's departure didn't come as a huge surprise to Ben. But then Leo only had one point of view—his own—which put him at a disadvantage at times like this when a modicum of empathy would have been useful.

"If she thinks for a second she's going to have Matt, I've got a news flash for her!" Leo shrieked, like the madman he was. "Matt is *my* goddamn *son*! *Mine Goddammit! Mine! Mine! Mine!*"

Leo Rolf's face and bald pate were beet red edging toward purple, the violence of his temper, as always, disconcerting to those who were sane. Ben was almost to the exit of the mammoth office overlooking the East River. "I'll see that Roman gets here ASAP, sir," he said, hoping like hell Leo didn't have a stroke right before his eyes. With Leo, there would always be that moment of hesitation about whether or not to call an ambulance. Like when Stalin lay dying and everyone in the politburo sat around playing cards instead of calling the doctor.

Leo Rolf was that kind of guy.

Not well loved.

But the perks of Ben's position were hard to pass up. Trips around the world in Leo's private jet, reservations at all the best hotels, meetings with world leaders who needed Leo's particular brand of financial acumen and contacts. Ben Connor figured in five years his stock portfolio would allow him to retire and live like a king.

The instant Ben exited what he had come to refer to as the loony bin, he felt his shoulder muscles release what felt like fifty pounds of tension. Exhaling a sigh of relief, he quickly moved to his desk and punched in Roman Novak's number on his speed dial. Roman was Leo's go-to man who operated on the fringes of the law and did what was required of him, no questions asked. He could hack into the Pentagon if necessary and had a couple times when Leo wanted to know about contract bids from competitors. The defense industry was big money for Leo. Not that his pharmaceutical stock wasn't doing well, too, along with his development sites on the East River and his new inroads into the Chinese market.

Roman picked up, curtailing Ben's musing. "Crisis time. Leo wants you here five minutes ago."

"What's up?"

Roman always spoke calmly, like nothing ever rattled him. Although, Ben thought, if he was as big as Roman, maybe he could afford to be calm, too. "Here's the picture." Ben didn't even try to sanitize the situation. In Roman's line of work he'd seen it all. "Leo had the locks on his apartment changed yesterday when Janie and Matt were at the gym. Funny—she got mad about it and took off with Matt. He wants you to find his son and bring him back. Janie is expendable, of course. Leo will fill you in when you get here."

"They left yesterday?"

"Apparently. He's in an explosive mood. Just a warning."

"I'll be there as soon as I can get through traffic."

Ben hid in his office until Roman arrived, praying Leo wouldn't shriek for him again. When Leo's eyes were bulging like that and he was approaching that shade of eggplant, he wasn't thinking too clearly. Ben didn't want to get fired for saying the wrong thing, and with Leo in one of his out-of-control moods, even commenting on the weather could be a major blunder.

When Roman Novak strode into the office twenty minutes later, Ben looked up and exhaled, "Thank God," like he'd been rescued from the Black Hole of Calcutta.

His relief was so obvious, Roman grinned. "Relax, kid. Leo's just like all the rest of the big shots. A bully when he has his money and backup behind him, but not so brave when it's mano a mano with someone his own size, if you know what I mean."

"Easy for you to say." Roman was a very large ex-NYPD detective who had boxed professionally as a youth. Still pretty much ripped beneath his custom Armani, he was capable of intimidating just about anyone.

Roman flashed a smile, all white teeth and good humor. "I hope you're stashing away some of Leo's money, kid. Then you can get out eventually, like his latest wife just did."

"I doubt he's planning on Janie getting out without a down-and-dirty slugfest. He's really pissed she took *his* son as he puts it."

"I always thought Leo had scored way above his pay grade with Janie. She's damned nice. Too bad he didn't have sense enough to know when he had a good thing. Don't let him give you a heart attack though. He's all bluster."

"That might be, but he's really into orbit over this. You know how he feels about his kids. Christ—the money he spent to gain custody of Sarah would have financed a third-world nation."

"And the only reason he finally won that case was because Lisa was stupid enough to do cocaine in front of a photographer. Dumb shit."

"She *was* a little ditzy."

"She's dumb as a post. Period. Little Janie has quite a few more smarts." Roman nodded toward Leo's office. "Tell him I'm here." Then, without waiting for Ben to make the call, he walked to the door, shoved it open and, entering the sunlit room with the East River view, said in his deep, calm voice, "Hey, dude, your fixer is here."

"It's about fucking time!"

"My price goes up when people scream at me," Roman murmured, shutting the door and standing perfectly still.

"Sorry." Leo waved his hands in a dismissive gesture. "I'm just so fucking teed off. Come, sit down." Another wave, indicating a chair. "You heard. Janie left with Matt."

"I heard you changed the locks on the apartment," Roman said, moving toward the chair.

Leo shrugged. "She began to bore me."

"That must mean you have someone else in mind."

Leo smiled faintly. "Maybe I do."

"You're gonna be right up there with Liz Taylor's marital record if you keep this up," Roman noted, sitting down. "Why the hell do you marry them all? It's the twenty-first century. Haven't you heard of cohabitation?"

"Call me old-fashioned."

More like controlling, Roman thought. Four times married and counting was not exactly what you'd call old-fashioned values. Unless you had Henry the Eighth in mind as a role model. "Whatever you say, Leo." He wasn't a therapist. "So what do you want from me?"

"Find her, naturally, and bring my son back."

"That could be construed as kidnapping."

"Don't shit me. Since when are you concerned with legalities?"

"Since I'd be scaring the hell out of your kid. He's pretty young to be yanked out of his mother's arms by a stranger."

"Bring them both back, then. I'll deal with her myself."

"Do you have any idea where they might have gone?"

"Not a clue." Leo grimaced. "That's why I need you."

Leaning back in his chair, Roman held Leo's gaze. "So who's the new woman?"

Leo smiled. "One of our interns."

"That's getting pretty young." Leo was officially late fifties but actually mid-sixties. Tanned and semitoned by a personal trainer, he liked to think he didn't look his age.

"So?"

Roman shrugged. "So nothing, I guess." He came to his feet. "I'll give you a call when I know something."

*As Roman exited Leo's office, Ben shot him a raised-*eyebrows look. "Has he calmed down?"

"Semi. Who's the new babe in his life?"

"Hannah Reiss. A tall, leggy blonde, big boobs—maybe real. She doesn't want to work all her life."

"I see. And Leo took the bait."

"She's good-looking, sharp, smooth as silk. Anyone would take the bait, but she didn't put out for anyone in middle management. She went straight to the top."

"Jeez. And I suppose he believes her when she tells him he's great in the sack."

"Fucking a. Leo eats up her phony flattery; they giggle on the phone. It's disgusting."

"You shouldn't listen in on conversations."

"You should talk. Anyway, it's self-preservation."

"You *have* lasted longer than the others."

Ben grinned. "I have the bloody record, and you know it."

Roman smiled. "Can't argue there. Not that I'm any different than anyone else. I put up with him and take his money, too, just like this new little Hannah Reiss is gonna do."

"She's not little. She's pushing five ten. Them together is like Tom Cruise and Katie Holmes. I figure any day now, Leo's going to get lifts. So, are you bringing his kid back or what?"

"I don't know. Maybe."

Ben's gaze narrowed. "You didn't tell him that."

"I don't tell him anything." Leo's go-to guy lifted his hand in a casual wave. "I'll stay in touch."

Eleven

That evening, after Matt had been tucked into bed, Liv and Janie sat on the porch, watching the moon come up and drinking a glass of wine.

"I really can't thank you enough for your hospitality, Liv. Matt adores your farm—your dogs and kittens and horses. It's perfect for him. I'm feeling as though I can really decompress here."

"You're more than welcome. And Matt's a darling—really—he's sweet as can be. There's a lake not far from here, too, if you get bored. They have swimming lessons in the summer for the kids. He might like that."

"Thanks. Maybe we'll try it. And thanks, too, for listening to me all day. I talked you to death, I know, but it's been quite a while since I could vent. Leo always had so much staff around, you were never sure if someone might be listening to your conversation."

"Not a problem. It sounds as though Leo's been a major pain."

"A vast understatement." Janie made a small moue. "I have a feeling he's found someone else, though. Not that I'm surprised."

"Since *you* were in the wings before he divorced his last wife, you probably shouldn't be."

Janie sighed faintly. "I know. I just thought maybe I'd be different. Not too bright of me, I suppose. Although, the way Leo's been screaming and carrying on and making my life difficult lately, I can't lie and say I'm heartbroken. It's actually a relief to have it over."

"What are the chances he might roll over on this divorce?"

Janie snorted.

"That's what I thought. His last custody fight was vicious." Liv smiled. "I hope you haven't done any drugs with photographers nearby."

"God no. I'm not that stupid. Lisa, on the other hand—well you saw what happened. She lost her daughter. I'm not about to do anything that'll jeopardize custody of Matt. There *is* another little thing, though, I probably should mention." Janie put up a calming hand. "Don't worry. It has nothing to do with drugs. And it's not actually *little*. It's life-sized and should arrive tomorrow."

"Okay, you have my interest. Just one question. Will anyone be going to jail for this *little thing*?"

"Technically, it's mine—so, no."

"Somehow that's not reassuring. How about in terms of the letter of the law? Will a court agree with you?"

"If possession is nine-tenths of the law, it will."

"Jeez," Liv muttered. "So what of Leo's did you steal?" Janie had always looked on things she wanted with a flexible attitude apropos actual ownership details. When they'd shared an apartment, Janie had always conveniently overlooked whose dress was whose. Or shoes. Or jewelry. Or on occasion even the money in Liv's wallet.

"We had Hockney paint portraits of us shortly after we were married. I just took mine with me, that's all. Leo's going to say he paid for them, but I figure they're half mine, and I took my half."

"*David* Hockney?"

Janie nodded.

"So this portrait you took is worth what? Two, three mil?"

"Probably," Janie said under her breath. "But why should I leave my portrait behind for Leo to sell or put into storage somewhere?"

"Weren't you locked out? How did you get your hands on it?"

"Because I'm a very lucky person, that's how," Janie brightly replied. "The portraits had just been sent to MoMA for an upcoming exhibit. I simply asked for mine back, although, I must say, the curator wasn't very gracious about it. I had to resort to screaming and threats." She smiled. "Men never like when women scream in public. He caved, and then I watched while they crated it up and personally saw it put in a FedEx truck. You'll really like it, by the way. I'm wearing my Rick Owens little black suit, and you know how his clothes all drape so naturally and flatter the body. I must say I look fabulous. I saw no reason to leave that gorgeous portrait behind."

Liv could see the headlines now: "Stolen Multimillion Dollar Painting Found in Minnesota Barn."

"How soon before Leo sends out the gendarmes for you or, more precisely, for Matt and the Hockney painting?"

"They're probably looking for us already. But, really, with our false passports and your remote location, I really think we're safe. As for the painting, Leo won't know I took it from MoMA. He's totally uninterested in museums, and the curator was too intimidated to even bring up the fact that I'd been there."

"That all sounds good," Liv politely replied, figuring harsh reality would impinge on Janie's dream world soon enough. Leo had been both relentless and ruthless in his last custody fight. There was no reason to think he'd be any different in Matt's case. But time enough for cynicism in the morning. Picking up the bottle of wine, she smiled. "More wine?"

"Yes, please. Your wine tastes so-o-o good. Do you have a marketer or an advertising agency working for you? I know a few people who could make you rich with this fabulous wine."

"Thanks," Liv said, refilling Janie's glass, "but I prefer my boutique label and hand-selling. This operation is more hobby than serious."

"You always did save all your money. I suppose you're set financially."

"I have enough to live on, which was the point of working so hard those years when I was in demand."

"But you quit long before you would have had to."

"As soon as my finances allowed, I was gone. That was the plan."

Janie sighed. "You always were so sensible. Unlike me. I haven't saved a penny."

"Don't sweat it. That's what a lawyer is for. He'll get you a nice settlement."

"So Brad says, although I'm not so sure. Leo always has to win at everything."

"He can't *always* win. He has to lose sometime."

"You think?"

Suddenly Janie looked frightened and unsure, her bravado gone. "You said you have a good lawyer. You have Matt with you. With luck, Leo won't find you here. I'd say you're holding a winning hand."

Janie's smile reappeared. "Thanks. You always could cheer me up. Remember that time they fired me from the soap, and you calmed me down and told me what to say to get my job back?"

"See, things *can* work out," Liv soothed. "They did then, and they will now. Don't worry. Call your lawyer in the morning, tell him you're safely settled in a *remote location*," she said with a grin. "But let him know you have that Hockney painting—if you haven't already told him. You don't want to be thrown in jail over some legal technicality. Leo would use it against you like he did with that photo of Lisa doing blow."

"You always think so rationally. Thanks for the good advice. What time is it, anyway? Can I still call Brad? He *did* say I could call him day or night," she added, answering her own question.

"Then call him. Ask him what to do with the painting. You'll sleep better knowing all the facts."

Twelve

Liv could have used some of her own advice about knowing the facts and sleeping better, because she was having serious trouble falling asleep. When she should have been getting a good night's rest for her busy day tomorrow, she was tossing and turning, kept awake by persistent memories of Jake Chambers looping through her brain.

When she shouldn't be thinking of him at all.

Because—realistically—she and Jake Chambers had had a good time, but that's all it was: a good time.

It would never do to become infatuated with him because he was incredible in bed. The long list of women before her who had enjoyed his sexual favors suggested infatuation would be a waste of time.

As for an actual relationship, it was not only ludicrous but lunatic to even contemplate such a thing after one night of sex, however mind-blowing.

There. Really. She was a mature adult. She was capable of separating lust from fantasy. More importantly, she did not, nor had she ever, had fantasies about *any* man. Period.

Maybe she could fall back on the same excuse as Jake. She was tired, not thinking straight. In the morning—if she could ever get to sleep—her world would return to normal. Her vineyard, winery, and the work she loved would suppress the tumultuous moonlight madness keeping her awake.

Jake had spent the day sleeping, so when he woke up at eight, he knew he was going to be up for the night. For the next few hours, he worked on some rough sketches for remodeling the restaurant. Nothing major. The main dining area didn't need much altering, but he would be adding the sports bar he'd always wanted, and that would entail more substantial changes. Walking downstairs, he eyeballed the dimensions of the spaces, the position of the windows overlooking the river, considered the possibility of adding a terrace outside, decided the east wall would probably have to be knocked out to make the bar area larger.

He wanted his River Joint to be like the bars he'd hung out in back home in Seattle: neighborhood places where people could relax, eat good food, visit with friends. He'd been thinking about his menu for a long time, probably as long as his discontent with the razzle-dazzle world he'd inhabited for so many years had been simmering in his brain. He wanted a menu heavy in *small plates* so customers could taste a variety of foods and flavors. And he wanted a bar menu that ran the gamut from Bud to private-label liquor with wines from speciality vineyards.

He made lists on top of lists, e-mailed more of his suppliers on the West Coast, decided about eleven that it wasn't too early to call some vineyards in France. An hour later, he set down the phone, having ordered several hundred cases of his favorite wines.

It was nearly midnight, he was hungry, and the small niggling thought he'd been able to keep at bay with constant activity suddenly surfaced.

He literally muttered, "No," aloud, rose from his chair overlooking the river, and hied himself upstairs to his kitchen. He'd make himself something to eat, then maybe go for a walk. He was *not* going to call Liv Bell only hours after leaving her. He wasn't some horny adolescent who couldn't control himself. So get a grip.

That stern admonition lasted ten minutes—maybe less. Whether he liked it or not, his cock had other ideas, and his sex drive being what it was, he struggled to keep himself in line. With considerable effort he restrained himself from calling her, flipping through the channels on cable instead, looking for distractions.

Wouldn't you know—nothing appealed.

For five minutes more, he tried to talk himself out of obsessing over having sex with Liv again. It was totally bizarre how he couldn't get her out of his mind. It wasn't as though he hadn't fucked plenty of beautiful, blonde models before.

So what was the freaking problem?

Was it some voodoo magic? Yeah, right.

Was he just flying high now that he was living his long-unrealized dream? Possibly.

Was Liv Bell hotter than other women? Absolutely.

So there. A simple answer. It was just pure lust. Nothing to angst over. He was experiencing basic male urges. Although his fierce impatience to assuage them did give him pause. For maybe another two seconds.

He glanced at the clock. Midnight. Fuck—it was late.

He picked up the phone anyway and hit 411 for information.

A few moments later, having received her number, he waited for the connection to click through.

Liv answered on the first ring.

"Did I wake you?"

"I should say yes, but no, you didn't. For some reason, I can't sleep." She wasn't about to say he was the reason nor that her pulse rate had accelerated big time on hearing his voice.

"Same here. Although I slept all day, so I'm not exactly tired. How are Janie and Matt doing?"

"Good. They're sleeping." Is that why he called? Hoping to talk to Janie?

"So what are you doing?"

"Trying to sleep."

"I've been thinking about you."

"I admit you've been in my thoughts, too."

"How far is it out there?"

"It's too far. An hour."

"I drive fast."

"You shouldn't. It's really late, and I have to work tomorrow."

"You mean it?"

"No."

"Give me directions."

She lay in bed after she hung up, shaking faintly, wondering what had come over her that the mere sound of his voice could make her feverish with longing. She'd never believed such feelings actually existed, that another person could provoke such spine-tingling sensations. When other women had talked about the breathless ecstasy some man provoked in them, she'd always thought they were overemotional wing nuts.

Apparently, she'd been wrong.

Which was good and bad. Good, because what she was feeling was fantastic. But not so good that she was wildly out of control.

She'd never been that kind of person.

The man behind the wheel of Chaz's silver gray BMW was speeding north with one eye out for the highway patrol. Less introspective by habit as well as circumstance—in this case, his rock-hard cock was serving as power player—he was pretty much focused on consummation. Issues of restraint or the lack thereof would have to wait until a more coolheaded time.

He glanced at the clock on the dash, flicked his gaze upward to check out the rearview mirror, then quickly surveying the wide-open road before him, punched the accelerator.

His voice of reason tried to make itself heard, clamoring, *Turn around, turn around, don't get involved!* But his libido was deaf to reason, or maybe the stereo, turned up high, drowned out admonitions to caution.

He had the windows down to the summer night, a prime song was singing the pleasures of foxy ladies and wild sex, and he was on his way to get some.

Let's see what this baby can do, he thought, flooring it.

What to wear, what to wear! Tossing the covers aside, Liv quickly rose from her bed and moved toward her closet, looking for inspiration. Should she greet him like this—naked? Or should she dress or wear a robe or maybe some sexy lingerie? Aaagh . . . stupid indecision, when in the past she wouldn't have given it a second thought. She would have welcomed him any which way. Dressed or undressed, sexy or not sexy, however the mood struck her. And now she was debating the minutia of sexual politesse as though she'd never had a man sleep over before.

Really, this was ridiculous.

She stopped just short of her closet, her decision made.

She'd put on an ordinary robe, like the blue seersucker one on her chair. Keep it casual. Don't make this something it isn't. Sex is sex is sex.

Or not, as it turned out.

Fortunately, it took Jake nearly an hour to reach Liv's farm, allowing her the opportunity to try on and discard a dozen different outfits. All of which were now—in her haste—tossed out of sight in her closet. Finally, glancing at the clock, she had no choice but to give it up and race downstairs. She wanted to wait on the porch in order not to wake Matt or Janie.

Just as she stepped outside, car headlights appeared at the entrance to her drive.

She stood at the top of the stairs as the car approached and came to rest at the edge of her lawn. She didn't move as Jake stepped out and walked toward her unless the faint tremble in her hands counted. When he stopped at the bottom of the stairs and smiled up at her, she thought she might come just looking at him. He was consummate male machismo limned by moonlight. Powerful and assured in what she was coming to recognize as his uniform of jeans and a white T-shirt, he looked up at her with lady-killer eyes.

"Nice," he said, indicating her dress with a lift of his hand. "The age of innocence in moonlight." Her eyelet dress was pure white virginal chic.

"Thanks." She tried to keep her voice placid like his but didn't quite succeed. She touched the Dolce and Gabbana ruffled skirt with a shaky hand. "I didn't know what to wear," she added with a whisper-soft naivete that matched her little-girl dress.

It shouldn't have mattered to him that she was skittish and trembling. He shouldn't have felt so pleased she was turned on. After all, he'd come for himself, not her. As always. And, as always, he'd remembered to bring something because women liked presents. "Here," he said, mounting the stairs, holding out his hand.

He came to rest beside her a moment later, and she saw a small cabochon emerald suspended from a slender braided gold chain lying on his open palm.

"Sorry, it's not something better." He shrugged. "There aren't any shops open this time of night except 7-Eleven. I used these in a promotion once."

Nice promotion, she thought, recognizing Bulgari. "You didn't have to—but thanks." She lifted the necklace from his palm. "I'll think of you when I wear it."

A small silence fell, the sounds of crickets and frogs suddenly shrill in the night.

Fuck it, he thought. This wasn't business as usual; he might as well be honest. "I tried to stay away," he said. "And yet . . ."

She nodded. "I know. I couldn't sleep because of you."

His smile suddenly flashed white in the moonlight. "Glad to hear it."

She wrinkled her nose. "I'm not sure I like feeling this way."

His smile this time was sexy and sweet; they were both on the same crazy wavelength. "Maybe I could make you feel better," he said soft and low.

She gazed up at him from under her lashes. "No doubt."

He grinned. "I'll have you know I broke all the speed limits getting here."

"So I should stop equivocating."

He held her gaze. "I didn't know you were."

"But then you don't know much about me."

"How about I'm willing to learn."

"You're way too smooth."

He shook his head. "Believe me, I've never raced to see a woman in the middle of the night."

"So I'm not the only one losing it."

"Hell, no. I've been trying not to call you since I woke up"— he glanced at his watch—"five hours ago. Unsuccessfully, as you can see."

She smiled for the first time since his arrival. "We have to be quiet with Janie and Matt in the house."

He grinned. "I'm not the one who screams when they come."

"Very funny."

"Look—they won't even know I'm here." He took her hand in his. "Show me your bedroom."

"I thought you might have been calling to talk to Janie," she noted as he held the door open for her.

"I told you I wasn't interested in Janie."

"I know."

"I meant it."

"I'm glad."

Then she put her finger to her lips as they approached the stairs, and they didn't speak again until she shut her bedroom door behind them.

"Nice," he said, indicating her room with a wave of his hand. "Everything in one place."

She had a small office in one corner: desk, computer, file cabinet, bulletin board with wine brochures and catalogues tacked up. Under the farmhouse eaves, she'd had bookshelves built, crowded now with to-read possibilities. A row of blooming white gloxinia lined the top of the shelves. Embroidered white-on-white linen curtains were open, the windows raised high to let in the warm night air.

And then there was her bed.

She'd found it in an antique store shortly after she'd bought her place. She hadn't been looking for a bed. She'd already bought a serviceable one that would do just fine. In fact, the only reason she'd gone into the store along the highway in Wisconsin was because the sign outside had heralded Lavazza espresso. Now, she wasn't into psychic events, but seeing that bed smack-dab in the middle of the store when she walked in qualified as a bona fide mystical experience. She'd immediately fallen in love with it. The enormous size and flamboyant scrollwork of twined branches and delicate leaves reminded her of some whimsical fantasy.

She'd asked the price and, thinking she must have heard wrong, asked again.

The owner explained that it had been part of a stage set for Sarah Bernhardt on one of her American tours, so the price was partially predicated on the celebrity factor. "Try it out," the store owner had pleasantly offered, as if the lady had known the supernatural was seriously at work in her store that day.

When Liv had lain on the bed, she'd felt as though the bed had been made for her or she for it—a feeling of inexplicable comfort and joy had melted through her senses. Not that she didn't remind herself that she already had a bed *and* she had better places to spend her money. Like on her vineyard.

But it's so you, a little voice inside her head had cooed. *And doesn't it make you feel incredibly, outrageously good?*

Liv's stop for espresso had ended up costing her ten thousand dollars.

"That's one big bed," Jake said. "It must have come up in pieces."

Wasn't that just like a man. Nothing about its sculptural beauty or antique patina. "Actually, I had the windows taken out and had it hoisted in."

"It's old, right?"

"Yes." No point in mentioning the divine Sarah, she figured when he was talking practicalities.

"It suits you. All sumptuous swank. And I can actually stretch out. Not that I'm tired," he said with a small smile.

She smiled back. "You had me worried there for a minute."

"Rest easy, babe. I am *so* primed."

A small silence fell.

"Sorry," he murmured. "I didn't mean to raise alarms."

"No, you didn't. Look." She held up her hand so he could see the tremor. "I might be past you when it comes to being primed."

Curling his hand around hers, he brought it to his mouth and brushed a gentle kiss over her knuckles. "Everything's on your terms, babe," he murmured, his dark gaze direct. "Tell me to stop, I'll stop."

"Don't stop," she whispered, remembering the rapturous feel of him, the hard-ramming size, his wanting what she wanted as often as she. "And thanks for coming up."

He lifted his shoulder in the merest shrug. "I couldn't stay away," he said gruffly.

"You would have liked to, though."

Another shrug. "Not really."

Her brows rose. "I've never had such reluctant sex before."

The wariness left his eyes, replaced by a more familiar amusement. "Wrong word, babe. This is about insatiable. That's what's bothering me."

"So don't let it."

He grinned. "You mean—as long as I'm here."

"And I couldn't sleep."

"Not to mention my cock had a mind of its own."

"There you go. Obviously, we have no choice."

He gave her a quick, decisive nod.

Something about his sudden certainty and assurance sent a little shiver up her spine. Or maybe it was him suddenly dragging her against his body and the hard imprint of his erection that inspired her response. Not that she needed evidence of his carnal urgency to goad her. She'd gone sleepless the last many hours thinking about him.

Thinking about sex with him.

Thinking about feeling *this* inside her. Rubbing against his cock, back and forth, back and forth, she purred in anticipation.

Her message came through loud and clear—as if he didn't know what she liked and how she liked it. Moving backward the few steps to the bed, he sank down, pulling her with him. Sprawled on his back, he settled her astride his hips with a casual strength, shoved her skirt aside, slid his hand between her legs, and glanced up with a smile. "Convenient," he murmured, running his fingers over her slick pussy hospitably devoid of panties. "No waiting."

"Plan ahead," she said on a suffocated breath, his virtuoso touch ramping up every sexual receptor in the immediate vicinity.

He grinned. "Because you can never wait."

"Give me a break," she said, spurred on by sharply necessitous, totally wanton urges. "I've been thinking about this . . . a lot."

"Same here." His gaze flicked downward to his erection stretching waist-high.

"Perfect then," she said with soft finality and, taking matters into her own hands, reached out and unzipped his jeans. High-strung, impatient—really pretty much like she always seemed to be with Jake Chambers—she drew out his engorged penis, the swollen gleaming crest and hard, unyielding length sending a rush of liquid longing through her cunt. Perhaps having been forced to wait so long, or maybe simply driven by outrageous lust, without thought for her most basic rule, she forced his stiff cock upright, positioned her throbbing ready-to-party sex over the head of his cock, and began easing downward.

"Hey, hey, hold on." Grabbing her around the waist, Jake stopped her. "Give me a second to get a condom."

"Thanks," she whispered shakily, falling back on his thighs.

"Not a problem," he said, casual and polite when he could have wondered whether she was trying to make trouble for him, when he really might have if it had been anyone other than the genuine, shoot-from-the-hip Miss Bell. "Two seconds, babe . . . that's all I need." He'd already pulled a condom from his jeans pocket and was ripping open the packet.

She unconsciously licked her lips as he rolled the condom down his better-than-any-vibrator extremely large erection.

"Done." Equally impatient, he quickly pulled her up on her knees, guided his erection to her sex with a delicate finesse, and slowly slid his cock inside her. Since he planned on fucking her— at the minimum—all night, he exercised caution, not about to abrade or chafe her sensitive tissue. Gauging the receptive elasticity of her tight, little cunt, he penetrated her with measured restraint even as her breathy moans urged him on.

"More, more . . . more," she begged, trying to break his tight grip on her hips, wanting to feel him deeper, faster. Wanting him to cram her full.

"Take it easy," he whispered, brushing her hands away. "We have all night."

"I don't want to wait." After hours of contemplating this, she needed surcease to her flame-hot cravings; she needed to feel more of his erection buried inside her. She needed to come— soon. "Jake, please—*hurry*," she cried, struggling to break his hold as her orgasm began—too early, too soon—before he was completely submerged.

Fully aware of what was happening, he immediately dropped his hands from her hips, and she impaled herself on his erection so swiftly, her bottom jarred his balls. Not that he was complaining; it was a very gratifying jolt. After which, he had the pleasure of watching her and—even better—feeling her ride his dick to a precipitous orgasm.

Unlike darling Livvi, he wasn't into speed and, rigid inside her, he remained motionless as she uttered breathy sighs of orgasmic content, and her last piquant flutters of pleasure dissipated.

When she finally opened her eyes, he smiled at her. "Better now?"

Stretching lazily, she ran her fingers through her pale, tousled hair. "You didn't come."

"There's plenty of time. I'm not going anywhere."

A slow smile lifted the corners of her mouth. "So I have this . . . here"—she wiggled slightly on his erection—"for as long as I want?"

He grinned. "We're here for you, babe." He traced the delicate outline of her mouth with a fingertip. "How about another quick one, then we'll get undressed and do some serious fucking."

Her smile was pure sunshine. "This must be one of those times when everything's going my way."

"This way?" He swung his hips upward.

She gasped faintly, caught her breath and, leaning forward, placed her palms on his chest. "And this way, too," she murmured, swinging her bottom in a lazy circular motion so they both felt every delectable nuance of sensation.

"Are you on the pill?"

She wrinkled her nose. "Side effects."

"Too bad." For the first time in his life, he considered going condom free, an impulse so incredibly rash he immediately called himself every kind of stupid.

"Too bad? You gotta be kidding."

His brows flickered. "Consider it a moment of insanity."

"Just so you know," she said carefully, "I don't do sex au naturel."

"Me either—normally. Don't worry. We're cool."

"I'm glad you're not completely cool," she murmured, sliding upward on his cock, slowly descending again. "I'm glad he's still fired up."

As she slipped into a languid up-and-down rhythm, Jake's eyes went shut. He could talk about taking it slow, but he'd been thinking about fucking her since he'd left her that morning, and present reality far exceeded any abstract contemplation. With a soft groan on a particularly deep downstroke, he gave himself up to the full gravitas of sensation. Not that he didn't intuitively gauge the progress of her next climax, particularly since he planned on matching her simulcast. Which he did, meeting her in a blast-off of such monumental proportions, he didn't actually hear her screams that time.

Neither moved for so long afterward, they could have been participants in a tableau vivant. Like in the red-light district of Amsterdam.

But Jake managed to pull himself together first, because he wasn't about to admit that something of a cataclysmic nature had occurred. Nor that his heart was still racing like he'd run twenty miles. Male survival instinct forced him to move and, lifting Liv up and away, he set her on the bed beside him.

"I can't talk," she said in a wispy breath, every nerve in her body aglow with glorious satisfaction.

"Don't worry—I didn't come here to chat," he drolly replied. Sitting up, he stripped off his condom and came to his feet. Hitching up his jeans, he walked into the adjoining bathroom, discarded the condom, washed himself off, zipped up and, standing in front of the mirror, stared at himself as though expecting some obvious change.

Nope. Excellent. See? A physical high, no matter how staggering, didn't amount to some grand metamorphosis. Liv Bell was just hotter than most women, that's all.

His five-second therapy session having put him back on track, he returned to the bedroom, his plans unaltered.

Fuck until you drop, and then go home.

With that in mind, he undressed, sat down on the bed, and began to unbutton the top of Liv's ruffled dress.

"I need a break." Her eyes were still at half-mast, her voice hushed. "That was one supercharged climax."

"I'll just get you ready," he said, slipping one of her arms free of the chemise top. "Then you tell me when you want my cock inside you again."

His deep voice was utterly composed, as though he was willing to play affable stud to her passions. Why was it then that she felt as though it was she who was submissive to him?

Why did she feel as though he was master of this game?

Worse, why did she want his cock inside her the moment he brought up the subject?

Rising on her elbows, she gave him a charged look.

"Here, let me get this off," he said, ignoring her stare, freeing her other arm.

"Something's different."

"You got that right." He smiled. "I'm trying to ignore it."

"This is just good sex, right?"

"Ideally, yes."

"Then why—"

"Let's not go there." He smiled. "You have nice freckles," he added, brushing his finger over her cheek.

"Are you changing the subject?"

"Yes, I am."

"Because?"

"Because I don't talk about stuff like this, let alone actually think about it."

"Just like a man," she said, suddenly smiling, relieved by his answer, reminded that her yin/yang considerations weren't a sensible train of thought.

"What can I say? Sex-change is not an option for me. Lift up, babe, and I'll pull down this dress."

"What if I said no?"

"I'd figure you were playing hard to get," he said, sliding the dress down her hips and legs and tossing aside Dolce and Gabbana's irreverent take on chastity.

"What if I meant it?"

"But you don't."

"Maybe I don't like smug men. Have you thought of that?"

"Not much, considering your nipples are really hard," he murmured, touching one tip with exquisite gentleness. "I think you want to get screwed again."

"Know-it-all. I *should* say no."

Why would you even want to? he thought, but since there was no point in being rude at this stage of the game, he said instead with a grin, "But you won't, cuz you're polite."

She wrinkled her nose. "I wish."

"It really doesn't matter. Come on, relax," he said, lifting her against the pillows. Gently spreading her legs, he kneeled between them, cupped her breasts in his palms, bent his head, and sucked first on one nipple then the other until her cunt was aching, throbbing, pulsing with every beat of her heart. Until it was only a question of whether she was going to come with or without him inside her.

For a fraction of a second, she debated her outrageous willingness or his outrageous appeal. But just as she was deciding she should be less slavishly under his spell, that she could control her desires if she only put her mind to it, he slipped two fingers in her so-*so*-ready-for-action vagina, a streak of ravenous lust ripped through her fevered senses, and there was no longer any question of going it alone. "Jake, *now*," she fervently cried.

"In a minute." His voice in contrast was serene. Then he went back to sucking her nipples and massaging her G-spot and clit while she panted and squirmed and pleaded. Stopping his feel-good therapy just nanoseconds short of her liftoff to climax, he sat back on his heels. "Hey, babe—intermission."

It took her a moment to respond, to put sound and words in some reasonable frame of reference when she was totally absorbed in sensation. When she finally realized what he was doing, she said, "Don't be a prick."

She was right, and if he'd not been struggling with his own ungovernable cravings, he might not have given in to his baser

instincts. It was probably some Neanderthal defense mechanism—
having to be in control. Moving off the bed, he held out his hand.
"Come here, and I'll be as nice as you want."

She scowled. "No."

He shouldn't have felt such a lecherous rush at her unwilling-
ness. "Come on. I'll fuck you. You want that, don't you?"

Her indecision was palpable.

"Think of it as part of the game."

"What if I don't like your game?"

He smiled. "But you do."

Damn him for looking like some female fantasy: tall, powerful, too good-looking for even a smidgen of humility, with a cock
that literally stretched from crotch to waist and could have been
an ad for Viagra, since it was hard forever.

As if he could read her mind, he lightly traced the length of
his erection with his fingertip.

"I'll do this to you later," she muttered.

"What?"

"Make you wait."

"But you don't have to wait." He crooked his finger.

She scowled. "I could use my vibrator."

"Do that when I'm not here."

"Don't sound so sensible when you're pissing me off."

"Come on."

Who could refuse? Maybe someone with zero libido. Hers,
unfortunately, was operating at maximum capacity. Moving to
the edge of the bed, she took his hand and came to her feet.

"Over here," he said, detouring long enough to pull a condom
from his jeans pocket. Drawing her to an upholstered chair near

the window, he turned it around so the chair back faced the room. "Bend over this."

She didn't move.

"Do what you're told, babe, and I'll put my cock in you and make you come."

"Fuck you," she muttered, glaring at him.

"Or I could fuck you," he gently observed.

He shouldn't have felt such elation as she complied, bending facedown over the chair back. But her submission struck some perverted chord, his cock surged higher, and in compensation for his brute behavior he promised himself she could come as many times as she wished.

He had the condom in place a second later and, moving up to her prominently displayed sex, he grazed the gleaming pink flesh of her vulva with the tip of his erection, tracing her slippery, wet cleft from top to bottom. "Now, if you ask real nice, I might—"

Surging upright, she spun around, swung at him furiously, and would have landed a square punch on the jaw if he hadn't quickly sidestepped. As it was, she left a streak of scratches down his cheek. "Get out!" she snapped.

"No." He held his arms out. "I won't move this time. Take your best shot."

"I could call the cops," she muttered, steamed and breathing hard.

"Be my guest, but I'd rather stay, and we could take advantage of this." He glanced downward, his upthrust penis hard against his stomach.

She didn't answer, but her gaze was directed at a point below his waist.

"Look, I was out of line," he said very, very softly. "It won't happen again."

"Damn right it won't," she said with a little pout.

He was pretty much home free at that point, but he knew better than to gloat. And bottom line, it was to his advantage as well to reach rapprochement. "Just an observation," he said, with utmost diplomacy, "and I offer it as a suggestion only, but if you'd care to give that chair a try, I can guarantee you'll like it."

"Is this in your play book?"

"I don't have a play book," he said, ultrapolitely. "Call it a hunch."

"Hmph."

"Come on, babe," he softly cajoled. "You and I both know we're operating under some goddamned irresistible mind fuck. I promise not to give orders."

She looked at his engorged cock, then at him, her gaze still partially shuttered. "So you're telling me this is going to feel better than usual."

"I have no idea about what's usual for you, but let's just say I'm pretty sure you'll like it. And I'm sorry, okay?" Although he was mostly sorry, she'd become an obsession for him.

She smiled faintly. "You can be damned polite."

"I usually am. That other stuff—consider it an aberration. Not to be repeated."

"Sounds good," she said briskly. "Show me what you've got."

Bitch. She was deliberately goading him. But never one to let anger get in the way of mind-blowing sex, he said, polite as hell, "Sure thing, sweetheart."

He was less polite a moment later as he rammed his cock into her cunt. Not that she seemed to mind, if her breathy cries were any indication. Nor did he get the feeling he'd be leaving any-time soon as she eagerly lifted her bottom in anticipation of his downstrokes, uttered high-pitched, feverish screams when he buried his cock in her, and came so many times he lost count.

Eventually, collapsed over the chair back, she whispered, "Stop."

Good, he thought. There was only so much wear and tear one condom could take. Not that he intended to be entirely selfless.

His own climax was relatively quick; he'd been curtailing his orgasm for damn near a record length of time. But quick didn't mean it didn't pack a wallop.

The record this time was one of intensity.

Like a stage-two hurricane.

Or a boiler exploding.

Or the exquisite feel of a woman who was doing a real number fucking up his purposefully independent life.

Not that he was giving much thought to cerebral issues when there were hours yet till morning. And he had plans.

Thirteen

Roman had interviewed the staff at Leo's apartment. The housekeeper knew something. But apparently, loyal to Janie, she was unwilling to divulge anything, even when he threatened her with calling the immigration authorities.

"Call them," she'd spat, meeting his hard stare. "I've seen worse than you before. Where I come from you can get killed for a chicken."

It was plain she wasn't going to talk. It was even plainer she disliked Leo. "Why do you work here?" he'd asked.

"Stupid question. For the money. I'm supporting my whole family back home."

He'd given up, figuring he could always return and threaten her again if he had to. Then he'd gone back to his office and set about tracking Janie's charge cards and phone records. (It wasn't just the NSA who could monitor your calls.) A short time later, he understood he could have saved himself the trouble of interviewing the staff. There it was, plain as day on her Verizon account.

A call at seven that morning to a number with a Minnesota area code.

Fourteen

Liv woke to the smell of bacon and maple syrup and the sound of conversation drifting up the stairs. Rolling over, she took note of her empty bed, put two and two together, and quickly ran through her options.

She could get up and join her guests downstairs.

That's what she *should* do. And if it wasn't—jeez—freaking seven o'clock in the morning, she might think about it. It looked as though she was going to owe Chris again today. After only three hours' sleep, there was no way she was going to be able to get out of bed, let alone meet her work crew in anything that resembled a conscious state.

Her obligations summarily canceled, she shut her eyes and went back to sleep.

• • •

"I think it's so sweet that you and Liv are friends," *Janie* said, smiling at Jake across the kitchen table. "I mean, really, how amazing is that, that my two *best* friends are enjoying each other's company." In deference to her son who was eating his apple-cinnamon French toast beside her, she conversed about the relationship in bland phrases.

"Yeah, how about that," Jake said in a tone of voice that would have warned off most reasonable people.

Janie's smile was guileless. As if she knew that he knew that she wasn't going to let him off that easy. "So tell me again how you met."

"Didn't you like the last answer?" he murmured drily.

"Darling, I want details, not some casual remark about some wine purchase."

"How about some other time." He flicked a glance at Matt.

She made a theatrical moue. "Very well, I'll give you a pass for now. But I want to know *everything*."

"As if."

"Remember, I can ask Liv," Janie purred.

Jake opened his mouth to speak, abruptly shut it and, quickly rising to his feet, crossed the kitchen to the screen door that opened onto the back porch. A large man had suddenly appeared on the other side of the screen. Even in the shadows of the honeysuckle vines that shaded the porch, Jake could make out the bulge under the man's right arm. "Looking for someone?" As if he didn't know. This was Leo Rolf's bloodhound.

"I'd like to talk to Mrs. Rolf."

"I'm not sure she wants to talk to you."

"Why don't you ask her?"

"You're good, Roman." Janie had come up and was standing at Jake's side. "I thought I'd done a better job of hiding."

"You don't have to give him the time of day," Jake muttered. "He's not the law."

Roman held his hands up. "I'm not taking sides. That's not my business. Just give me a few minutes, Janie. I guarantee I'm harmless."

Janie gave him an assessing look. "I'm assuming Leo sent you. With him behind this visit, I'm not so sure . . ."

"Leo might be paying for the charter plane, but *I'm* not for sale. You're perfectly safe."

"Leo's a grade-A prick. Just so you know where I stand." Janie spoke softly so Matt wouldn't hear, although her son was thoroughly engrossed in the adventures of Sponge Bob Square Pants on the kitchen TV.

"No argument there." Roman smiled. "I doubt you'd find many who'd disagree. You have a lawyer, I presume. Call him; I'll talk to him first. He can vet me."

Janie's mouth twitched in indecision, not that she thought Roman was actually dangerous. But her husband was. "Oh, very well," she said. She turned to Jake. "Would you watch Matt for a few minutes? I won't be long."

"Not a problem." Jake didn't anticipate Janie's abduction. If precedent held, Leo Rolf wanted his kid, not his wife.

Roman opened the screen door and stepped aside.

Janie gave him another assessing look as she walked through the doorway. "Have you been here all night?"

"More or less."

He hoped the man hadn't been taking pictures, Jake thought as he retraced his steps and sat down at the kitchen table. The bedroom curtains had been open. Not that he was seriously concerned. Janie was the man's target, not Liv. He glanced at Matt, who hadn't even noticed his mother was gone, entertained as he was by Sponge Bob. Then Jake checked out the clock on the stove. Still too early to wake up Liv, although he was sorely tempted.

His psyche was running pedal to the metal on high-octane lust. And while that sensation was way outside any normal paradigm, it wasn't as though he could turn it off. Somehow Liv had gotten under his skin. Not that her can't-get-enough-of-sex wasn't a major attraction. Duh. In fact, if he wasn't in charge of a three-year-old hooked on cartoons, he'd go upstairs right now.

Then, out of the blue—as if he were being compensated for having lived a stellar life—a young woman with short dark hair, jeans, and a faded red T-shirt walked into the kitchen from the old parlor and said, "Hi, Chris tells me there's a little boy here who likes kittens."

Matt swung around, wide-eyed at the word *kittens*. Sponge Bob dropped from his radar, and like every little kid who's been snapped out of his cartoon trance, he said, "Huh?"

"I think you might have a customer," Jake said, smiling and coming to his feet.

"Great." She put out her hand as she reached the table. "I'm Amy, Chris's wife."

"Jake Chambers. And this is Matt," he added, grabbing a napkin and quickly wiping the syrup from the boy's mouth.

"So how about it, Matt?" Amy knelt down beside his chair. "Would you like to go out and see the kittens?"

"I wuv kittens," Matt said gravely.

Amy looked up at Jake. "Is it okay if I take him to the barn?"

"His mom's on the back porch talking to someone, but I'm sure it's fine. I'll let her know Matt's with you."

"Let's go, kiddo," Amy said, lifting Matt down from his chair and coming to her feet. She took his hand. "We'll be in the barn if you need us." She smiled at Matt. "Right?"

"Wight."

Amy and Matt left hand in hand, going out the way she'd come in. The front door slammed a moment later, and Jake found himself alone. Chris's wife hadn't asked who he was or why he was here. Either gossip traveled fast, or there were often strange men in Liv's kitchen.

Did it matter?

Not unless he'd completely lost his mind.

Which he hadn't.

So now what?

As if he didn't know, when fate had handed him this really sweet deal.

Although Liv did need her sleep.

Damn.

How nice did he want to be?

He glanced out the kitchen window. The couple sitting side by side on the porch swing seemed to be getting along mighty swell if Janie's body language and flirtatious smile meant anything. From the look of things, Janie didn't need his protection.

He was pretty much off the hook all around.

Although if he were truly sensible, he'd drive back to the cities and work on getting his restaurant ready to roll. Or better yet, go home and sleep. He was running on adrenaline and not much else.

With his current obsession in bed upstairs, however, he was more inclined to endorse that old saw about time enough to sleep in the grave. It couldn't hurt to go upstairs and just *see* if Liv might be awake, could it?

The question wasn't seriously open to debate.

Not when he was this horny.

Walking to the back door, Jake opened it enough to explain to Janie that Matt had gone with Amy to look at the kittens. "I'll be upstairs if you need me."

Janie smiled. "Thanks, Jake. And Roman's being very understanding, so don't worry about me."

Perfect, because he really didn't want to worry about her. "See you later, then."

"Roman might stay for a few days," Janie added.

"Don't tell me. Tell Liv."

"I thought you might tell her since you're going upstairs. She won't mind, I know." Janie turned to smile at Roman. "We've been friends forever."

"If it's a problem, I can stay at a motel," Roman politely offered.

"Don't be silly. Liv has plenty of room in this old farmhouse. Doesn't she, Jake?"

Since he'd only seen Liv's bedroom, the kitchen, and not much else, Janie was asking the wrong person. "I'm going to stay out of this. Check with Liv when she wakes up."

Janie turned a quick smile on Roman. "As you see, Jake's mantra is *Never get involved*. Isn't that so, darling?" she trilled.

Jake rolled his eyes, shut the door, and left Janie to her machinations. Roman looked as though he could handle whatever Janie dished out.

Picking up the serving plate of remaining French toast, he added a few pieces of bacon, warmed it all in the microwave, grabbed a fork and the syrup bottle, and headed upstairs. Whistling.

Christ, he'd never been the whistling type before.

He felt like he was in Mayberry.

Although his version was definitely X-rated.

Fifteen

"I so appreciate your understanding," Janie murmured, lifting her eyes to Roman, hoping she was properly conveying a look of tender regard and gratitude.

Roman smiled at her drama. "Just for the record, my motives aren't completely altruistic."

"I didn't expect they were." Her lashes fluttered demurely before rising to frame a coquettish gaze. "If there's anything at all you want from me, just let me know."

He laughed. "Cut the theatrics, Janie. We're both way past those games."

She pouted prettily. "But I truly mean it, Roman. Sincerely."

He wasn't about to say something rude when he wasn't entirely sure why he was doing what he was doing. Nor how long he'd continue operating outside Leo's jurisdiction. "I still might take you back to New York," he warned.

She knew better, even if he didn't. She had no intention of going back to New York. But rather than argue uselessly, she smiled. "I understand. I have no expectations one way or the other."

"Just so everything is clear."

"Perfectly. Although, I know there's another woman involved with Leo, so I want you to know where *I* stand. I'll go to the mat before I let some strange woman raise my child. Just so everything is *clear*," she mimicked.

He smiled faintly. "Got it."

"And I'm not stupid like Lisa."

"No one's as stupid as Lisa."

"Anyway, thanks for the reprieve, however long," she noted. "And while you're here, I was thinking maybe we'd have time to—" Roman cut her off with a raised hand.

Pulling out his phone from his pocket, he flipped it open. "I'm listening."

"You're gonna get a call from Leo. He's barking orders as usual. Let me know where you are when you get the chance." His assistant, Vinnie, never minced words.

"Will do." Roman shut the phone but kept it in his hand. "Leo's about to call. I'll take the cell off vibrate and put it on speakerphone for your edification," he added with a grin.

Janie wrinkled her nose. "Hearing him will ruin my day."

"Better to hear him than see him," Roman brusquely declared. When the anticipated ring occurred, Roman answered. "Morning, Leo. How's it going?"

"Where the fuck are you?" Leo bellowed, his thunderous voice rending the hushed, honeysuckle-scented air.

"Pretty much nowhere at the moment. I'm lost in a corn-field."

"What the *fuck*?" Another barrage of invective ravaged the morning calm. "Why in hell did the bitch run to ground in the country?"

"I'm not sure yet. I'm working on it."

"Well, work harder, *dammit*! I want results! I want my son back! ASAP! Do you fucking *understand*?"

"Tone it down, Leo," Roman said, soft as silk. "You don't pay me enough to take crap from you."

"Sorry. No offense, okay?" A rare sycophantic note briefly colored Leo's voice before his tone shifted back to its normal blare. "But I want my son back sooner rather than later! The bitch can't hide forever! Goddamn it! Find her!"

"As soon as I know something, I'll give you a call." Unruffled, Roman gave away nothing.

"If you need more money, just say so. My kid is worth any price—you know that. Call me—day or night. And fucking hurry!"

The line went dead.

"He never says good-bye," Janie muttered. "The prick."

"If it's any consolation, he's not a happy man." Leaning back against the swing, Roman slipped the phone into his jacket pocket and stretched out his long legs in a lazy sprawl. "The guy's gonna have a major stroke someday."

"I didn't have a clue what he was really like." Janie grimaced. "I didn't hear him scream until after Matt was born. Believe me, it was a major shock."

"He must have been on his best behavior for quite awhile."

"Almost a year," she replied. "Until he went ballistic that first time, I'd believed him when he said his previous wives had been bitches from hell. All I'd ever experienced from him was kindness and an interest in pleasing me. But when he went Jekyll and Hyde on me, I knew I'd made a terrible mistake."

"The three wives before you probably came to the same conclusion."

She shook her head. "If only I'd known, as they say. I thought at first I might have said or done something to initiate his rage. When the tirades only escalated, I knew it had nothing to do with me. Mazie stepped in at that point and helped run interference."

"Your housekeeper."

"She was my absolute savior."

"I interviewed her, along with the rest of the staff. She told me to go to hell."

Janie smiled. "I can always depend on Mazie to protect me. And perhaps you as well?" She gazed up at him from under her lashes. "Possibly?"

His brows rose. "Anything's possible."

"Seriously, you can't really consider bringing Matt back to a man like Leo."

"That's not my bailiwick. I'm no psychologist."

"Neither am I, but I know what's good for my son."

"I can't make any promises. Let's just leave it at that."

Janie touched his arm lightly. "I'm grateful for any consideration you might give to me." But before she could elaborate further, a Federal Express truck came roaring up the driveway, and her expression and demeanor instantly changed. "Oh, wonderful! It's here! I probably should have mentioned that I took my Hockney portrait when I left," she said in a rush. Leaping from the swing, she raced for the stairs.

"So I can expect another irate call from Leo." Roman was fast on his feet for a big man. He caught up with Janie before she reached the stairs.

"I don't think so. Leo doesn't pay attention to paintings." She smiled up at him. "And what good would my portrait be to the new Mrs. Rolf?"

Grand theft might be more of a problem than the new Mrs. Rolf, Roman thought. But then again, he hadn't really expected a trouble-free assignment. "You're gonna need some help with that thing," Roman said. He'd seen the size of the full length portrait at the apartment.

"Thanks, I do," Janie cheerfully noted, waving at the FedEx driver as he came to a stop at the edge of the lawn. "I already told Liv about the painting, and she said something about her barn," Janie added, descending the stairs. "I'm guessing there's plenty of room for it there."

"The driver can swing over to the barn."

"How clever," she brightly said, offering him a dazzling smile. "You are, you know. And good-looking, too."

He frowned. "Don't. Okay?"

"I don't care. It's true."

"Yeah, yeah." He raised his voice so the driver could hear. "Take it to the barn. Over there." Roman pointed. "Come on, Janie." He held out his hand. "And no more bullshit, okay? I've heard it all. I'm here just getting the lay of the land. So let's just talk about the weather or something."

"Whatever you say," Janie replied sweetly.

"And how about a normal tone of voice," he said with a grin.

"Isn't it a lovely day in the country?" Janie smiled. "How's that?"

Roman surveyed the green, rolling countryside and exhaled softly. "It *is* a damned lovely day. And you know what else? It's fucking *peaceful*."

For a man who had seen all there was to see of the sordid underbelly of the world, perhaps he, more than most, could appreciate serenity.

Sixteen

Jake had just walked into Liv's bedroom and quietly shut the door in order not to disturb her when the phone rang.

Coming awake, Liv saw him first and smiled.

He nodded at the phone. "Want me to get it?"

"I'd better. I wouldn't want to explain to my mom what you were doing here at this hour of the morning." Reaching for the bedside phone, she picked it up, glanced at the caller ID, said, "False alarm," and lying back down, hit the Talk button. "It's way too early, Shelly."

"Speak for yourself. I've been at work for two hours."

"That's because you're driven to succeed. Kindly keep in mind when you have these early morning impulses, I'm semi-retired."

"I haven't heard from you since you so rudely left us in the lurch at Taglio's. He must be good."

After a moment's hesitation in which Liv debated lying, she said, "He is."

"Tell me every little detail, or I'll come out there tonight and see for myself."

"Don't waste your time."

"So he's not there?"

Silence.

"I knew it," Shelly crowed. "Whenever you talk like someone's around, someone's around."

"Okay, so you win the prize. I'll call you later."

"Is he in bed with you?"

"Good-bye, Shelly."

"Let me say hi."

"We're not in the eighth grade. Otherwise, I would."

"Selfish."

"You betcha." Liv hung up the phone. "It was Shelly," she said.

"I heard."

"She's embarrassing."

He grinned. "What are friends for?"

"She wants to meet you."

"Is she as good-looking as you?"

"Why?"

"Just curious."

"No you're not. That's a typical man question."

He laughed. "Look, I was just teasing. I'm not even remotely curious."

"I shouldn't care."

"And I should be curious."

"So this is strange."

"I think we've already established that. The question is not over the strangeness, but the resulting consequences. And with that in mind, I'm here to tell you that Janie is busy with the detective her husband sent out from New York. Matt is looking at kittens in the barn with Amy, and we are conveniently alone for at least—"

"Long enough," Liv interrupted, grinning. "Do I have time to eat that French toast you're holding?"

"Sure. What I have in mind won't take long." His smile was wicked. "Let me rephrase that. The first time won't take long. The rest depends on whether we're left alone or not."

"It's my house."

"I didn't want to say it, but yes, it is."

"So I may do as I please."

"Or occasionally as I please."

"Why don't we discuss that after I eat." She held out her hand, suddenly ravenous. Or maybe the sight and smell of apple-cinnamon French toast and bacon had triggered all her taste receptors.

"Yes, ma'am," he drawled, pushing away from the door.

"If I didn't know better, I might think you're actually submissive."

"I wasn't under the impression you were looking for that kind of man."

"Smart-ass."

"Just checking." He smiled faintly as he handed her the plate. "Would you like me to feed you?"

"If I wasn't starving, I'd say yes. It sounds like fun. But since I am, I'll pass this time."

It didn't matter; he wasn't in a hurry. He figured the kittens would prove entertaining for some time. As for Janie, she'd been working that private eye to the max. He didn't anticipate Janie needing company anytime soon. Uncorking the syrup, he held the bottle over the plate. "Say when."

He poured and poured, looked up in query, then poured some more.

"When," Liv finally said.

"You like French toast with your syrup, I see."

"It's syrup from my maple trees. Jeez, how do you get the bacon to stay so flat?" The four pieces framing the French toast were picture perfect.

"The right pan, the right temperature, and years of practice."

"You'll have to show me. My bacon is always a tangled mess."

"But then you're not the patient sort."

She glanced up, a piece of bacon halfway to her mouth. "Is that a slur?"

"Did I imply I was looking for a patient woman?"

She smiled, took a bite of bacon, and said, "Good," between chews. "Because you're way too hot. What can I say?"

He smiled. "You're my aphrodisiac of choice, too, babe." Sitting on the edge of the bed, he waited while she ate, feeling oddly content. As though he might have made the right choice coming out here to Minnesota. All the tension commensurate with his West Coast life had disappeared into the ether. Not that a ton of orgasms weren't likely to prove relaxing.

"These apple slices are heavenly—all buttery and caramelly. I suppose those take patience, too," she said with a grin.

His brows lifted ever so faintly. "Never rush anything, babe. That's the secret."

"You're good at not rushing in more ways than one."

Her smile was definitely enticing, her lips shiny with syrup and allure. "Pleasure shouldn't be a race. It should be more like a marathon." He smiled. "Circumstances allowing, of course."

"And your judgment is superb in every instance," she murmured.

He grinned. "You're just easy to read."

"You mean you're not psychic?"

"With your one-track mind, I don't have to be." His dick swelled larger as memories of last night inundated his brain, her fondness for sex a real turn-on. Shifting slightly to give his hard-on growing room, he said with observable constraint, "Are you about done?"

Her aquamarine gaze met his from under her lashes. "Should I be?"

He found it necessary to clear his throat before replying. "That'd be great," he said tautly.

She held out the plate.

Taking it, he glanced at the door. "I should lock the door."

"If only. There's no key. It's long gone."

"I'll shove a chair under the doorknob if that's okay with you. With a three-year-old around." He shrugged.

"Be my guest."

As he rose, set the plate aside, picked up a chair, and moved toward the door, Liv lay against her pillows watching him, feeling an extraordinary degree of satisfaction and contentment. He'd allowed her to sleep, brought her breakfast in bed, and was now about to further reward her with sex. Was she basking in the sweet clover of life or what? "You're spoiling me," she murmured. "All the fabulous food . . . and you . . . and him." She nodded at his blatant erection as he'd half-turned at her words of approval. She grinned. "It's all quite heady."

"My pleasure." A smile warmed his eyes. "And it's not as though I don't get spoiled in return."

"This is all *waaay* too perfect. When does the tornado hit?"

"Cynic. Maybe life's always good." Shoving the chair in place, he moved back to the flamboyant bed.

Her gaze narrowed. "Pul-ease."

"Okay, so it's not always this fine," he said, sitting beside her. "But what the hey—let's take advantage of"—his brows rose—"whatever this is."

She was mildly unnerved by the degree of happiness he inspired. And it wasn't just his cooking or his sexual skills. He was different from the other men she'd known. Sweeter, kinder, truly obliging, conveying pleasure with a kind of deft benevolence. "I have to brush my teeth," she abruptly muttered, and throwing back the covers, jumped out of the other side of the bed.

"Was it something I said?" he drolly inquired.

She spun around. "I'm beginning to want you too much. I don't like it." Snappish, taut words. Turning away, she walked to the bathroom and once inside, slammed the door shut.

He didn't quite know if her combatant statements pleased or displeased him.

On the other hand, he'd always subscribed to the theory that introspection was much overrated. Particularly in his dealings with women. Furthermore, his long-held belief in that principle had always served him well. So no way was he going to enter any labyrinthine web of emotional curiosity, even if Liv was more intriguing than most.

Shit always happened.

He never made plans when it came to women.

He didn't even *think* of making plans.

It was safer that way.

By the time Liv returned to the bedroom, she'd had sufficient opportunity to lecture herself sternly about confusing sex with affection. As she'd brushed her teeth, she'd looked into the mirror and chided herself for being stupid. Everyone knew that honesty and openness were bad karma when it came to sexual fun and games.

What had she been thinking?

"I'm good now," she declared, smiling her camera-ready smile as she walked out of the bathroom, wearing a robe now as though in added defense against her outrageous desires. "Forgive my lapse of judgment. I talk too much."

"Hey—say whatever you want."

Her brows rose in perfect arches. "Because you don't really listen anyway?"

"I didn't say that."

"It looked like you wanted to."

"Unless you're a mind-reader, you don't know what I wanted to do." He grinned. "Except that." He held out his hand. "And I want you too much, too. We're both a little goofy. No sense in making a federal case about it."

"Exactly." He made it so easy to go with the flow. He knew all the right moves. Better not to question how many women it had taken to acquire such practiced charm.

As her hand slipped into his, he pulled her between his legs and lifted his face. "Kiss me now that you've brushed your teeth."

She grinned. "Where?"

He grinned back. "We'll do that later. Right now"—he pointed to his mouth—"here."

In the confirmed goofiness of their moods, their kiss was extra sweet and then not so sweet and ultimately a kind of melting ravishment that left them both breathless and wanting more.

"I'm too old to waste time kissing," he said, panting, lifting her off his lap and jerking off his T-shirt and tossing it.

"And I'm too sexed-up." After a night of orgasms, all her senses were heightened, her body seething for his touch, overstimulated, eager, impatient. She reached for the tie on her robe. "Nice T-shirt," she said with a nod toward the rumpled garment on the floor.

"I found it in the back closet," he said, standing to take off his jeans. "I like your logo."

Her Liv Bell Wines T-shirts were promo items; she had stacks. "A friend of mine's a graphic artist. Keep it and think of me."

"Right now I can't *stop* thinking of you. It's like I'm fifteen again and horny as hell." His jeans and boxers discarded, he dropped back onto the bed and stretched out.

"Lucky me to be able to take advantage of your horniness."

He opened his arms and smiled up at her. "Come on down, babe. We're open for business."

She leaped at him, giddy, infatuated, as willing as he to give in to her vaulting desires, no longer questioning what she was feeling. He was the cherry on the top of her sundae, the frosting on her cake of life, the man who could ring all her bells.

He caught her in midair and lowered her gently until she lay on him, warming all his senses, gratifying a newly susceptible contentment he'd not been aware he possessed. Framing her face in his hands, he just looked at her for a moment, taking in her fresh-faced beauty: the rosy-pink softness of her full lips, the green blue of her straightforward gaze, the smattering of freckles across her fine nose and cheeks that made her look younger than she was.

She could have asked what he was thinking, but on her own emotional roller coaster ride, she held her tongue. She couldn't possibly talk about feeling something more than sexual attraction. He'd bolt for the door. "Hey," she finally whispered. "Don't forget how greedy I am."

His smile was instant.

Practiced, she thought, but engaging and full of charm.

"I haven't forgotten," he said smoothly, focused once again, rolling her under him in a smooth, supple movement that belied his size and weight. "You'll be wanting a few orgasms first to take off the edge, and then we'll play."

Seventeen

It was four in the afternoon when Jake woke with a start.

He lay very still, his heart pounding, his fight-or-flight reflex on red alert at the unusual circumstances. He couldn't remember the last time he'd actually *slept* the day away with a woman after sex. Fuck.

With every primal impulse exhorting him to flee, he quickly considered his options. Go or stay? With his libido operating at the max, it was a five-second smack-down.

Any and all perceived liabilities were kayoed.

Major horniness the winner.

And bottom line, he reminded himself—Liv wasn't the clingy type. She was a self-reliant, independent woman who had a life of her own. He wasn't in danger of losing his free agent status.

His pulse rate began to subside, the hair on the back of his neck settled into place, his tension abated. It wasn't the end of the world that he'd dozed off. After two nights of hot sex and little sleep, not to mention a morning romp, anyone would have done as much.

Having rationalized his squeamishness, he decided he might as well take advantage of his sound decision-making skills. Rolling over on his side, he took in the fine view. Liv was sleeping on her back, her hands flung over her head, the gentle rise and fall of her breasts inviting his touch. Unconsciously flexing his fingers, he recalled the feel of that ripe, pliant flesh. Not a single silicone insert to jar one's fingertips; just fucking made-to-be-sucked world class tits.

His cock apparently shared his enthusiasm for her boobs, jacking up into action mode with renewed energy after a well-deserved rest.

So the question was, should he let her sleep or not?

Did she need her rest, or would she rather wake up with a cock inside her?

Liv had kicked away the sheets in the warmth of the day, exposing her faint bikini line at hip and thigh. She apparently tanned topless; he hadn't noticed before. Or maybe he'd just been too busy chasing orgasms to pay attention.

There was no question, though, why she'd been a top model for so long. Liv was quintessentially female. Lithe, curvaceous, fresh-faced and—he smiled—gung ho about sex.

Not to mention she liked his cooking.

Or more to the point, he liked cooking for her.

If he'd been attuned to the warning bells in the distant reaches of his brain—currently muted by lust—he'd have noticed the unprecedented phrase, *He liked cooking for her.*

But he didn't for the above mentioned reasons.

Instead, he found himself suddenly occupied with the thought of food and a possible supper menu, when he should have been in his car driving home.

Even more strangely, he didn't give a rat's ass that he was veering off his well-trodden path of male independence.

In fact, he had more or less decided to wake Liv and ask her whether she wanted hot or cold food for supper. He found he was starved. And no wonder; he hadn't eaten since breakfast.

"I'm hungry," Liv murmured, her eyes still shut.

He smiled, not even questioning the bull's-eye eeriness of her comment in light of their felicitous affinity. "And I'm planning our supper menu."

Her eyes snapped open. "Are you going to stay and cook?"

"You betcha."

"I am *one lucky woman*," she whispered, her lashes framing the smile in her eyes. "Let me count the ways . . ."

"Amen, babe." His voice was gentle, his mouth as he leaned over to brush her lips gentler still. Then, unnerved by the wave of tenderness spiking through his senses, he quickly pulled away. "How would you like to be my sous-chef?"

"I'd be honored," she replied, picking up on his ultracasual tone. She had no more intention than he of giving in to dewy-eyed feelings, no matter the sweetness of his kiss. Not when he literally made women squeal in excitement when they saw him. God's truth. She'd seen him on *Entertainment Tonight* when his L.A. restaurant had opened. He'd been all preternaturally cool eye candy while the women in the opening night crowd had screamed like crazed groupies.

"Feel like a shower first?"

Dragged back from the video clip in her mind, she looked blank. "Huh?"

"Would you like a shower first?" Polite and tactful, like he'd seen that blank look before. Like he was used to women zoning out at the sight of him.

"God, yes. I reek of sex." So she'd joined the line of groupies. Not that she had a single regret when she was the happy recipient of super sex à la Jake Chambers.

Their shower took slightly longer than anticipated, primed as they were for sex. But even hungry sex eventually gave way to more potent hunger pangs.

"How about a rain check, babe," Jake finally murmured, water streaming down his face. "I'm getting weak from starvation."

She hesitated, then decided she couldn't be completely selfish forever. "Sure," she agreed, although nothing about him appeared to have weakened—neither his hard cock nor his strong arms holding her impaled on his erection.

"Down you go, then." Unlacing her legs from around his waist, he set her on her feet. Stripping off his condom, he pulled the shower curtain aside, pitched the condom into the wastebasket under the sink, and turned back to her with the kind of focused energy she'd come to know. "Need a last rinse?"

She nodded, thinking she could use his undivided attention for the next week or so as well. But still rational enough not to utter such heresy, she dutifully waited to be rinsed off.

Nudging her legs apart, he hosed her down with the flexible shower hose, did the same for himself, and hung the shower head back in place.

"I'm sooo lazy," she murmured as he turned off the water and reached for a towel. "Where do you get your energy?"

He grinned. "I'm driven by hunger, babe. And I don't need any help with cooking. Just keep me company. I'll make us a mojito—if you have the liquor. They're perfect on a hot day like this."

"I should feel guilty letting you do all the work."

She'd given him the ride of his life; she deserved a rest. "Not a problem," he said. Lifting her onto the tub rug, he rubbed her down with a towel, then gave her a light slap on her butt. "Go get dressed."

Exhausted by more nonstop, wild sex than she'd ever had the good fortune to experience before, she moved at a snail's pace.

Jake was dressed long before she. Wordlessly brushing away her fingers from her languorous buttoning of her blouse, he took over.

"Jeez, you're wired," she murmured, perfectly willing to stand still and let him do all the work.

"I'm in a hurry for food, babe. Shorts or jeans?" he added, patting the last blouse button in place.

"Shorts. Over there." She pointed.

Whipping a pair of lime-green shorts from the back of a chair, he kneeled at her feet. "Left foot," he said, then, "right foot," his voice quiet and calm, like he had everything under control. But his actions were crisp and swift, her shorts pulled up and zipped in record time. Standing before her, he gave her a questioning look. "Shoes or no shoes?"

"No shoes."

"I knew that." The fact that he did warmed his previously unassailable heart. Not that he was about to seriously acknowledge the fact. He waved at the door. "After you, babe."

· · ·

That they were in accord—in more than sexual passion— was apparent as Jake prepared supper. They immediately fell into a cozy, comfortable companionship as though they'd often worked in the kitchen together. Between sipping on her mojito, Liv fetched items Jake needed from the fridge or pantry, set the table with the odd dishes and glassware she collected, brought up some wine from her cellar. They conversed about nothing with ease, agreeing or disagreeing with equal amity, smiling at each other with great frequency. Feeling outrageously happy.

Janie, Matt, and Roman returned from the barn midway through the preparations. "I told you." Janie shot a glance at Roman. "We could smell supper clear out to the barn," she added, smiling at Jake.

"Sit down, have a drink. We're almost ready to eat. Hey, babe." Jake smiled at Liv. "Think you can mix a couple drinks?"

"You're better, but I'll try."

"You're plenty good at other things," he said with a wink. "Just remember to muddle the mint."

Janie took note of the warm intimacy between her friends, the affection in Jake's voice particularly significant. "You two seem to be getting along nicely," she murmured archly.

Liv pretended not to understand. "Jake got hungry," she replied. "So I'm fetching and carrying. It's about all my amateur status allows."

"I don't know about *amateur*."

Liv blushed at his sexy intonation. "So tell me, Matt," she said, quickly changing the subject. "Did you enjoy playing with the kittens?"

"Amy an' me named 'em." Matt gave Liv a solemn look. "She said you dudn't mind."

"I don't mind at all. I bet they like their new names."

A smile suddenly lit his chubby face. "Day do. Wots and wots." He pointed at the TV. "Tartoons on?"

Saved by a child's short attention span, Liv busied herself finding the remote. "Come, sit here." Liv pulled out a chair for Matt near the TV. "Let's find you some cartoons you like. We have ten channels, you know?"

Matt's eyes lit up, and he jumped up on the chair upholstered with a chicken print fabric.

"I'll make the drinks," Jake offered, turning the heat down on his red sauce as Liv flicked on the TV. He glanced at Janie and Roman. "Two?"

Janie's hand went up, Roman nodded in the affirmative, and in short order Jake produced another round of drinks.

Roman had discarded his sport coat and Glock somewhere in the course of the day. His shirtsleeves were rolled up, his mood no longer wary, his lounging pose as he sat down at the table, relaxed.

Janie's actress persona had reverted to an authenticity that was rarely in evidence. For the first time in years, the faint echo of a West Texas drawl could be heard, Liv noticed as she rejoined the adults. Raised dirt poor, Janie had worked hard to erase any trace of her hardscrabble past. Why she'd decided to jettison her affectations today piqued Liv's interest.

Not that Liv wasn't aware that a heavy dose of mojo was in the air.

Maybe some odd confluence of planets and galaxies had prompted everyone's diverse moods. Whatever the voodoo reasons, the odd mix of supper guests, all remarkably different in background and circumstance, found common ground and agreeable conversation in Liv's kitchen.

Roman entertained them with hair-raising stories of real-life villains and heroes from his years as a detective. The good guys always won, the bad guys got their just desserts. And Janie took it all in with rapt, adoring attention.

Liv wondered whether Janie's interest was genuine or feigned. After all, Roman had been sent here to find her. But in her current benign frame of mind, Liv was willing to give a nod not only to Janie's benevolence but to wish her all the Pollyanna luck in the world. Not that Janie wouldn't need a boatload with Leo out to get her.

While everyone drank and talked, Jake smoothly orchestrated supper, working swiftly and competently like the professional he was. In what seemed a very short time, he wiped his hands on a towel, tossed it aside, and announced, "I'll open the wine, and then we're all set."

Eighteen

In the peak of summer, most kitchens had the necessary items for tomato sauce, so Jake decided on a first course of penne in pomodoro sauce. He filleted plum tomatoes, slivered garlic, picked some basil from a pot on Liv's back step, opened a can of Italian plum tomatoes, one of paste, then swirled and simmered and seasoned the sauce until the taste was to his liking. Cooking al dente penne, he drained it quickly into a colander and, still dripping the starchy pasta water, dumped it into the waiting sauce. Tossing it with a few splashes more of extra-virgin olive oil, he served it, knowing in his heart of hearts, he'd nailed it.

His companions agreed, their praise effusive as they enthusiastically relished the flavorful dish. By the time they'd savored the last bite of their first course, everyone was on their second glass of Liv's full-bodied red, and conversation and alcohol-fueled appetites increased exponentially.

A bottle of Liv's dry white wine accompanied the second course of *salade niçoise*—Jake's menu choices determined by what was available in the larder of a woman who didn't regularly cook. In the hands of a master, canned tuna and anchovies, hard-boiled eggs, potatoes, tomatoes, olives, red onion, and green beans quickly came together in a delectable taste of summer. Jake's vinaigrette was basic: Dijon mustard and sherry vinegar, whisked together, olive oil added a little at a time, then minced garlic, salt, and pepper to taste.

The presentation, however, was far from basic, the salad artfully arranged on a large platter, each colorful morsel gleaming temptingly from a light drizzle of vinaigrette.

Everyone was silent for a time as they ate, only soft *mmmmms* of content audible as the succulent flavors melded and tantalized taste buds—every bite fresh, vibrant, crunchy, clean-tasting.

While Matt had eaten all his pasta, he eyed the salad suspiciously and only ate select items, mainly potatoes. But when it came to dessert, Jake had produced a winner for all ages.

Finding a bowl of cherries in the fridge, he'd pitted and halved them, simmered them with sugar and a little water, and spooned them warm over vanilla ice cream. He would have added a few tablespoons of kirsch for flavor if Matt hadn't been there. But in deference to a child's palate, he didn't.

By the time everyone was enjoying their dessert, Liv was thoroughly convinced that having a live-in chef was right up there on the top of her list of pleasures—along with prime sex. Whether it rated first or second was still under debate. Not that her faculties were debate-sharp at this point. Between the drinks and awesome food, not to mention Jake's can't-keep-your-eyes-off-him good looks, she was drifting somewhere between euphoria and a ride on the gravy train.

This state of mind caused her to be just a tad slow on the up-take when Shelly walked through her back door. Liv's first thought was: it was *way* too early for Shelly to make it this far north. She shot a glance at the clock. *Six-fifteen?* Like way, *way* too early. Shelly was always the last to leave work.

Every inch the polished professional in a fawn-colored suit, heels, and sleek, blonde, not-a-hair-out-of-place coif, Shelly smiled at Liv. "I tried calling," she blandly lied, "but no one answered. Am I too late for supper? It smells delicious."

In her blissed-out torpor, Liv was still trying to sort the dis-crepancies of time, distance, and Shelly's surprising appearance. Since her brain synapses weren't currently operating at optimum levels, the sorting was less than speedy.

"It's not too late at all," Jake said, smoothly coming to the rescue. Rising, he pulled out an extra chair. "Please, sit down." He put out his hand. "I'm Jake Chambers."

"Shelly Parks." Walking forward, she shook Jake's hand. "A real pleasure," she said like she really meant it. "Now I under-stand why Liv's been incommunicado."

"Shelly, let me introduce my friend, Janie," Liv interjected, getting her brain up to speed, desperate to avoid more of Shelly's embarrassing comments. "Janie Rolf, Shelly. This is Janie's son, Matt." Liv waved her hand toward Roman. "And another friend, Roman Novak."

Roman came to his feet and shook Shelly's hand, while Janie looked up with a measured gaze. "Hello," she said cooly. She'd not yet made up her mind whether Shelly was competition or not.

"It's a pleasure to meet everyone," Shelly murmured, ignoring Janie's assessing gaze. In her business, assessment was de rigueur if one wished to survive. "It was soooo hot in town, I thought it might be cooler up here," she prevaricated, as she took a seat at the table. "You painted your kitchen chairs again," she added, smiling at Liv. "I like the wild colors."

"Thanks. You left work early." Nothing like a couple mojitos and wine to obliterate tact.

"I had a good day. Made a ton of money for everyone, myself included. I thought, what the hey . . . the company can get along without me for awhile."

Okay. So Shelly and the truth weren't tracking tonight, Liv decided. Although what did she expect? She'd be just as nosy if Shelly dropped out of sight with a new guy. "Shelly's a futures trader," Liv said, opting for forgiveness and good manners. "She keeps the wheels of commerce greased."

Slipping her suit jacket off, Shelly smiled. "I'm addicted to the game—what can I say. And I apologize for dropping in unexpectedly," she added, hanging her jacket on the back of her chair.

"What do you know about offshore accounts?" Janie abruptly asked, although her voice was ultracasual. "Or is that something outside your field?"

"I know a little." Shelly waggled her right hand. "They're legal in some instances, but ethically—not so much. The IRS would like to get their hands on the billions they're losing in taxes with those accounts. They're beginning to crack down here and there. What do you want to know?"

"I'll bet I can find you Sponge Bob on TV, Matt." Roman gave Janie a warning look. "Or would you rather see a Disney movie?" he asked, lifting the young boy from his chair.

As Roman carried Matt away from the table, Janie leaned forward slightly. "I was just wondering. For instance, if someone was getting cash from, say, the Isle of Man on a regular basis . . . would that be legal?"

Roman glanced back and gruffly said, "Watch it."

"It's just a general query," Janie said with a dismissive shrug. "People talk at cocktail parties . . . about their stocks and, well, these offshore accounts. I was just curious."

"Legalities can always be parsed," Shelly noted. "And they often are with these offshore accounts." She'd seen the interchange between Janie and the large man who looked like he could snap anyone's neck without breaking a sweat. She chose her words carefully. "If you had specifics, I might be able to give you a more definitive answer. Or if I couldn't, I know a corporate tax lawyer who could."

"Never mind," Janie said with a careless wave of her hand. "Although, should I need more information at a later date, perhaps I could give you a call."

"Certainly, anytime. By the way, I loved that soap you starred in. You were great."

Janie adored flattery. "It was a few years back, but thanks," she murmured, preening.

"You had a fabulous part. Tammy Winthrop was a woman who went after what she wanted. How cool is that?"

And truer than you think, Liv reflected, privy to Janie's leave-no-stone-unturned pursuit of Leo.

"Didn't you marry—what was his name—the big-time developer?"

"Leo Rolf."

"That's the one. Good for you. Money makes the world go round."

Roman frowned as he returned to the table.

Liv looked at Janie.

Janie looked at Roman.

Jake set the penne in front of Shelly. "Bon appetit," he said into the silence.

"I stuck my foot in my mouth, didn't I?" Shelly scanned the faces around the table, their unease palpable.

After a lengthy moment, Janie softly sighed. "Actually, I've left Leo. I'm in hiding here."

"And I barged right in. Sorry." Shelly tipped her head in Janie's direction. "But don't worry. I won't breathe a word to anyone."

"I'd appreciate it if you'd forget you ever saw Janie." The threat in Roman's deep voice was unmistakable. "Leo doesn't believe in playing by the rules."

Shelly figured Leo Rolf might have his hands full if Roman Novak was protecting his estranged wife. "Trust me; I'm dependable. As for rotten divorces," she added tersely, "believe me, I could write the book."

Roman smiled.

Was that tight-lipped smile threatening or sympathetic? Shelly wasn't sure.

"Just so there's no misunderstanding," Roman added, his tone softer now, only a hint of a growl evident, "Janie isn't here. She's never been here. You didn't see her."

Shelly nodded. "Understood. Leo Rolf's last divorce made the papers in Minnesota, too."

"Look, I can vouch for Shelly's discretion," Liv said. "Enough already about life's problems." She turned to Shelly. "Now, eat your pasta before it gets cold. And no more talk about vile Leo," she added, surveying her companions. "It's ruining my good mood."

"We wouldn't want that to happen, since I have plans," Jake murmured with a shameless grin. He held up a wine bottle. "Who needs a refill?"

After topping off everyone's glass, Jake launched into a story about a celebrity chef of TV fame who had drunk one too many of his signature POM martinis and had nearly burned down the studio along with the head of the network, who happened to be there for promo shots.

Janie chimed in next with a humorous story about her first audition in Hollywood, followed by another of Roman's vivid descriptions of vice and politics, New York style.

As the conversation continued apace, the focus on less angst-ridden topics, Shelly finished her second course. By that point, she'd come to the conclusion that both Liv and Janie would without a doubt be enjoying themselves tonight. Jake was charming and heart-poundingly handsome, not to mention he knew his way around females. Roman was all hard-bodied, larger-than-life machismo, coiled tight as a drum. His disciplined constraint was intriguing. Or frightening. She hadn't quite decided which.

Not that Janie appeared intimidated.

Maybe she was too Midwestern, Shelly thought. Big-city detectives with hard eyes, however entertaining their stories, weren't the norm in her—granted—probably unworldly sphere.

After finishing dessert, however, and numerous glasses of wine, her reservations were largely dispelled, and everyone had been categorized as charming to the core.

"Stay the night," Liv offered after Janie left to put Matt to bed. "You shouldn't drive after drinking anyway."

"I don't know. I have to get up real early."

"I'll set the alarm. You can sleep in the downstairs bedroom where it's extra quiet."

"And then I won't wake you when I leave," Shelly noted with a grin.

Liv grinned back. "That, too. But stay. McKinley and McKinley wouldn't like it if you were picked up for a DUI. Bad for their image."

This would have been an opportune moment for Jake to say, "I'm going back to the city. I'll drive you." He'd even run the idea through his mind a couple times. God knows, every sensible brain cell was telling him to get out of Dodge. If he actually stayed a second night, he'd be setting some alarming, possibly dire record. He didn't do sleep-overs. It had always been his cardinal rule.

And now, he couldn't bring himself to say those few simple words: *I gotta go*.

Instead, he poured himself another glass of Liv's wine. A good wine, perhaps someday even a great wine. Not that he was about to disclose his personal judgments on the subject. Both her red and white were remarkably balanced and smooth for (1) a boondocks wine-growing region of the world, (2) a brand-new vineyard, and (3) hybrid grapes no one had ever heard of.

"Let's play charades," Janie suggested brightly as she returned from tucking Matt into bed. "I adore charades."

Maybe because her entire life was a charade, Jake thought, immediately blaming his churlishness on his inability to do what he should do. Like leave.

Liv looked at Jake.

He grimaced.

Roman shrugged.

Shelly said, "I love charades, too!"

And three out of five adults inwardly groaned.

Nineteen

"You were unbelievably polite," Liv murmured as she walked toward her bed and Jake shut the bedroom door behind him. "Thanks."

"How long could charades last? I figured. Who knew," he said with a scowl. "But—hey—it's over, and you're my prize."

"At least Shelly and Janie had fun," Liv murmured, dropping backward onto her bed in free fall.

"That's because Janie loves to be center stage. I don't know about Shelly. What's her problem?"

"She's a frustrated drama queen. She used to perform in local theater before her job began to consume her. But she makes tons of money, so there's compensation for her long hours."

"She was up here pretty early tonight."

"And we both know why."

He smiled. "Just checking."

"You can't blame her. I haven't been in seclusion like this before."

His brows rose. "Ever?"

"I should say no, but I lie so poorly, so yes. I do not as a rule engage in unending, unremitting, till-the-cows-come-home sex. I have no explanation."

"That makes two of us."

Her brows rose.

"All of the above, okay?"

"I shouldn't be pleased, but I am. I thought perhaps you were just referring to not having an explanation."

"I have a busy life, babe. Fucking nonstop isn't part of my normal schedule. Not when I have to get out three hundred meals in two restaurants every night."

"That's nice," she murmured, smiling.

He'd never seen such a sexy smile. Correction: all her smiles were sexy, which meant he was obviously crazed. And liable to walk over the edge if he wasn't careful. *Shit, shit, shit.*

Striding to a chair across the room, he dropped into it. He needed to distance himself from the object of his obsession, try to arrive at some rational explanation for what the hell was going on, and—mostly—talk himself into leaving.

"What are you doing over there? You're too far away," Liv murmured soft as silk, ignoring his sulky gaze, slowly unzipping her shorts.

"Fucking witch," he muttered, but he was smiling.

"If we're talking witchcraft, I empathize completely. And I don't even believe in that hocus-pocus. But whatever's going on here is unreal."

"No shit. I'm gonna wear myself out fucking you."

"While I have to think about actually going to work again someday."

"This is crazy," he said with a sigh.

"I agree."

But she'd slipped her shorts down her legs as she'd spoken, and her little white lace panties with the purple bows were fully engaging his attention. He lifted his chin the merest distance. "Take them off," he said, gruffly.

"What if I don't want to?"

"You don't have a choice."

"You're going to make me?" she whispered.

"No doubt in my mind."

"I'm getting really wet from you talking like that."

"Good. It'll make it easier to slide my cock into your tight little cunt." He reached for the zipper on his jeans. "Come here."

She should have at least hesitated, but he'd pulled out his erection that was swelling before her eyes and her addictive senses wouldn't allow her to equivocate.

"That's a good girl," he said with a tight-lipped smile as she slipped off her panties and rose from the bed, his mood further darkening as he wondered if she was equally obliging to every guy who showed up in her bedroom. "Bring that ripe, juicy cunt over here where it'll do me some good."

"Or where you'll do *me* some good." His taunting tone struck a raw nerve.

"That's a given. You can't ever get enough, can you?"

She could have explained that he was the exception, that not getting enough was unique to him. But she didn't feel like explaining when he was appraising her like she was a commodity or a means to an end. Or a convenience for his present lecherous appetites. "Don't look at me like that," she said sulkily, stopping before she reached him.

"Don't tell me *don't*," he said, lunging forward, grabbing her wrist, and jerking her forward.

She struggled against his hold. "I'll scream and embarrass you or—" Her words died in her throat. He'd jammed two fingers palm deep up her vagina.

"Or what, sweetheart?" he whispered, gently moving his fingers inside her. "Maybe come in the next few seconds?" She was wetter than wet, her clit engorged and rampant, her breathing labored: all the signs of an approaching orgasm so familiar to him right there under his fingertips. He could have stopped what he was doing and leveled the playing field. And if he hadn't been slave to his own ungovernable desires, he might have. But he didn't want to give her a chance to resist. He wanted her to want him as much as he wanted her. Without restraint or limits. Persistently, unremittingly. *Now*.

He reached for a condom even before the last quivering flutters of her climax quieted. Ripping the packet open with his teeth, he lifted her unresisting body and seated her on his knees. As she drifted in that half world of postcoital enchantment, he sheathed his cock with record speed, swept her up once again, and deposited her on his throbbing dick in one fell swoop.

There was no question about leisurely sex this time. He raised and lowered her on his erection at breakneck speed, his biceps and pecs flexing and contracting with brute power, her pliant, yielding flesh engulfing him in snug, blissful welcome. Toward the end, she was beginning to pick up the pace on her own, but he didn't feel like waiting. His demons wouldn't allow it. He came in a selfish, pissed-off, jet-propelled, slam-bang orgasm.

Seconds later, nostrils flaring, they confronted each other at close range.

"Thanks for nothing," she spat, her face only inches away.

"Don't worry," he said, insolently. "The night's still young."

"What makes you think you're staying the night?"

"This," he said, shoving his hand down between them and brushing her clit with a featherlight touch. "This little baby wants more."

She shut her eyes against the feverish rapture, calling herself every name in the book for not having any sense of propriety or self-discipline when it came to Jake Chambers. Damn him! Try as she might, she couldn't resist; worse, she could feel tears welling in her eyes because she wanted him and didn't want to want him this dreadfully. Great—now she was going to cry like a baby over sex!

She tried to think of something else in an effort to quell her tears.

But considering her current position, it was hard to think of anything but the fact that his cock was still inside her. She wanted it there. And she was an idiot.

He saw the tears when she opened her eyes and felt instant remorse.

"Sweetheart, I'm sorry," he whispered, brushing away the wetness spilling down her cheeks. "You're driving me crazy, and I'm taking it out on you." Holding her close, he gently kissed her eyelids and nose and lips. "I'll make it up to you. I'll make it all go away. I promise."

She sniffled and tried to smile and eventually slid her arms around his neck and kissed him back because she could no more subdue her screwy, fanatical feelings than he.

"Tell me you forgive me," he murmured sometime later, tracing the pale curve of her brow with his fingertip.

She nodded and blew out a small breath. "You should go, but I don't want you to go, and I don't have a clue why. Maybe we could just agree this is beyond reason and leave it at that."

"Agreed." He would have agreed that the world was flat if she'd smile again.

"Okay." She smiled—a weather-permitting smile, but nevertheless a smile. "Would it be my turn again, then?"

"It's your turn all night if you wish." He suddenly felt unburdened, swept away by an unalloyed sense of well-being and good cheer. "Consider me at your disposal."

"Oh my God. Did you feel that?" Her vagina had done a quick little tango step at that remark about him being at her disposal.

"Yep." How could he not with the strength of that vaginal flourish moving up his cock. "Give me a few seconds to clean up," he said, lifting her off his lap, "and then we'll see about sweet-talking your little pussy into an orgasm or two."

He was a master of sweet talk as it turned out.

Although darling Livvi had a certain competence when it came to sexual address, too.

And the remainder of the night was given over to a particularly endearing and affectionate form of communication.

Twenty

The knock on the door was loud.

And early.

Liv glanced at the bedside clock. Seven. Jeez—who was knocking on her door at this time of the morning?

"Don't answer it," Jake mumbled, his face buried in his pillow. "They'll go away."

But Liv was already reaching for her robe hanging on the bedpost. "I can see a car in the drive from the window. Maybe it's someone I know."

Reaching the window, she surveyed the expanse of gravel fronting her backyard. "Holy shit." Two county police cars were parked there.

"What's up?" Jake rolled out of bed, his brain's warning system switching on at her sharp expletive.

"The county mounties are paying a call." She tossed her robe aside, figuring clothes were required for this encounter.

"Here?" He dropped back onto the bed, his sleep-deprived senses overriding his brain's warning system.

"No, Siberia." She pulled a T-shirt from her dresser drawer.

O-kaaay . . . that was sarcasm. Coming to his feet in a surge of conciliatory good manners, he reached for his jeans. "Let me go talk to them. I'll tell them you're not home. They'll go away, and we can get back to sleep. Oh, shit." He felt the adrenaline rush as his brain cells engaged with reality. "This is about Janie and Matt. It's not about you. Look, stay here. See that no one comes out. I'll handle this. In my business I deal with security types all the time."

Pulling his T-shirt over his head, he was halfway to the door when Liv caught up and grabbed his arm. "Wait. It'll be better if I go out there. I know the county mounties. You don't. Also, this isn't the big city where your expertise with security types matters."

"Who cares whether you know these guys or not if Leo sent them? By the way, just how well do you know these guys?" His voice had taken on an edge.

"Is this where I say, 'It's none of your business'?" Her voice was equally sharp.

"I'd like a better answer."

"And I'm not giving you one."

Another knock on the door brought them back to the issue at hand.

"Sorry," Jake said. "I'm losing it."

"I apologize, too." She smiled. "And I lost it a long time ago."

"Since we're both semirational once again, may I politely point out that I could very easily deal with these deputies. I'll say you're on vacation. I'm house-sitting. I'll tell them to come back in a week." He figured he might be better with bullshit than she, seeing how he spent his whole life dishing it out to rich customers who all expected personalized service.

"My car's out there."

"So? You took a plane."

"Look, I grew up with these guys. They're good kids." She picked up the shorts she'd tossed on the floor last night. "And if this is about Leo, I guarantee you, his reach doesn't have the same power out here as in New York. This is the hinterland where no one's ever heard of him," she added, stepping into the shorts. "So be a dear and warn Janie." She zipped the zipper. "Then come down and see how I'm doing."

He hesitated for the briefest second. "Okay," he said, clipped and low. "We'll do it your way."

She lifted her brows. "That sounds as though you don't normally utter that phrase."

"You got that right," he muttered, still not sure he couldn't handle the situation better.

Another round of knocking echoed through the house.

Jake's jaw twitched, then he reached out and opened the bedroom door. "Go."

They met Roman in the hall.

"I told Janie to stay in her bedroom," Roman said, his voice taut. "Matt's still sleeping."

"Liv thinks she might be able to talk these guys into going away," Jake explained.

"Could be." Roman nodded toward the stairs. "Better go before they wake up Matt. We'll watch your back."

"Please, don't say that. I've never in my entire life needed anyone to watch my back. Okay?"

Roman and Jake exchanged glances.

"And don't do that either," Liv muttered. "You're creeping me out. It's only the diaper patrol outside. I've known these guys from day one of their deputy jobs. Neither is over twenty-three, and the only reason they have these cushy, do-nothing jobs is because their daddies have money and connections in the county. We have no crime around here unless you count the occasional fight that breaks out at closing time at a local bar. So trust me. I'll handle this."

Quickly running her fingers through her hair, she ran down the stairs.

When she walked barefoot out onto her back porch a few moments later—like all farmhouses, traffic flowed through the kitchen—she resembled a fresh-faced farmer's daughter, all rosy-cheeked, pale tousled hair, leggy beauty, and a winning smile.

Watching from the kitchen window, Jake took note of the dropped jaws and open mouths as Liv came into view. The two deputies almost fell backward down the steps, practically doing a Keystone Kops pratfall before coming to rest on the sidewalk below. An older man in an Italian suit standing on the lawn, however, gave no visible reaction, unless the slight swing of his briefcase indicated a tightening of his grip on the handle.

The suit must be Leo's man.

And that guy didn't look as though he could be talked out of much of anything. His face was expressionless, his thinning hair cut short, his skin tanned to an acceptable, not-too-dark, PC shade. He was middle height, middle-aged, and toned. A white-shoe lawyer from the look of it rather than a goon, but obviously a man willing to do whatever it took to please his client if this crack-of-dawn visit was any indication.

"Morning, Wayne, Arlen," Liv said, her smile in place as she descended the back steps. "What can I do for you?"

"Sorry about the early hour," Wayne Stensberg said, his round face flushing red. Hitching up his belt, he shifted from foot to foot and looked as though he wished he were somewhere else.

Liv shrugged faintly. "It's not a problem. I'm always up early."

"The thing is," Arlen Christensen muttered, touching his holstered firearm as though to remind himself that he was a lawman, "this lawyer from New York wants us to deliver a summons."

Liv offered them a wide-eyed look. "A summons for me? Whatever for?"

"Nah, it ain't for you, Liv. This guy says you have a lady visitor here."

She shook her head. "He's wrong. I'm here alone." Her mouth lifted in the faintest of smiles. "Well, not precisely alone." She nodded toward Jake's BMW, Roman's car fortunately somewhere else. She'd never seen it. "A boyfriend stayed over last night."

Both deputies turned red, their imaginations running wild after Liv's remark about her boyfriend sleeping over.

Arlen regained his composure first, although he had to clear his throat a couple times before any words came out. "I'd say we're pretty much done here, then." He nudged his partner with his elbow. "Let's go." Drawing himself up to his full five-foot ten-inch height as though to add significance to his decision, he added politely, "Real sorry to bother you so early in the morning."

"Whose shoes are those?"

Everyone turned at the sharp question.

The thin-lipped lawyer was pointing his right index finger at a spot on the lawn.

Liv's heart sank. There were Matt's red sandals, a vivid splash of color against the green grass. He must have left them there when he'd swung on the basswood tree's rope swing.

"Those must be my neighbor boy's," she said, nervously watching the well-dressed man walk over to the sandals and pick them up. "Gracie brought Ryan over the other day," she went on, smiling at the deputies who knew Gracie as well as she did.

"Prada."

The cool voice was in contrast to the triumph in the man's eyes as he held up the sandals and nailed Liv with a victorious look.

"We have Prada in Minnesota." She forced her voice to a calmness she didn't in the least feel.

"The boy's here. I know it," Leo's lawyer rapped out. He nodded at the deputies. "Serve the papers."

"Are the papers for me?" Liv was relatively sure they couldn't serve Leo's papers to just anyone.

Wayne lifted the sheaf of papers he held and, gazing at them, read, "Janie Tabor Rolf. Some custody papers, I think," he added. Giving the lawyer, who had treated them like hired help from the moment he'd walked into their small office, a resentful look,

Wayne jabbed his finger toward Liv. "This here ain't Janie Tabor," he said, his voice loud enough to carry across the lawn. "New York," he muttered under his breath. "Cranky fuck. Beg pardon, Liv," he murmured, his gaze apologetic. "But we had to at least drive him over here. The idiot was screamin' something fierce."

"I understand. It's not your fault. And if there was anyone here besides me and my—ah—friend," she murmured, "I'd be the first to cooperate."

"We know that," Arlen replied, clearly sympathetic. "The guy's a nutcase," he added, careful to keep his voice down. "Threatening and carrying on like he owns the world. Hey, Mr New York—you want a ride back?" he shouted, indicating his car with a jerk of his thumb. "Or you can walk back to town if you want. Wayne and me are leavin'."

Red-faced with fury, the man, who looked vastly out of place in the country in his Italian suit, stomped back to one of the cars, got in, and slammed the door.

"Wanna flip who drives that one?" Wayne grumbled. The man had gotten into his car.

"I'll drive the prick if you buy at Smitty's tonight," Arlen offered.

"You got yourself a deal! I'll buy coffee at Mae's, too, as soon as we dump this piece of shit."

"Sweet."

The two young deputies high-fived each other and, with a wave for Liv, strolled back to their cars.

Liv remained on the sidewalk until the two police cars disappeared from sight down her driveway. Then, realizing she'd been holding her breath, she exhaled softly and turned back to her house.

"You were impressive, babe," Jake drawled as she walked into the kitchen a few moments later. "That big-city lawyer's spitting nails about now."

"Wayne and Arlen are nice guys. I was pretty confident they'd listen to reason."

"They were serving custody papers, weren't they?"

Liv turned at the sound of Janie's voice and saw her standing in the doorway to the kitchen, Roman at her side like her Pretorian guard. "I think so. Wayne mentioned custody papers."

"This might be a good time to move on," Roman observed. Leo wasn't a patient man. He'd put someone else on the hunt who'd found the same phone records as he.

"Or perhaps time to give Leo a call," Janie countered determinedly. "I don't feel like running every time one of his goons shows up. I really like it here. It's peaceful." She smiled at Liv. "Who would think I'd like peaceful? But I do."

"Leo might not operate so legally next time," Roman warned. "He sent me out here to snatch Matt and bring him back."

"I know." Janie patted his arm. "I knew why you'd come. I also had a pretty good idea you couldn't do what Leo wanted." Roman had always been nicer to her than he would have had to be as Leo's hired gun, taking time when they met to engage her in conversation.

"My personal feelings aside, I'd still recommend finding a better refuge. Leo won't give up. He's putting plan B in action as we speak. That's my professional opinion, and I know him better than you." Dipping his head, Roman held Janie's gaze. "I know a lotta things you don't *want* to know about him."

"But then *you* don't know that I have something of Leo's he's going to want back *very* badly." She hadn't told anyone about it.

Not Brad or Liv, not Roman who, until last night, had been only a possible in terms of reliability.

A new degree of admiration gleamed in Roman's eyes. "Is that a fact?" he murmured.

Janie grinned. "Yes, indeedy. I have some excellent leverage. I hadn't planned on using it unless it was absolutely necessary. But if Leo wants to play hardball starting at square one, I'm more than willing." She took Roman's hand. "Come, I'll show you." She turned to smile at Liv and Jake. "If you'll excuse us."

"That was all very mysterious and cheerful," Jake murmured, watching the couple walk away.

"Whatever it is, I don't want to know," Liv said firmly. "With Leo Rolf, ignorance is bliss, believe me. There is nothing about that man that withstands close scrutiny."

Jake knew some foul things about Leo but kept them to himself. Time enough to reveal the sordid details should Janie need help in divorce court. "How about close scrutiny and me?" Jake playfully inquired.

"Now, that's entirely different," she said, gazing up at him from under her lashes, her smile pure seduction.

"Not that I shouldn't go home."

"I know. And I should be out in my vineyard, working."

"So what're we gonna do?"

"How tired are you?"

"I'm never that tired."

"I was hoping you weren't."

"I knew you were hoping that."

"Don't think you know everything about me."

"I've got a feeling I'm gettin' close to knowing everything about you."

"Sex-wise you mean."

"No, I meant your favorite CDs."

"Just for that, I may not want to have sex with you."

"That'll be the day."

"You think I can't go without sex?"

"Yeah."

She saw the certainty in his eyes, heard it in his voice, realized he might understand her better than she understood herself. "It's all your fault." A flat, almost resentful note in her voice.

"I know how you feel," he grumbled, a scowl drawing his dark brows together. "I've been trying to leave before I even got here."

She suddenly grinned. "It's not as though it's the worst problem in the world, I suppose, what with the Middle East currently going up in flames."

A smile slowly formed on his mouth. "I guess. Put it in perspective—right? But I'm tellin' you, this is sorta getting out of hand."

She slid her fingers through his. "Could we talk about this later?"

"After you come?"

"And after you come."

His grip tightened, and he jerked her against his body, his free hand skimming down her back, cupping her bottom, holding her hard against his cock. "What if I feel like doing it right here?"

"You can't."

"I can do anything I want." Putting action to words, he pulled her toward the pantry, opened the door, shoved her in, and shut the door behind them.

"Really, Jake . . . wouldn't it be more comfortable—" He'd

pushed her up against the door and was unzipping her shorts. "What if someone came in?"

"Like who?"

"Like anyone or may—"

He kissed her hard, stopping her objections, which weren't very convincing anyway, since she'd begun moving her hips in a show-me-what-you've-got way. Although even if her protests had been convincing, he might not have noticed, since he was busy shoving her shorts down her legs.

"Jake—stop!" This time there was no question she meant it.

"Uh-uh." That male-brain single-focus thing was operating at the max. He lifted her up, kicked away her shorts, and ran his middle finger down her cleft in a practiced checking-on-progress stroke.

It took her a moment to drag her senses back to reality after his titillating scouting maneuver. But once back on track, she said, heatedly, "Stop! You don't have a condom!"

"Don't worry, baby. I won't come in you."

He was stroking her clitoris, every one of her sexual receptors was panting in response, sending competing messages to her brain apropos the importance of condoms. And when she should be responsible and engaged, her brain seemed to be turning to mush.

He was unzipped a second later and forcing her thighs apart with his muscular thighs, pushing his swollen cock up into her with his own very specific style of engagement. Propelling her up on her toes, he grunted in satisfaction as he thrust in up to the hilt and lifted her completely off her feet. As she started to fall, he quickly slid his hands under her bottom, picked her up, wrapped her legs around his waist and, without missing a beat, swung his hips out and drove back in again hard, hard, *hard*.

Leaning into her, he pressed her back against the door while she clung to him and met each pounding, fevered thrust.

"What are you doing getting fucked in your pantry?" he said, thickly. "I thought you didn't want to."

"Screw you," she muttered, rankled at his knowing tone, chafing as well that she wanted him with an almost unfathomable intensity.

They could have been animals mating, she thought, her panting, him growling, each uttering guttural, throaty moans deep in their throats. Mere days ago, she couldn't have contemplated such outrageously wanton feelings, no more than she could have considered overlooking the lack of a condom. And here she was, throwing caution to the winds just to feel the raw, feverish pleasure he so casually offered.

How did he inspire this overwrought nymphomania? Was it him or her or some odd, compelling combination of the two?

His arms abruptly tightened.

As if she was alert to his every mood, she looked up.

He smiled faintly, neither resentful nor ruffled—other than sexually. He was exclusively focused on getting off. "No rush," he politely said. "Just wondering." He'd actually considered coming in her, a notion so shocking it had sent his adrenaline into the stratosphere, instantly clearing his mind. On the other hand, he couldn't last forever.

"Are you waiting for me?" Her gaze was heated, her voice breathy with need, issues of unfathomable need obliterated by more gratifying sensations.

"Take your time."

He didn't mean it. "You come. I can wait," she said, inexplicably willing to subordinate her pleasure to his like some harem slave or vassal handmaiden from ages past.

"Uh-uh . . . we'll both come; I'll fill you full of my sperm," he said, his voice a low, sexy rasp. "That way I'll leave my mark on you, and other men will know you're taken—that you're my property. No one else will be able to screw you—just me. Only I can cram my cock in you and make you scream for more. Would you like that?"

The pulsing ache inside her had reached fever pitch at his words, the entire focus of her senses on his cock sliding in and out of her flame-hot vagina.

"Answer me," he growled, "or I'll take it out."

"Yes, yes—please don't!"

"Good girl. Here, babe—you can have it back."

She gasped, the jolt of his cock hitting bottom spiking through her brain, the aftermath rippling outward in concentric waves of heated bliss.

"Maybe I should keep you tied to my bed," he murmured, "so you'll always be there to fuck me. Then when I come home, you'll be waiting for me, with your cunt wet with longing. I'll ram my big stiff prick into your tight little pussy and fill you with come over and over again. How would you like that? Would you like me to fill you to overflowing?"

She wasn't able to answer. She was climaxing.

Like he wanted.

And just in the nick of time, he determined, jerking out and coming all over her stomach.

After he'd found some paper towels and wiped off and wiped her off, he helped her on with her shorts. Patting the zipper in place, he dropped a kiss on her nose. "Thanks, babe. I needed that."

"As if I didn't. By the way, you're good," she said with a sunny smile. "You should do phone sex."

He grinned. "Just for you, I'm on call twenty-four/seven."

Twenty-one

Having been shown Janie's ace in the hole, Roman was sitting beside her on her bed, discarding all of the contingency plans having to do with Leo's physical well-being that were racing through his brain. "Are you sure you want to talk to Leo?" he muttered, irrationally feeling as though Janie needed protection even across the phone lines. Or maybe not so irrationally; Leo was without scruples. "I could give him the bad news."

"I'm so pissed right now, I'm in the mood to tell him *myself* what he's up against. Look"—she held out her hand—"I'm shaking, I'm so pissed. If he thinks he's taking Matt from me, I'm going to personally clue him in."

"At least let me patch you through to him via my office. I'll call Vinnie, and he can set it up. Leo won't be able to trace the call that way." He shrugged. "Not that it much matters, I suppose, after our recent visit from his stooge."

"No, you're right. Why make it easy for him? Call Vinnie. I'll take great pleasure in telling Leo to leave me alone—and the sooner he knows it, the better." She exhaled softly. "I actually thought I might not have to threaten him. I thought maybe he'd be agreeable about the divorce. We could deal through our lawyers, come up with some congenial settlement." She snorted. "How's that for naive?"

"Leo's Leo," Roman simply said as he dialed his office. "A leopard doesn't change his spots. And Leo's been pushing people around for a long time. Hey, Vinnie, roll me over to Leo Rolf's office. And FYI, as of now, we're off the prick's payroll. Right. Don't talk to him unless you clear it with me." He held the phone to his ear and listened, then spoke crisply. "Ben, Roman here. Is Leo there? Okay, put on your flak jacket and put me through." Roman chuckled. "Fuck no. Why should I tell you? You're gonna listen anyway. Now, do it, okay? I'm in a hurry."

"Where the fuck are you!!!"

Leo's fury bounced off the bedroom walls.

Holding the phone away from his ear, Roman said, "None of your business. I'm not working for you anymore."

"Then you owe me for your *goddamn plane ride*!"

"Shut up and listen, Leo. And just a word to the wise. Don't fuck with me. You'll lose. Now, Janie's here. She wants to talk to you."

"You're screwing my *wife*! I can't frigging *believe* it. I'll sue your ass! I'll see that you *never work in this town again*! I'll—"

"Shut the fuck up, or I might put a bullet through your head and save everyone a lotta trouble. Now here's Janie." Roman handed her his cell phone.

"I don't appreciate your lawyer showing up here at the crack of dawn, you prick," Janie snapped.

Leo was still debating the degree of danger he might be in after Roman's threat; it took him a moment to gather his thoughts.

"Leo, dammit, are you there?"

"I heard you," he murmured, deciding he'd hire bodyguards for protection. His momentary fear resolved, his voice returned to its normal bullying tenor. "Now, listen to me, you worthless cunt. I'm getting custody of Matt, and there's nothing on God's green earth that you can do to stop me. You can't afford to take me on in court, and I have enough money to stay in litigation for years. So listen up, you greedy bitch. Do as you're told, and I might give you enough money to live in the style to which you were accustomed. How much can a fucking trailer cost?"

"Are you finished, you impotent old fart? Because I happen to have the means to put you in jail." After his allusion to trailers, Janie's temper was red-hot. She'd worked hard and long to guarantee she'd never be poor again. No way would she let Leo destroy what it had taken her years to accomplish. "For your information, I have a flash drive from your personal computer. I copied all your files, Leo. Every last one. The ones with the Isle of Man accounts. The ones with the Cayman Islands accounts. The list of those black-box companies and dummy corporations. I dumped everything, Leo. Every last red cent of your illicit operations and bank account numbers is in my hands. So fuck you."

"I'll *kill* you!" Leo shrieked.

"Even if you do, you'll still go to jail," Janie said, cool as ice. "If I die or disappear, a friend has orders to mail the flash drive to the attorney general of New York, the IRS, and every newspaper on the East Coast. You have yourself a good day, Leo, and leave me the fuck alone."

"Wait, wait, don't hang up. Let's talk about this."

"There's nothing to say."

"For one thing," Leo smoothly noted, careful to keep his voice restrained, "if I go to jail and they confiscate all my property, you won't get anything. Have you thought of that?"

"Of course. Here's the way I see it, Leo. You don't want to go to jail a lot more than I want your money. So I'm pretty sure I'm holding a better hand than you. My suggestion to you would be"—her voice took on a crisp cadence—"get your lawyers to draw up divorce and custody papers ASAP, giving me full custody of Matt. Along with that, I want fifty million. It's not complicated. So let me know when the papers are ready to sign. You can leave a message at Roman's office. In the meantime, enjoy your life."

Snapping the phone shut, she shivered uncontrollably.

"Hey, hey, everything's good," Roman murmured, taking his phone from her white-knuckled grip, tossing it aside, drawing her into his arms, and holding her close. "I'm pretty sure you ruined Leo's day."

"Better his than mine," Janie whispered, feeling the tension drain from her body with Roman's arms around her. "And thank you for your support and kindness." She looked up and smiled. "And thank you for last night. I haven't had great sex for a very long time."

"You shouldn't marry old men."

"Tell me about it."

Roman smiled faintly. "In that case, you might not mind knowing that Leo has a new girlfriend."

Janie grimaced. "I figured. I wish her luck. She's going to need it." Resting her cheek against Roman's chest, she sighed. "I was so stupid, wasn't I? Like a damned lamb to the slaughter."

"Don't beat yourself up. You weren't the first woman to succumb to Leo's lavish lifestyle. There were a few before you."

She glanced up. "Did you spy on his other wives, too?"

"Naturally. Not that it's an excuse, but the others were pretty damned mercenary. You, however, still had a modicum of sweet, small-town girl in you when I first met you. To be honest, it surprised me." He didn't say he'd always wished her the best—an anomaly for a cynical soul like him. He'd never been given to benevolence. "Anyway," he said, changing the subject to something less angst-filled, "you should think about what you want to do in terms of your and Matt's safety."

"I was hoping you might stay with us until everything is resolved."

"You did, did you?"

"I'd pay you for your time, of course," she quickly offered, uncertain of how to interpret his brusque reply.

His gaze narrowed. "With what?"

"Hey!" She shoved him away, distancing herself on the bed. "Don't you dare even think what you're thinking! I have money!"

"Calm down. I'm not impugning your character." He blew out a breath, cracked his knuckles, half-rose, sat back down again, and stared at the toes of his custom shoes. "I've been all about business for so long I don't know anything else," he said gruffly. "I didn't think I had any functioning feelings left. When you come up through the vice squad like I did, then go private and deal with every lowlife, rich and poor, you get numb. You just do your job and don't ask questions." He turned his head marginally in Janie's direction and looked at her from under his lashes. "You don't have to pay me with anything. Not money, not you, not a smile or a kind word. I'll stay because I want to. There," he muttered. "We're done."

"You're really a good person, Roman. I mean it," Janie added softly. "It's been a long time since a man's done anything for me without wanting something in return."

"Let's not talk about that." He knew she'd pulled herself up from poverty; he also knew she hadn't always been particular about the methods she used.

She smiled, liking that he preferred not seeing the skeletons in her closet. More importantly, she liked that he didn't want something from her. "Do you think we could stay here in the country for a while at least? It's sort of like a little bit of paradise: strife-free, laid back, away from everything icky."

He laughed, understanding the ickiness of the world better than most. "Sure, why not. Let me make a few calls, and when Matt wakes up, we'll take him somewhere fun. There has to be a park or something around here."

When he said really sweet things like that, she found herself beginning to feel something way beyond gratitude. Or maybe it was just that anyone who was good to Matt touched her heart. Leo had never actually played with his son. He'd just hired nannies and tutors, clowns and pony rides on birthdays. Roman's kindness to Matt was profoundly moving.

Although on a purely selfish level, Roman was also a major turn-on sexually. Like he was *enormous* and after being with Leo, she was dying for a big, husky man who could last.

And could Roman *last*.

Really, a holiday in the country was just what she needed.

On several levels.

All of them sure to prove highly satisfying.

Twenty-two

Leo strode through Ben's office in an obvious hurry. "I'll be out for the rest of the day," he snapped. "And I won't be taking messages."

The outer door slammed behind him, and Ben Connor leaned back in his chair and murmured an explosive, "God damn!"

The phone conversation he'd just overheard made him decide to get his financial ducks in a row. Like cashing in his stock in Leo's companies, for starters. Janie wasn't going to go down without a knock-down, drag-out fight. And from what he'd just heard, it wasn't entirely clear who might win.

Unless Leo recovered that flash drive, he was screwed. Royally.

If Leo was sensible, he'd give Janie a generous settlement, get the flash drive back, and get on with his life. But knowing his boss, Ben didn't think that was likely.

For one thing, Leo wasn't rational.

For another, he didn't like to lose.

Ever.

The detritus in terms of human misery and looted companies Leo had left in his wake were testament to his ruthlessness. Which thought prompted Ben to make sure he didn't join that woeful debris. Flipping through his Rolodex, he dialed his broker. That Cal was also his ex–college roommate was reassuring. The kind of divestiture he was planning might raise questions with anyone other than a trusted friend. He'd give Cal enough information so he understood that Leo might be going through an expensive divorce. The real story would have to wait until such a time as Leo was indicted, and if that never happened, so much the better for his own long-term plans.

Ben had always understood that he wasn't working for a saint. Not that saints were much in evidence in corporate America. The camel-through-the-eye-of-a-needle thing that had been around for a couple thousand years, a case in point. "Cal—Ben here. How're you doing? I'm good—good. Yeah, yeah, still hanging in there. I'm chasing down the record. Yeah, no shit. Anyway, I have some trades I'd like you to handle. I want to move some of my portfolio to safer ground. Cash maybe—no, I'm not skipping the country. I'm just in a cautious mood."

Twenty-three

While Ben Connor was seeing that his financial security wouldn't suffer because of his boss's malfeasance, Leo was driving through the Lincoln Tunnel heading for Jersey.

Due to the confidential nature of his upcoming meeting, Leo had dispensed with his driver. He was also using a nondescript sedan for the same reason. Being inconspicuous was essential.

The neighborhood restaurant he walked into some forty minutes later had just opened for the day; the waiters were setting up for lunch. The manager behind the cash register acknowledged him with the merest nod, then pointed to a table at the rear of the room where two men were seated.

When Leo sat down, the younger of the two men silently rose and walked away.

"What can I do for you, Leo? It's been a while." The well-dressed, older man with manicured nails, close-cropped gray hair, and a Florida tan smiled faintly. "I was thinking you might have found new facilitators."

Leo shook his head. "Everything's been running smoothly—at least up until now. I haven't needed your services. By the way, thanks for your prompt response. I appreciate it."

"You sounded as though you needed something in a hurry."

"I do. The usual terms?"

"The same. Cash. Untraceable. We'll pick it up."

"My wife just left with my son. I want him back."

"Sorry. We don't mess with women or children."

"I know, I know. I'll deal with that myself. What I need from you is a little something she took with her when she left—a flash drive from my personal computer. She copied all my files. I need that flash drive back. And I need it quickly."

"That's why I don't like computers. Nothing's safe," the man grumbled. "With all these crazy kid hackers or the feds sticking their noses in everyone's business, better an accountant or tax attorney you can trust."

Leo frowned. Far be it for him to argue with a man whose operation was still essentially brown-bagging it; international banking was slightly more complicated. "My computer files are more personal than anything else," he lied. "But still, I wouldn't want her to sell them to the highest bidder."

The gray-haired man grinned. "She got your Bangkok pictures?"

"She has a little bit of everything, I'm afraid." Another lie, not that it mattered with either one of them. "Can you help me out or not?"

Leo's facilitator flicked his manicured fingers in a dismissive gesture. "Of course. Where do we pick up this flash drive?"

"In Minnesota. But I don't want my son frightened. So no rough stuff—just a quick snatch and run."

"Look, no offense, but I doubt your wife is going to just hand it over."

"I know. Work it out any way you have to. Just so no one lays a hand on Matt, and I'm fine. Understood?"

"We're businessmen just like you, Leo. We don't get physical. People understand they're better off cooperating with us. It's that simple."

Leo nodded. "Good. Perfect. You always come through, Carmine. I appreciate it. Here's the address. Let me know when you want me to pick up my package and where you want your payment delivered. It's a pleasure doing business with you."

"Likewise."

As Leo left the restaurant, the man at the table watched him, a smirk on his face. *Dumb fuck*, he thought. *Why does the stupid shit keep marrying the broads?*

Twenty-four

"Leo, darling, I hate to see you so upset." Hannah Reiss glanced at herself in the mirrored wall opposite her. Thank God she looked good, even in this terrible light in this horrid dive that Leo insisted had the best steaks in town. "Not that you don't have every right," she added, taking pains to make her voice softly sincere. "For that woman to take your son from you is . . . really . . . criminal."

"Damn right it is. But she'll get hers," Leo grunted, flicking a glance upward from his twenty-two-ounce steak. "You're not eating. Don't you like your steak?"

Good God, would the man not talk with his mouth full? She forced a smile. "I love my steak, darling, but we had cake and ice cream for Chelsea's birthday just before I left work. Do you remember Chelsea? She's in accounting."

"The fat broad with no tits?"

"She's not exactly what you'd call fat, dear."

"Fuck if she isn't. But Jeff tells me she's practically a human calculator. So she stays, fat or not."

Now, Hannah Reiss had spent her entire life doing her own kind of calculating. In her case, it had entailed selecting the right friends in high school, the right extracurricular community activities, such as reading to the blind, volunteering at the local hospital, driving elderly people to church on Sunday. (It wasn't her fault the nursing home van had stopped running and some of her passengers had passed out in the hundred-degree heat; the girl at Baskin-Robbins should have made her banana split faster. But her father had taken care of that little imbroglio, and really, what was all the fuss about? No one had actually died.) So with her high school record pristine thanks to her daddy's intervention, college admission officials were duly impressed, and she was accepted at the right college where she took the right classes (preferably where professors gave grades for sex), and graduated magna cum laude. After graduation, she applied at companies with the best potential for advancement. That Leo Rolf was known for his roving eye figured, if not exclusively, pertinently in her decision to take an entry-level job at Rolf Enterprises for a lesser salary than she would have liked.

Now, if she could continue to stomach Leo's numerous vulgarities, her life would proceed very much as she'd planned. She would become wife number five . . . and if Leo happened to keel over during sex in the not too distant future, she would gladly become a rich young widow. "You know, I think I'll take this delicious steak home and enjoy it later," she said sweetly. *Or flush it down the garbage disposal.*

"Want another martini?" Rolf snapped his fingers at the waiter. "They make the best martinis here. Just a smell of vermouth—that's the secret. We'll take two more," he brusquely said at the young waiter's approach. "And bring the bread pudding while you're at it—lots of whipped cream. I don't want a couple little dabs. Okay?"

With barely concealed loathing, the waiter said, "Yes, sir. Lots of whipped cream it is." The waitstaff always drew straws for Leo Rolf. No one wanted to serve him.

"And coffee," Leo barked. "A big cup. None of that sissy demitasse shit. Lots of sugar, too!"

The clientele in the hundred-year-old steakhouse was, like Leo, not here for ambience or a fusion menu. Only a few patrons even glanced up at Leo's shouted orders. They were here for meat and martinis, and Murphy's Steakhouse delivered. Everything else was an afterthought.

"I never get tired of Murphy's," Leo murmured, pushing his plate away and leaning back in his chair with a satisfied sigh. "A steak and a martini." He winked at Hannah. "And a piece of ass afterward. Hell, life doesn't get much better."

Maybe she could slowly poison his martinis, Hannah thought, not sure she could manage a lengthy sojourn as wife to this boorish lout. "I enjoy your company, too, Leo. You're just as charming as everyone always says."

"They say that?" he grunted, picking his teeth with a toothpick.

"Of course, darling. You're universally known for your charming manner," she went on, doing her best to overlook the dribble of spit sliding down his chin. "You put people at ease," she went on gamely. "You can talk to anyone on any subject" (as long as it's about him—or him—or, for a change, him). "Dex said the other day that you're the smartest man he's ever met."

"I've done okay for myself, I guess," Leo said smugly, setting the toothpick on his plate and wiping his mouth with his napkin.

Thank God for small favors. He'd used his napkin instead of the back of his hand. "You've done more than okay, darling," Hannah said, feeling as though she would be pushing a huge rock uphill until this evening ended. "You're at the absolute top of your game. No one knows how to make things happen when it comes to deal-making better than you."

"Speaking of making things happen. You look sexy as hell in that hot-pink suit. You're gonna have to take that off for me real soon."

She always cringed at the thought of having sex with him. When he took off his clothes, he was hideously wrinkled and flabby, despite his personal trainer. And if he lasted thirty seconds before he came, it was practically a record. The flip side and the only side that mattered, however, was that he was fabulously wealthy. "I'm tingly just thinking about it," she murmured, offering him the tantalizing smile she'd been practicing before the mirror since high school. "And for your information," she purred, "my lingerie is hot-pink, too."

"To go with your hot cunt," he said with a leer just as the waiter returned with their martinis.

Having seen his share of rich old men with beautiful young women, the waiter didn't so much as blink as he set the glasses on the table. "Coffee and dessert will be up shortly, sir."

"Here's to us, babe," Leo cheerfully said, ignoring the waiter and lifting his martini glass to Hannah. "And to the rest of the evening."

Hannah smiled and raised her glass. "You don't know how much I'm looking forward to it, darling."

And to the day that lovely pink diamond engagement ring she'd seen at Tiffany's was slipped on her finger.

As for her sex life, those bodyguards Leo had just hired might be willing to do a few things for her as well. A little extra overtime on the side, as it were. Leo always immediately fell asleep after he climaxed, leaving her totally unsatisfied.

And dying to get off.

She stole a glance at the next table, where the two buff young bodyguards were seated, all stern-faced and alert, scanning the room just like those CIA men did in movies. Really, the one closest to them could have been a model, he was so handsome. He reminded her a little of those Abercrombie & Fitch boys, only he was clearly a *man*.

What would he do if she brushed up against him in the elevator?

Better yet, why didn't she invite them *both* into her bed some night when Leo was dead to the world?

That delicious thought kept a smile on her face for the remainder of the meal, and when she *accidently* tripped getting into the car outside the restaurant, she made sure Mr. Abercrombie was standing close enough to catch her.

She smiled as he helped her into the car a moment later. "Thank you. I must have drunk more than I thought," she said, squeezing his hand in what could have been simple gratitude.

"Not a problem, miss. Anytime."

His middle finger slid over her palm. There was no doubt. "How polite you are," she murmured, taking her seat, a little jolt of lust warming her senses.

"Yes, miss." He released her hand and stepped back.

Had she been mistaken? Was it simply a meaningless stroke of his hand?

"If you ever need anything, miss, Bo and I are here to serve you."

"Thank you. Leo, your bodyguards are the most polite young men," she said, turning her smile on Leo as the two men moved to take their seats in the front of the limo. "What agency sent them?"

"Fuck if I know. Ask Ben. He takes care of that shit." Leo rubbed his stomach and grimaced. "I shouldn't have had that third martini. I'm going to call it a night, babe. Sorry, but you're going to have to wait to get laid." Leaning forward, he tapped on the glass behind his driver's head. "Take me home, Tommie, and then take the lady home." Falling back against the seat, he muttered, "Maybe it's all the stress with my bitch wife. Chriiist. As if I don't have enough on my plate without having to chase her down."

"Poor dear," Hannah murmured, stroking Leo's arm. "If there's anything I can do, just let me know. I feel just terrible for you."

"Thanks, babe. It's all in the bag though. Soon the problem will be solved."

"To your satisfaction, I hope." Janie's rather sordid background had always made her a complete unknown to Hannah. Unpredictable. Impossible to read. Even harder to understand.

"Of course to my satisfaction," Leo said with a snort. "Is there any other way?"

Twenty-five

While Hannah Reiss was trying to play all her cards right and possibly score with Leo's bodyguards in the bargain, those seated at Liv's kitchen table were enjoying another fabulous dinner, compliments of Jake Chambers.

Matt was eating his second chocolate chip cookie, while the adults were sipping chilled coffee and Kahlua with a dollop of whipped cream much superior to that served at Murphy's Steakhouse.

Roman, Janie, and Matt had spent the day at the beach. Liv and Jake had spent the day in bed until such a time as extreme hunger forced them to rise. After a quick trip to the local co-op grocery store, Jake made Southern fried pickle spears for an appetizer; a baby beet, heirloom tomato, and fig salad; and pulled pork with barbecue sauce served on homemade focaccia bread.

Everyone was stuffed, content, and practically speechless from a sense of well-being. The warm summer evening insinuated itself into the kitchen through the open windows and door, while the frogs and crickets sang their nightly chorus.

"You're sunburned," Liv murmured, only half-lifting her hand in Janie's direction, overcome as she was with balmy lethargy.

"That's a great beach so close to your house, and I'm just a little pink. It's nothing," Janie airily added, smiling up at Roman. "We're going back tomorrow, aren't we?"

"Whatever you say, boss."

The blatant absurdity between Roman's formidable seen-it-all detective persona and his quiet acquiescence made Liv smile. She turned to Jake and sportively asked, "Why aren't you so amenable?"

He looked amused. "I beg your pardon? Have I ever said no to you?"

Liv's gaze flicked to Matt in warning. "I was just teasing."

He grinned. "I wasn't. Not that I'm complaining. In fact—"

"Stop," she hissed, her gaze darting to Matt again. But the little boy was totally engrossed in picking chocolate chips out of his cookie.

"I was only going to say that I find your company extremely pleasant in every way," Jake said with a lazy smile.

"And I yours," Liv replied as smoothly, relieved that no one at the table was even listening. Janie and Roman were talking softly to each other; Matt had completely decimated his cookie and was now intent on pushing the crumbs into a pile on the very edge of the table.

Taking note of Liv's quick survey, Jake softly drawled, "See, I didn't embarrass you. They don't even know we're here."

"Fortunately."

His mouth quirked into a faint smile. "You—the shy type?"

"Please." Her brows flickered. "Stop it."

"Yes, ma'am."

An irrepressible grin appeared. "You're impossible."

He slid lower in his chair, looked at her from under his lashes, and said in a low voice pithy with ambivalence, "Perhaps—but never with you."

"Allow me to decide that," she said with deliberate lightness, knowing if she had half a brain she'd never lose sight of the fact that the past few days were nothing more than fun and games. Which meant she'd best curb any thoughts she might have about wanting him to stay.

It suddenly felt like déjà vu, as though she'd been here before at her kitchen table on another summer night. And Jake had been staring at her with that same intense scrutiny.

"Mama, will you read me da moon book again donight?" Matt asked, sending the cookie crumbs flying with a wild sweep of his hand.

Janie looked up. "Of course, dear. Are you finished eating? If you are," she said, ignoring the mess he'd made like someone with a household staff might, "we'll go upstairs and read."

"Me done." Matt jumped to the floor. "I wuv dat book."

When Janie rose from her chair, Roman stood. "I'll come listen, too." As Matt came hurtling past on his way to the stairs, Roman scooped him up in his arms and tossed him over his shoulder to the squealing delight of one three-year-old little boy.

"That's turning out to be a real interesting trio," Liv murmured, her gaze on her retiring guests. She preferred talking about safer subjects in her current overly sensitive, déjà vu mood.

"I hope Janie doesn't fuck him over," Jake remarked, his voice carefully neutral, as though he, too, understood the necessity for a shift in conversation.

"I'd guess Roman can take care of himself."

"Let's hope so. I wouldn't want to see him get pissed."

"It's really nice of him, though, to help out Janie. Or give her moral support or whatever. She can use some sympathy in what will probably turn out to be a nasty divorce."

"I'd say Janie has Leo in a box." Janie had explained about taking the computer files.

"Let's hope so. His last wife didn't fare too well."

A small silence fell.

They'd both run out of miscellaneous topics.

"I think I should head home," Jake finally said into the lengthening silence. "It's been a while since I checked my voice mail and stuff."

They both knew he could check his voice mail from anywhere, but his remark wasn't unexpected. In fact, Liv was surprised he'd stayed as long as he had. Surprised and hugely gratified sexually. But really . . .

They were both adults.

They both understood this couldn't go on forever.

"Thanks for driving up. Your visit was"—she smiled—"exceptional in every way."

"I agree."

"And thank you, too, for all the wonderful meals."

"My pleasure. Stop in next time you're in town."

"I will."

Leaning over, he kissed her lightly on the cheek before coming to his feet. "Sorry about leaving you with the dishes."

"Don't be. You can't be expected to make the meal and clean up, too."

Lifting his hand in a casual wave, he walked to the door. As he pushed the screen door open, he turned back. "I had a *really* good time," he said, his voice hushed and low.

She smiled. "Me, too."

The screen door slammed shut a second later, and she heard his footsteps cross the porch, then only silence as he moved away from the house.

A car firing up echoed in the stillness a moment later, the sweep of headlights flitted across her kitchen windows, and then the soft roar of the BMW slowly diminished as he drove away.

She didn't feel sad.

She didn't feel happy.

Instead, she experienced some middle ground of feeling: a gentle satisfaction and contentment. As though, well-stocked with orgasms and sexual pleasures, should a period of prolonged abstinence befall her, she would remain calm and unruffled.

Jake, on the other hand, wasn't sure he could withstand *any* abstinence when it came to Liv Bell. Even before he reached the freeway—a mere seven miles away—he was thinking about screwing her again, his powerful cravings fucking with his brain big time.

Jerking his hand off the wheel, he stabbed the stereo On button and, cranking the sound up high, resorted to his tried-and-true method of amnesia, male style. Loud music and high speed had always been the perfect combination to take his mind off things he wanted to forget. Something about the compelling need to stay alive always obliterated lesser issues.

He scanned the highway for cops.

None.

He punched the accelerator and, with the music blasting, headed home.

Once there, Jake immediately began answering his phone messages. Christ, he had a lot of people needing him to make their decisions. Luckily, his restaurants were well-oiled machines that ran despite his employees' occasional uncertainties.

A dozen calls later and everyone's questions were answered. Peace and tranquillity were restored to his West Coast operations. Not that he dared take a break or relax, or he knew exactly what he'd do.

Get in his car and drive back up north.

Despite the hour, he began calling the contractors Chaz had recommended. All they could do was tell him to go to hell. But since the men were all friends of Chaz's, they were more than willing to discuss Jake's building project, late hour or not.

Jake set up three early morning appointments for the next day.

Insurance, as it were, to make certain he stayed in town tonight and didn't cave and drive back out to Liv's. To that end, he decided it would be best not to stay in the apartment. He'd tour some of the bars downtown. Chaz had left him a lengthy list. He apparently knew every bartender at every happening place in the city.

Jake drank more than he should that night, politely brushed off a considerable number of women hitting on him, and felt curiously detached from the buzz and hustle of the crowds when loud music and bar noise were his normal comfort zone.

He actually made his way home before closing time.

This from a man who regularly joined his crew in after-close partying.

Less familiar with sleep deprivation, Liv found herself struggling to stay awake once Jake left. After cleaning up the debris from dinner, she went upstairs. Janie et al. were out of sight in their rooms as she moved down the hall to her room. Collapsing on her bed a moment later, she turned on the TV, but even knowing *The Daily Show*, her favorite program, was about to come on wasn't enough to keep her eyes open. TiVo to the rescue, she decided and flicked off the television.

Eight uninterrupted hours later, she woke refreshed.

So refreshed and together that she could even placidly consider life without Jake Chambers's brand of fabulous sex.

And seriously, her life was beaucoup busy, she reminded herself. Particularly now, with her added houseguests. More particularly since she'd not so much as stepped foot in her vineyard for days. She really didn't have the leisure to give herself up to amorous play ad infinitum.

On that rational note, she left her bed, showered, dressed, and, after making herself a latte, carried it with her out to the barn.

With the sun warm on her face, chirruping birdsong sweet in her ears, she inhaled the fresh morning air and felt gloriously alive.

Really, was life good or what?

"Don't smirk," she said to Chris, who was smirking big time as she walked into his office in the barn.

"Can't I be happy to see you again?"

"And don't say *again* in that insinuating way."

But her voice was so obviously cheerful, Chris knew she was teasing. "Whatever you say, boss. Come see our new museum piece," he said, getting up from his desk and nodding toward the back of the barn. "It classes up the neighborhood, but I'm not sure it should be out here in the dust and flies."

"Janie took her painting out of the packing?"

"She didn't, but I did, along with that big guy. Your friend likes to give orders. You should talk to her though. Seriously, the painting's too valuable to be out here without any protection."

"How big is it? Do I have room in the house?"

"It's frigging big, but it might fit in your parlor. The ceilings are higher there."

"Wow," Liv murmured, as she rounded the last horse stall—the barn now home to only two horses—and came face-to-face with Hockney's portrait of Janie dressed to the teeth in a sophisticated evening suit. The pricey artwork looked grandly out of place. "That's almost more than life-sized."

"Yep."

Chris was right. Janie's insurance company would be apoplectic if they saw it now. "Okay, I'll talk to her. We'll find someplace for it in the house. And with luck, the cops won't come looking for it. On the other hand, it's not precisely my problem. So—tell me what I missed."

"Everything's looking good. The crews have been busy cultivating. We had rain, so we didn't have to irrigate, the temperatures have been ideal, even the bugs—or lack of bugs—have been cooperating."

"Perfect. I appreciate your stepping in." In his baggy shorts, Converse sneakers, and spiky blond hair, Chris looked more like a skateboarder than a vintner. But he was a rising young star in the business, urban image or not, and he was also a superb farm manager.

"Not a problem, Liv. And FYI, it looks as though we're going to have our best harvest yet. We might very well end up with a drool-inducing vintage this year."

"Really—*really*? Wonderful! Thanks to your expertise, of course."

"Yeah, well, the soil left behind by the glaciers has a thing or two to do with it, too. But we're on the verge." He dipped his head. "Are you back on schedule work-wise or what?"

"Definitely. I'll be up in the mornings and out here early. It's good to be back." And she really meant it; getting things right in her vineyard was in the same category as great sex. Or maybe she'd waited for this enviable stage so long, she enjoyed it more than most. Or maybe she was just practical.

After all, while Jake Chambers was synonymous with great sex, he wasn't looking for permanence.

She would be wise not to forget that.

Twenty-six

Jake woke with a colossal hangover, the sound of the alarm jarring his brain. He lunged for the clock radio, grunted as agonizing pain spiked through his head, and slammed his hand down on the Off button just as a wave of nausea hit him.

Falling back, he shut his eyes.

Jesus. That made his churning stomach worse. Opening his eyes, he dragged himself into a sitting position on the edge of the bed and waited for the world to stop spinning. He might have dozed off again, he wasn't sure, but when he came to again, taking his head in his hands, he carefully rose to his feet. Steady. Stars flashed and popped before his eyes. He did that deep breathing thing until they disappeared. Then, dropping his hands, he cautiously moved his head left and right. Okay, that was working.

Now, if he could walk without hurling, he'd try to find the Vicodin he kept for times like this.

Since he'd hardly unpacked, it took him longer than he would have liked to ferret out his hangover remedy. But dire necessity prevailed, and two Vicodin later, he navigated the route to the kitchen and made himself café au lait with six sugars. After his chemical and caffeine fix had worked its magic, he showered, shaved, dressed, ate some toast, and felt almost normal. Okay, he couldn't lie; he wasn't in shape to run any marathon. But everything else was definitely on the rise.

Descending the stairs to the ground floor, he stopped on the bottom landing to take in the panoramic view of the mighty Mississippi flowing by the restaurant's window wall. Sun sparkled off the water, runners and walkers were taking advantage of the meandering path on the opposite bank, water poured over the dam in a white-water torrent, the scene vibrant and alive. There was something restorative in the view—a tonic perhaps—or a reminder of the simple beauties of life.

Speaking of beauty, his new restaurant was going to be one awesome place to hang out once the dust settled.

Now, which contractor was scheduled first this morning?

The following days saw major changes in Jake's River Joint as work crews demolished and plumbed, wired and rewired, took out windows for new windows, power-blasted the original brick walls of the old mill, and cleaned the kitchen to pristine splendor.

Each day was a three-ring circus of activity, with Jake's participation indispensable for decisions large and small. Suppliers, wholesalers, decorators, and construction managers all needed him to tell them what went where and when. Not that he didn't welcome the tumult. It kept his mind off Liv.

However, once the work crews left at the end of the day, he was alone, and things always turned dicey. He'd find himself obsessing again about pretty much one thing. Or person. Or whatever designation best characterized his bizarre craving.

If he was actually introspective—which he wasn't—he would have described his craving as lust: a perfectly understandable concept for him. Didn't someone once say an accommodating vice was preferable to a more obstinate virtue? He would have agreed. As for harboring feelings of affection for Liv, he wasn't ready to acknowledge anything of the kind.

Every evening, he'd force himself to focus on the project he'd come here to accomplish—like open a restaurant. Meeting Liv had thrown him off track for a few days, but he was back on schedule, and he had every intention of staying there. After all, getting a restaurant up and running was normally a smoothly run operation for him. Hadn't he always prided himself on his ability to concentrate on business, regardless of distractions?

So, stay on task.

Self-lectures and warnings notwithstanding, he still found himself constantly daydreaming about Liv at night when he should be concentrating on the next day's work schedule. It seemed as though every little thing reminded him of her, whether he was trying to decide on the type of outdoor tables and flowers for the window boxes, or the color of bathroom tile, or the dimensions of the new dining room carpet. It was insane.

It was even more disturbing to think about sleeping in the Bollywood bed. Although that emotional can of worms at least made sense. His memories of her in that bed were totally erotic. Just remembering them gave him a hard-on.

So after that first night when he'd fallen into bed drunk, he'd chosen to sleep on the couch. Or semisleep. That was the best he could do with lascivious images of Liv looping through his brain.

Christ, he felt like he was losing it.

While Jake was overseeing the construction on his River Joint and struggling to maintain his equilibrium, Roman, Janie, and Matt were enjoying a little bit of paradise—in their case consisting of children's activities in the daytime and adult pleasures at night. Matt was thriving and happy with two adults inclined to give in to his every whim. Janie basked under Roman's tender accommodation and didn't even once think about Leo's nastiness. Roman took pleasure in one day at a time; he'd learned a long time ago that it never paid to plan.

Liv and Chris worked long hours seeing that the grapes were nurtured with loving care in hopes that Chris's anticipated first world class vintage would materialize. One and all missed the in-home chef, but generally by the time Liv returned from the fields and Janie's group arrived home after their amusements, it was too late to even think about cooking.

"We found the nicest little restaurant not too far from here," Janie cheerfully announced the second day. "They have chicken-fried steak that reminds me of Texas. And Roman says their cabbage rolls are almost as good as his grandmother's."

"I wike da cheese mac," Matt had chimed in.

And Nickie's Diner replaced Jake's meals for Liv's guests.

Liv would make herself a sandwich or omelet or eat some fruit and cheese when she came in for supper. Then she'd drink a glass of wine and spend the night catching up on her TV watching. She was fine, she told herself. She liked her life. She'd been alone here for years. If she needed some nightlife, she could always go into town and hang out with Shelly et al. Ah—denial.

Jake was less in denial and consequently less laid-back. He couldn't remember when he'd spent time alone, his schedule the last twenty years essentially seven-nights-a-week work in the mass hysteria of a commercial kitchen.

He tried to tell himself that he was long overdue for peace and tranquillity. He even tried to believe it.

But when platitudes no longer staved off the potent force of his libido, he'd go downstairs, pick up one of the sledgehammers left behind by the demolition crew, and take out his frustration on the wall that was being razed between the restaurant and the new bar.

He'd smash cement block, brick, and old lathe and plaster until he could no longer lift his arms, then he'd drag himself back upstairs, collapse on the couch, and try to find something to further distract him from his out-of-control desires. Reading a book wasn't in the cards. He was too jumpy. TV became his mindless fallback, which meant he ended up watching a ton of dreck on cable.

One night, very late, when sleep was more elusive than usual— okay, impossible—he sat down and made a list of the relevant liabilities apropos a relationship with Liv. This from a man who'd never even considered an actual relationship with a woman. Nor had he ever done anything so truly lame since he'd written that poem to Dede Orlando in the seventh grade. Which only went to show the extent of his lust or Liv's frigging appeal; he wasn't sure of the pecking order on that one.

Anyway, on the very top of his list of liabilities he scrawled: "I won't be here long. Six months at best."

Second, he wrote: "Liv is passionate about her vineyard and settled in for the long haul. Seriously. No ambivalence there."

Third: He didn't do relationships.

Fourth: He'd never done relationships.

Fifth—shit, his brain was caught in a useless groove.

So, okay, there it was. He wasn't available. Now, if only his libido was equally reasonable about that long-held belief.

Fuck. His damned libido didn't give a shit about lists or availability or beliefs of any shape or form. It just kept telling him to get in his car, drive to Liv's, and do what he wanted to do.

He figured he was becoming pretty well unglued when he was talking to himself and—worse—answering back. But grim, dogged self-control managed to get him through another night.

Just barely.

Okay, so the sex channels helped.

But the next morning, after greeting the work crews and running over the schedule with the project manager, he said in what he hoped was a mild, restrained tone of voice, "I'll be gone today. If you need anything, call my cell." He counted to ten real, real slowly on his way out the door, hoping to rachet down his champing-at-the-bit horniness.

Five minutes later, he was on the freeway, heading north.

He probably shouldn't have stopped for an espresso, he was already strung out, but it was an hour drive. He'd have time to calm down.

Twenty-seven

Jake saw the late-model four-door sedan with New York plates parked on the shoulder of the road just south of Liv's driveway and slowed down to look. It was empty. Knowing Leo's killer instinct, understanding Janie had something of his he wanted, Jake pulled his car into the turnaround where Liv's driveway met the county road and parked. Getting out, he opened his trunk, pulled out his tire iron, and wished he had something more substantial as a weapon.

A car like that—undistinguished, with New York plates, parked away from the house—was disquieting.

Was it one of Leo's photographers like the one who had taken the clandestine picture of Lisa that had irrevocably damaged her custody fight?

Was it another of Leo's lawyers hoping to hand Janie a summons before she could react?

Was it another PI to replace Roman?

Although why any of those people would drive all the way from New York when they could fly didn't make sense.

Shit.

There were men who would want to remain anonymous. Men who didn't like to be hassled by airport security. Men who liked to bring weapons with them when they traveled.

He should probably call 911, he thought, but having seen Wayne and Arlen, he wasn't so sure they'd be useful. And in the event the stranger in the neighborhood wasn't necessarily dangerous but rather someone sent by Leo, perhaps he'd better check it out first. Or better yet, maybe Roman already had the situation under control, and nothing would be gained by bringing in the local gendarmes.

Walking up the drive, Jake was careful to stay out of sight. Fortunately, the driveway had been planted on either side with Douglas fir a century ago and the large evergreens offered concealment. As he approached the house, he scanned the building and windows. Nothing.

But the front door was open he saw as he circled the house, and it was never open. It was rarely used. Moving forward in a crouch, he stationed himself beneath one of the parlor windows that was open.

Not a sound. Debating whether to enter the house from the kitchen, he suddenly heard a muttered curse, the Jersey accent unmistakable. Then Janie's voice drifted through the open window.

"I told you, I don't know what you're talking about. My husband's hallucinating. You came out here on a wild-goose chase."

Jesus, he had to give Janie credit for having balls. Most people didn't talk like that to what he suspected were goons for hire.

"Shut the fuck up, bitch. Hey, Joey!" the Jersey voice shouted. "Find anything?"

Jake heard only a muffled reply from where he was standing, but someone named Joey had apparently entered the room, because the answering voice was close. While he wasn't particularly in favor of everyone bearing arms in America, right now Jake wouldn't have minded a nice forty-five in his hand. But that option not currently available, he carefully maneuvered himself into a concealed position near the open front door. Liv's two large ivy topiaries bordering the door offered him both cover and a view of the parlor.

Christ, some guy was pointing a handgun at Janie and Roman, who were seated side by side on the sofa. Even with the man's back to him, Jake had the impression he'd come from central casting for *The Sopranos*. He was short, stocky, with dark hair—on his arms and fingers, too. And his feet were planted in the wide stance of a street fighter.

A second man was taller but just as fit. Joey, perhaps. He stood in the open archway between the parlor and hall, a tennis bracelet of megasized diamonds hanging from his outstretched finger.

"We got extras on this trip, Paulie. Is this a beauty or what?"

"It's great, but not what we came for. Did you look everywhere up there?"

"Trashed the place. Nuthin." Joey slipped the bracelet into his pants pocket. "It looks like we might have to get the little lady to talk," he murmured, leering at Janie. "Not that I mind that one fucking bit."

Roman shifted on the sofa, his eyes narrow slits. "Don't touch her," he growled.

"And what the fuck are you gonna do about it, dude? Take a bullet for her?"

"I don't have anything," Janie said, her voice sulky and pissed. "So do what you have to do. I can't give you what I don't have."

Janie's in-your-face attitude wasn't helping, Jake thought. This whole scene was going to get ugly real fast, and waiting for Janie to get beaten up didn't seem like a good idea. It looked like now or never had arrived.

Leaping through the open door with the tire iron raised, Jake lunged at the man with the gun.

The instant Jake sprinted through the doorway, Roman bolted up from the couch and flung himself at Joey, hitting him with a hard, flying tackle.

Paulie crumpled to the floor under the force of Jake's blow.

Roman finished off Joey with a quick one-two punch.

Both wiseguys were out for the count.

"Thanks," Roman murmured, shooting Jake a smile before deftly going through Joey's pockets and pulling out a handgun.

"No problem. Have these goons been here long?" Picking up Paulie's weapon, Jake backed to the door and scanned the yard. "Are there more out there?"

"Hard to tell." Roman turned to smile at Janie. "You okay, baby?"

"I'm good." Janie smiled back.

"I don't suppose you know where Liv has some rope?" Roman said to Jake.

"Uh-uh. Shouldn't we call law enforcement?"

"No! Don't!" Janie cried. "I mean can't we just send these idiots back where they came from?" she added in a less vehement tone. "Leo's checkmated at this point, and I don't want any publicity that might screw up my settlement. If the police get involved, Leo might be implicated. He obviously sent these men, since they wanted the flash drive. Can't you find someone to get them out of here, Roman? Like Harvey Keitel did in *Pulp Fiction*? Or can't someone put them in a barrel or something and send them away like they did Jimmy Hoffa?"

"I don't actually off people, baby, unless they're coming at me with an AK-47 and there's no other way to stop them," Roman said gently. "I don't do cold blood."

"Well, these men certainly weren't very nice to me."

Roman tried not to smile. "We'll figure out something."

"Something that won't generate any bad publicity for Leo until I have custody of Matt and my money."

You had to admire a woman who could keep her eye on the bottom line when she'd only narrowly missed a beating. "They're starting to come around," Roman murmured, shifting his grip on the handgun as the two wiseguys began to moan. "Why don't I see if I can find someone around here who can take these guys off our hands."

"Don't bother, ass wipe," a gruff voice snarled from the direction of the front door. "Now drop your piece, or your friend here is gonna have a hole in his head." His handgun was pressed into Jake's neck. "You, too, dude. Drop it."

Jake had gone rigid as the cold steel struck his skin. *Crap. Isn't that the way*, he thought, letting his weapon drop to the floor. Just when things were going good.

As Roman carefully set his gun down on the floor, Joey gingerly pushed up on one elbow. "Fucking a," he muttered, scowling at the man holding Jake hostage. "It took you long enough."

"I can't help you two are wusses. I was just watching some kid riding a horse out there for a minute. My grandpa used to take me to the races. I love horses."

"Fuck you and your horses." Struggling to his feet, Joey picked up his handgun. "And fuck your grandpa, too."

"Leave my grandpa out of it, you prick. Can't you two take care of yerselves? I gotta come save your asses?"

"Shut the fuck up, Nick. We still got unfinished business here. For starters, this asshole who coldcocked me," Joey muttered, eyeing Roman malevolently.

"Look, I'll give you what you came for," Janie blurted out, in fear for Matt's safety now that he'd been seen, frightened for Roman as well. "The flash drive's upstairs. I'll go and get it."

"So you like this guy, hey?" Joey said, his smile wicked. "How much do you like him, baby? Enough to do me a favor?"

"You touch her, you're dead," Roman said, his voice cold as the grave.

"You'll be dead first, buddy."

"You won't squeeze off a second round before I have my hands around your neck. And one round won't stop me, *buddy*." There was no mistaking the threat was lethal.

"Come on, Joey. Chill out fer Chris' sake. The bitch offered us what we want. Watch these two," he added, shoving Jake in toward Roman. "I'll go upstairs with her. Come on, babe, lead the way."

By the time Janie and Nick returned, Paulie was on his feet as well. But he looked pale, the gash on his head from the tire iron trailing blood over his hair and neck onto his shirt collar.

"Mission accomplished, guys! We're outta here," Nick declared cheerfully, his hand holding the flash drive held aloft. "It was a pleasure, folks." He bowed mockingly. "And fucking relax, Joey. We were supposed to do this job all nice and polite, anyway. Don't even think of screwing things up."

Twenty-eight

"Sorry about the flash drive, baby," Roman said, watching Leo's hired guns walk away down the drive, concerned that they might have detoured to the riding ring at the barn. "I'll get their license plate number and have them stopped."

"Like I'm so stupid I only have one."

Roman spun around. "You're shittin' me."

"Now why would I do that?" Janie said with a smile. "I have two more copies."

So much for a license plate number, Roman thought, giving her a thumbs-up. "Way to go. You fooled the hell out of me."

"I knew I couldn't make it look too easy, or they'd be suspicious. I apologize for putting you and Jake in danger. But I had to make it look real." She smiled. "After those goons bring their prize back to Leo, I can hardly *wait* for his gloating phone call."

"I don't want to rain on your parade, Janie, but a man like Leo Rolf isn't going to suffer defeat kindly. You'll have more visitors once the bad news makes it to New York. I think everyone should clear out for awhile."

Roman nodded. "Jake's right. Don't look so surprised, baby. Leo's life is at stake, and he knows it. Between jail and you, it's no contest."

"My aunt has a cabin not too far from here," Jake said. "No one's used it for years. It doesn't have a connection to any of us. We could go there."

"Sounds good," Roman said with a done-deal decisiveness. "Then in a few days, we'll check in with Leo. Boy Scout that I am, I just *happen* to have my rerouting equipment with me. We can call him from—say—Rio or Tokyo. That should keep him from sending anyone here again."

"You're so clever, darling." Janie gave him an affectionate look. "But could we call him from Paris? Leo knows I adore Paris."

Roman shrugged. "Wherever. You name it."

"And you're a darling, Jake, to offer us safe haven," Janie said effusively, her spirits high. "I won't have to worry a second about Matt. Although Leo's priorities seem to be his bank account first. The awful men weren't even interested in Matt—*thank God*! So, let's see . . . I'll quickly check on Matt, then I'll come back and pack. Oh, dear." Janie frowned. "What about Liv? She's *not* going to want to leave her gardening or . . . grapes or whatever. She's out there working from morning to night."

"We'll explain. She'll understand." Roman shot a look at Jake and grinned. "Or rather, you'll explain. Here's where the rubber meets the road. Are you a smooth talker or what? You'd better be, 'cause it's up to you to convince her."

For a flashing moment Jake debated saying, *None of this is my problem.* "I'll do my best," he said instead, overcome by a curious sense of right-minded justice. Leo Rolf was long overdue for a smack-down and—what the hell—why not lend a hand?

Roman nodded at Jake. "There's no doubt in my mind you can do it. Hey, Janie, tell Matt he can go swimming every day," he said, as she began moving away. His gaze swung to Jake again. "There's swimming there, right?"

"It's a spring-fed lake. The swimming's good."

"Perfect!" Janie waved. "I'll be back in a minute. This summer's turning out to be really, *really* fun!"

"You gotta give her credit," Jake murmured as Janie walked away. "She's not easily intimidated. Even by wiseguys."

"She's one tough lady," Roman agreed proudly. "Leo's got his hands full this go round."

"Couldn't happen to a nicer guy," Jake sarcastically replied. "Now to talk Liv into leaving. She's not going to want to."

"Speaking of leaving, I didn't think you were coming back."

"I wasn't planning to."

"But?"

"What can I say? Lust trumps logic every time."

"There's no women in town?"

Jake made a wry face. "Don't even go there."

Roman put up his hands. "Forget I said anything. Bottom line though, we're in debt to your libidinous urges. It saved our asses."

"Almost saved your asses. Janie was the one who came through."

Roman grinned. "She played that little shell game to the hilt, didn't she? Leo's gonna be pissed when he finds out he's got zero for leverage."

"By the time he figures it out, you'd better have the draw-bridge up. He's one cold-hearted prick."

"You know him?"

"Nah—but I saw him in action once years ago. I was touring Asian restaurants with some friends. We were at a bar in Bangkok, and there was Leo buying himself a young boy. Since Rolf's face had been splashed all over the papers back home with his divorce from that Goldman Sachs high flyer, I recognized him. The kid was terrified. It was grim. How in hell can he con so many women into marrying him?"

"It's his money they're marrying. Although, I'm not sure about Janie. According to her, he was actually real nice for almost a year."

"Fucking sociopath."

"And that's the good part," Roman muttered. "He's corrupt to the core. Not that I can profess to piety or virtue. People don't hire me to help their grannies cross the street."

"You changed your mind about taking down Janie, though."

Roman shrugged. "I probably wasn't ever planning on fol-lowing Leo's instructions. You should see the equipment I brought along." He smiled. "Need anyone wire-tapped?"

"I wish I did, with an offer like that," Jake quipped. Then he blew out a breath. "I suppose I'd better go find Liv and give her the bad news."

"That you're back or that she has to leave?" Roman looked amused.

"Probably both. And the problem is, I'm not good at kiss-ing ass."

Roman gave him a sportive look. "Doesn't it depend on how much you want what you want?"

Jake laughed. "Okay, so I'm gonna kiss ass."

"Good idea." Roman's brows flickered. "Who knows? If you play your cards right, she might reciprocate."

Jake held up his hands, fingers crossed. "I guess that's what I'm here for. Mutual, reciprocal fun and games."

"Best reason in the world to drive this far." Roman gave Jake a finger-gun salute. "Good luck."

Twenty-nine

Jake walked to the hill behind the farmhouse to survey the acres of rolling terrain that constituted Liv's vineyard. The field to the south had three work crews cultivating the grapes, the field to the east was being irrigated by huge sprinklers, the vines to the north at first seemed devoid of workers. Until he caught a glimpse of Liv's pale hair glistening in the sun.

She and a man in a baseball cap were at the far end of the field hoeing, the rhythmic rise and fall of their hoes evidence of seasoned hands.

It always amazed him that Liv worked the fields like her crews. He didn't actually know any women who'd take on that degree of physical labor. Not that women chefs in his kitchens weren't equal to men when it came to diligence and energy, but farm work seemed different somehow, requiring another kind of strength and stamina reminiscent of a simpler life he'd never experienced. All this fresh air and sunshine was far removed from the fevered pace and sweltering heat of the kitchens he called home.

Maybe it was the strangeness of her world that appealed. He smiled. Yeah, right. She could live in an igloo or yurt, and she'd still make him salivate. His craving for her had nothing to do with her lifestyle or geographical location.

It had to do with fucking his brains out.

There it was, plain and simple.

So, did he apologize for not calling her or pretend it didn't matter that he hadn't called? What level of nonchalance would be acceptable? Had she just been into the sexual fun and games like him? Did it matter to her who was participating in her orgasms? Had she even noticed that he was gone?

He took a breath, exhaled, and began walking.

Time to find out.

It took him long enough to cross the yard and field that his arrival was no surprise. Everyone had plenty of time to school their expressions.

As Jake walked up, Liv and her partner stopped working.

"You're back," she said with a polite smile, brushing the hair out of her face with a gloved hand.

That was easy, Jake thought. *Not an iota of temper in her welcome.* He smiled back. "I missed you." Or, more accurately, sex with her.

"How nice. I don't think you've met my vintner, Chris Holloway. Chris, Jake Chambers."

As Jake shook Chris's hand and said hello, he was taking issue with Liv's ultracasual response. *How nice? What the fuck did that mean?* Did men make pilgrimages out here to see her with such regularity, he was just another guy lost in the crowd? Was she getting it on with this Chris guy, and his arrival got in the way? Did he *care* if he was in the way? Dumb question.

"Could I talk to you for a minute?" he said, keeping his voice mild with effort. "There was a little dustup at your house a few minutes ago. Everything's fine now, but Roman thought I should come out and tell you about it."

"Trouble with Leo?"

"Right."

Liv turned to her companion. "If you'll give me a minute, Chris."

"Do you need any help?"

"No." Jake's tone wasn't precisely unfriendly, but then again, no one would have mistaken it for cordial.

"Thank you, Chris," Liv interposed, her smile camera-ready. "I'll deal with this."

"Why don't I head back to the office and order those sprinkler heads we need? I'll see you back there."

"Good idea. This shouldn't take long."

Or maybe it will, Jake reflected, smiling like a politician just waiting for the crowd to disperse so he could quit smiling.

As Chris walked away, Liv turned to Jake with a frown. "I don't need you to answer for me. Understand?"

"Sorry."

"No you're not."

"I wish I was a better actor then."

"Just for the record, I don't take instructions from anyone."

His brows rose faintly. "I don't know about that."

"I'm talking about the real world, okay? Sex is different. Are we clear on our relative positions?"

"Yes, ma'am."

"And don't give me that cowboy shit," she muttered. But he looked beaucoup sexy, smiling at her like that with his head dipped slightly so he was looking at her from under his dark lashes. "So, let's cut to the chase." Her voice was brisk with resolve. "I have a pretty good idea why you came back. But that aside, how about giving me the scoop on this so-called dustup."

He was on notice to get down to business, and not the sexual kind. So he explained the problem in a similarly clear, brisk tone. "I saw a car with New York plates at the end of your drive and found a situation unfolding at your house. One of Leo's wiseguys was threatening Roman and Janie with a gun. Another guy was upstairs tearing your house apart, looking for the flash drive. I knocked out one dude with my tire iron; Roman decked the other one, and if a third goon hadn't opportunely arrived, it would have been over. The new wiseguy mentioned watching Matt riding a horse. Janie panicked, gave up the flash drive, and they left—mission accomplished," he finished, feeling as though his explanation was brief and succinct enough to pass muster with her.

"I just knew there'd be trouble with Leo," Liv said with a sigh of disgust. "I suppose it was just a matter of time. Was anyone hurt?"

"Just Leo's hired guns. Everyone else is fine."

"But Leo has what he wants now," she said grimly.

"Uh-uh." Jake grinned. "Janie has two more copies."

"You're kidding!"

"Nope. She's still in the game."

"Good for her! Now, that's positive news!" Liv should have known Janie's manipulative mind would have had a backup plan. Janie hadn't clawed her way up from poverty by her looks alone. There were thousands of women as beautiful as she who were still waiting tables in L.A.

"There is a slight problem however . . ."

She grimaced. "Why am I not surprised?"

"Probably because you know what Leo's like. Once he discovers he's been fucked over, there's gonna be more badasses sent out here. So the consensus is that everyone should vacate the premises for a short while at least. I told Janie my place at Deer Lake is available."

"Oh, jeez," Liv grumbled. "It's prime growing season for me. It's the worst possible time for me to walk away from my vineyard."

"I understand. I'd even suggest hiring security, but these wiseguys Leo employs might be out of the locals' league."

"This is a real pain," Liv said, sourly. "Everyone can't just leave the vineyard. It's impossible."

"Maybe Janie could contact Leo before his hired guns get back to New York and let him know the flash drive he's getting is useless. They could hash out a settlement with their lawyers, and this might all blow over in a few days."

"If you believe that, let me tell you about some land I have for sale in Florida. If you recall, Leo contested his last wife's settlement for over two years."

"This time he's facing major jail time, though, if that flash drive gets out. He's going to want to settle."

"Okay, okay, I get the message." She scowled at Jake. "I don't actually have a choice, do I?"

"Not really," he gently replied.

"Can I blame you?" she sullenly inquired.

"If it helps, sure." He smiled. "But Janie's your friend, too. I don't know if I want to take the entire blame for her poor marriage decisions."

"Don't be reasonable right now," Liv muttered. "I'm not in the mood."

"I understand."

"And don't sound so damned calm, either. The grapes this season are going to be our best ever. And now I have to just walk away and let everything go to hell?"

Her voice had risen markedly; he knew better than to reply.

Only the breeze rustling the grape leaves breached the silence.

Christ, she looked good, he thought. Her cheeks were faintly flushed with anger, her pale hair a tangle of curls, her bare arms and legs tanned and toned, her lush bottom lip pouty. And sexy. "Look, is there a back way into your land?" he inquired. "If there is, maybe we could check on things from time to time. Or if you want, we could call the sheriff and have him patrol your land."

"If only. We have six deputies in the entire county."

"Look," he said, quietly, clearly willing to be accommodating. "Tell me what you want me to do, and I'll do it."

At a loss, she shook her head. "I don't know what to do. Leo's a prick, though; that I do know. And I suppose if Janie and Matt are at risk, I have to help in any way I can."

"That's my call, too."

Lips pursed, she met his gaze. "This isn't exactly good timing for you, either, is it? You're trying to work on your restaurant."

"What can I say? Shit happens."

Her smile this time was warmer than it had been. "You're too damned reasonable."

"Sorry."

Her brows lifted faintly, and she studied him for a lengthy moment. "I didn't think you were coming back."

He hesitated briefly before saying, "Neither did I."

A grin lit up her face. "So you really did miss me."

"More than you know," he murmured with an answering grin.

"I probably shouldn't say it, but same here. I haven't been sleeping too well."

"I probably shouldn't say it, but I've hardly slept at all."

"So you've been thinking about me," she purred.

"More or less constantly. And for your information, it's annoyed the hell out of me."

"So I maybe should compensate you in some way—you know—for your annoyance."

His smile was wicked. "We could talk about it."

"Talk?"

"Whatever. You decide."

"I already have," she murmured. "Come." She put out her hand. "We'll go fill Chris in on all the sordid details, and then we'll deal with our mutual annoyances and/or desires."

His hand closed over hers as she moved away. "Deal-making. Sounds good." He grinned. "FYI, I'm gonna be a pushover on these negotiations."

"For some reason I thought you might be."

"Does my impatience show?"

She laughed. "Like flashing neon. Which reminds me—on other more practical matters—we'd better get Janie's splashy

Hockney painting out of the barn. She doesn't think Leo will notice it's gone, but I'm not so sure." She turned to him. "Do you have room at Deer Lake for a bigger than life–sized painting?"

"It's an old place. The ceilings are pretty high. We'll figure out something."

"If it's old, does it have those nice porches?"

"Wraparound screened porches, babe. Does that make you happy?"

"Yeah. And you coming back makes me happier."

"I'm glad."

She shot him a look. "Is this a karmic moment of complete harmony?"

"It sure feels like it."

"Yeah it does," she murmured, swinging his hand, deciding this wasn't the time to look a gift horse in the mouth. "Most definitely."

Thirty

Jake's aunt's place on Deer Lake was what would have been called a cottage at the turn of the century. The large, two-story Victorian house was poised on the heights overlooking the lake, the grass newly mowed, the flower gardens immaculate, the siding freshly painted in a typical turn-of-the-century color: pale blue with white trim.

"Someone's definitely paying to keep this place maintained," Liv murmured as she stepped out of Jake's car. "It's beautiful."

"Thanks. It looks the same as ever," he said with a noticeable satisfaction. "I spent some happy summers here as a kid. Come on in, we'll give Aiko a call and tell her how good everything's looking." He nodded at Matt, who was running toward the lake, Janie and Roman in hot pursuit. "I know *someone* who's gonna like it here."

"You think?" Janie had complained they'd had to literally drag Matt out of the water whenever they wanted to come back from the beach.

"I'm not a betting man, but I'd bet on that one. Let's get the place open before Chris and Amy get here. We'll find a place for that painting." Chris and Amy were bringing the Hockney painting and Janie's considerable luggage in the back of their pickup truck.

After unearthing the key from under some gingerbread trim on the back porch, Jake opened the door and walked in. The kitchen was huge, and with the exception of new appliances, it appeared largely untouched since the house had been built. A large wooden table, used as a work surface from the evidence of hard wear apparent on its maple top, held center stage. Surrounded by chairs, it must have served for informal dining as well.

"I love old houses," Liv murmured, thinking of all the people who must have gathered around that table over the years. "I bought my farm largely because of the house. Think of the memories."

"Including mine," Jake agreeably said. "I like that nothing's changed. I like that it's been in the same family all these years. My uncle's grandfather built it in 1904. The date's penciled on a closet wall upstairs." He held out his hand. "Come. I'll give you the grand tour."

· "A workman left his signature on a timber in my barn, too," Liv said, following Jake into the dining room. "Every time I see it I feel connected to the history of my place. Wow—is that a real Remington sculpture?"

"I don't know—maybe—actually, I think it is."

Apparently the original owner had a couple of nickels to rub together, Liv decided. Not that a lake cottage of this size didn't give one a clue.

They moved through a dining room with a built-in buffet and sideboard that were fashionable at the turn of the century and entered an enormous bow-shaped room that conformed to the curvature of the lakeshore. A wall of windows offered glorious, panoramic views of the lake.

"How lovely," Liv said, with a modicum of awe. The cabin she'd spent summers in as a child would have fit in this room. Not to mention the furniture looked like something out of an old *Country Life* magazine: soft sofas and easy chairs covered in subtlely faded chintz that probably was made to look that way from the beginning; fringed footstools; embroidered dog pillows here and there. In other words, posh.

"The upstairs isn't so decorated," Jake said, recognizing the note of wonder in her voice. "It's more summer camp stuff."

He took her upstairs to see the bedrooms on the second and third floors.

"Summer camp it might be," Liv noted, as they returned to the ground floor. "But it's definitely not Girl Scout camp on Fenske Lake." The decor reminded her more of a Martha Stewart summer camp: the kind with painted metal beds, white wainscoting, linen curtains, homespun bedspreads, woven rugs, and wicker furniture, all color-coordinated with the paint on the walls. "Everything's so perfect. It looks as though it's hardly been used."

"Actually, it has been. But my aunt had all the bed linens and curtains redone ten years ago or so, and lately, there haven't been many guests."

"If I have to be away from my vines," Liv said with an approving survey of her surroundings, "I certainly can't complain about the accommodations."

"Hopefully, this won't be a lengthy stay. Leo should be calling soon." Jake shrugged. "He can decide to settle or not, and I'm guessing he'll settle."

"I don't know if I'm that optimistic. Still, Roman knows the man better than we, and *he* seems to think Leo will panic."

"Fucking a. Wouldn't you?"

"I guess. So what—two, three days?"

"Sounds about right. Which doesn't give us much time for a vacation," he said with a grin.

"I hope your idea of a vacation and mine are the same," she murmured, smiling back.

"I guarantee they are."

"Such assurance." But her voice was sportive rather than displeased.

"Let's just say, I've gotten to know you. And since I braved armed desperadoes to be with you," he said, grinning, "I'm figuring we might as well have a good time. Sit down, relax; I'll go get us some food. Then no one has to go anywhere for however long."

"So we could, like, stay in bed and we wouldn't starve."

"You read my mind, babe. Let me call my aunt, and then I'll hit the road."

"I'll come with you. There's no way I can relax anyway—what with wiseguys on the prowl and the enticing prospect of lurid sex with you revving up my psyche."

Jake looked up from dialing the phone, one dark brow cocked. "Lurid?"

She grinned. "I meant it in the very nicest way."

Jake gave her one of those amused, whatever-you-say-babe looks, then said, "Hey, Aiko, guess where I am?"

After Jake's aunt in Seattle was thanked for her hospitality, Jake made a quick call to Eduardo. He didn't explain why he needed him to come to Minneapolis; he only said, "Something's come up. I need help. Bring out the usual crew tomorrow." And he hung up.

Apparently the two men weren't the chatty type, or maybe the usual crew was always held in readiness for such eventualities, Liv decided. But any further speculation had to wait, for the moment Jake put down the phone, he said briskly, "Let's go tell everyone we're going for supplies."

The rest of the party had settled in down by the lake. They were given a heads-up on the run to the grocery store and offered their pick of bedrooms, save for the one at the head of the stairs that had been Jake's as a child. "It shouldn't take us long at the store," he finished.

"Tet me tandy," Matt shouted from where he was digging a hole in the sand. "An ice ceam!"

"Just a little," Janie noted. "Any kind. He doesn't care. And maybe a bottle of champagne. You know"—Janie smiled—"to celebrate Leo's denouement."

By the time Janie was finished adding to her list of necessities, Jake was nodding his head and thinking, *If I can remember it all.* But he only smiled and said, "We'll be back soon," waved, and he and Liv walked away.

"I really like that bedroom of yours—the porch, all those windows, the view." Liv was lying back in the car seat, her bare

feet up on the dash, the breeze from the open window ruffling her hair, bliss inundating her senses.

"That was my room as a kid. What can I say—it brings back fond memories."

How darling. How sweet. How perfectly adorable, she thought, thoroughly awash in Pollyanna feelings when she should be up-tight about wiseguys and her languishing vineyards. Instead of succumbing completely to Jake's intrinsic darlingness, she should be worried about losing her grape crop—*not* drifting in some I'm-in-heaven parallel universe. "I'll bet you slept on that bed-room porch when it was hot," she murmured, imagining the dar-ling boy—or maybe the even more darling teenage heartthrob—sleeping there on a hot summer night.

"Yeah. Without air you had to."

His matter-of-fact response was transposed by her euphoric mind-set into a tantalizingly macho reply. Blunt, pithy, incisive, *all* male. A tiny quiver of desire warmed her senses at the thought of the coming night. "Could we sleep on the porch tonight?"

He grinned. "If you promise not to scream."

She gave him a sulky look. "Be reasonable."

"Seriously. Sound travels across the lake—especially at night. I don't want the cops coming to check on us."

Such brusque manliness only stirred her desires. Like, me Tarzan, you Jane. Like she was getting weak with longing just thinking about his hard-muscled virility and amazing stamina. Not that it would do to concede to such yearnings when they were only minutes away from the grocery store. "Tell me," she said on a small, suffocated breath. "How did an aunt from Seattle happen to settle at Deer Lake?"

He shot her a look, her voice patently restive.

"I was just wondering," she said lamely, unable to think of a more clever response when she was semifrenzied. "I mean, really, I want to know," she managed to say with a slightly more decisive inflection.

"Aiko and my uncle were married while he was an exchange student in Japan," Jake offered, careful to speak in a mild tone of voice. If she wanted what he thought she wanted—from a practical point of view—he'd rather wait until after shopping. "When they returned to Minneapolis, she opened the first Japanese restaurant in the city. A few years later, my uncle Joe had a job offer in Seattle. They moved, Aiko opened a restaurant there, my mom came over on a visitor's visa, met my dad, and that's pretty much it. You're from around here, right?" *Talk to me, babe,* he thought. *I'm too tall to even think about fucking in this small car.*

Be mature. Act like an adult, Liv cautioned herself. Sex right now was out of the question anyway. Not that her body was completely willing to acquiesce, but she tamped down her lust with effort and gave Jake the short version of her life. She described her family: her mom and dad who'd retired to a lake nearby, her sister, Lila, and husband, Larry, who owned a dairy farm nearby, and their two kids who would be three and four next year. "So everyone's close. And we all get along, which is nice. I can't remember—do you have siblings?"

He had always been super easy to talk to. He was a good listener who asked pertinent but not overly inquisitive questions, and before too long, Liv had relaxed once again against the pricey leather seat. Jake should be a therapist, she thought; their conversation was soothing, tranquilizing, evoking warm, cozy feelings apropos family and childhood memories. It was pleasant and odd at the same time, because she'd never before felt like bringing a guy she was sleeping with home to meet her family, and now . . .

Wonder of wonders—Jake Chambers was a possible.

Not that she was about to mention her unusual feelings.

No point in scaring him off.

Especially before they slept on the porch.

Although it didn't help her strength of purpose that their grocery shopping turned out to be one of those déjà vu experiences—like they'd done it a thousand times before. Nor did it help her tenuous self-control when he'd lean over from time to time and kiss her. He didn't even care if people were looking. The first time he did it in the produce aisle, she'd panicked, her eyes flaring wide, and he'd only said, "Relax. No one knows us."

By the time they reached the checkout counters, it was only a question of where they could have sex—not when. "Stand in front of me," he whispered. "Or I'll embarrass myself."

"You shouldn't have kissed me so much," she whispered back. "I'm about to lose it."

"Think of something gross. We'll be out of here in ten minutes."

"Ten minutes!" she shrieked, or shrieked as much as one could when they were whispering.

Shutting his eyes, he took a deep breath, opened his eyes, and said, terse and low, "Help me unload this cart, and then we'll test out that backseat."

"We can't!" she whispered frantically enough that the checkout girl looked up and gave them a slow once-over.

"Damn right we can," Jake muttered, ignoring the checkout girl, currently in the mood to ignore the world at large. For a fraction of a second he debated saying, *I'll be back for the cart*, and dragging Liv out to the car. But then all his years of training kicked in, and he decided the ice cream and Popsicles would melt into a puddle before he returned.

Or maybe Liv's petrified expression stopped him.

Shoving his hand into the cart, he grabbed the closest item, slapped it on the conveyer belt, and hastily unloaded the groceries.

A short time later, as they walked from the store, Jake tossed the car keys to Liv. "I'll throw these groceries in the trunk. Turn the air on full blast."

Liv made a moue. "We probably should wait."

"Too late, babe. Come on," he said with a grin, "I'll make it worth your while."

"There're people everywhere." His make-it-worth-your-while phrase was doing a number on her reservations, however.

"No one can see, baby. The windows are tinted." Reservations weren't on his radar with his libido in high gear. "Turn on the air, make yourself comfortable in the backseat, and I'll see you in five."

He always was so assured and on mission, although she couldn't discount her own explosive passions. She could have said no with more conviction. She could have seriously protested. As if—when he was mere feet away and radiating sexual charisma big time. He was the kind of man for whom the phrase, *Lead us not into temptation*, had been coined.

She smiled faintly.

No point in dwelling on the downside, when the upside was oh so close.

And oh so gratifying.

Jake had his own fleeting moment of indecision as he was stacking the bags in the trunk, knowing what the temperature would be in a car trunk parked on an asphalt lot at midday. But *fleeting* was the operative word.

Banging the trunk shut, he moved around the car, opened the back door, and stood transfixed. "Whoa," he breathed, arrested by the voluptuous image of sexual availability.

"Is something wrong?" *Please don't say you've changed your mind now*, Liv thought, every amorous nerve in her body on full alert and waiting.

"No. You just look good enough to eat, although," he muttered with a flicker of his brows, "this small backseat isn't going to offer any smorgasbord opportunities." Liv was half-leaning against the opposite door, nude from the waist down and—if her heated gaze was any indication—anxious.

"I don't care—really." A small breathy sound.

He smiled as he maneuvered his way into the backseat. "Lucky I know what you do care about."

She gave him a quick, chin-up, liberated-woman look. "I'm not going to apologize."

"Nor should you, baby. We're both in the same boat," he murmured, trying to find some room for his long legs. "Actually, this backseat is smaller than a boat. But, hey, the mood I'm in, I could fuck you in the backseat of a MINI Cooper."

Just to make sure he wouldn't break an arm later trying to dig a condom from his jeans pocket, he took one out in advance.

"My apologies for destroying the romance, but in light of the cramped quarters, I'm puttin' this on first."

"If I was looking for romance, it might matter. However," Liv said with a grin, "I'm way past that road sign."

He looked up, his task accomplished. "So, is Candy Land just around the corner?"

"Yup and I'm traveling fast."

"That's what I like about you; I hardly have to do a thing."

Just let me look at you, she felt like saying. He was the sexiest man alive. "It works for me," she said instead, smiling faintly.

"Let's see how well it works," he murmured, slipping his hands under her knees, pulling her downward, and climbing between her legs. "If I begin to crush you, punch me, and I'll stop."

"Sure I will."

"I mean it," he said, kicking the door accidentally, cursing, finally adjusting his hips so his cock was where it had to be and beginning to ease forward.

"Whatever you say—oh God . . . oh God—yesssss . . ."

No one spoke after that, unless heavy breathing and euphoric utterances counted. The windows steamed up, the groceries in the trunk melted, a young couple nudged each other when they walked by and smiled knowingly.

Not that the outside world intruded into the backseat of the silver gray BMW. Nor did reflections or considerations of any kind intervene in the purely physical pleasure consuming the attention of the two people in the car.

Since Liv was into multiple orgasms, Jake played the gentleman, more inclined than ever to be polite now that she'd welcomed him back into her life. Before long, however, even with air-conditioning, they were both slick with sweat or, in Jake's case, dripping with sweat.

After Liv had come twice, he figured he'd been well-mannered long enough. "This is it, babe. My legs are going numb," he muttered. "One last time."

It was a very nice welcome home, despite the cramped quarters and sauna temperatures. It was the nicest orgasmic welcome he'd ever received.

He kissed her afterward, a serious, meaningful kiss. The kind of kiss he'd never bestowed on a woman before. Not that he noticed or cared. Or maybe it just felt so damned good, he was willing to overlook ominous possibilities like commitment for the first time in his life.

Liv understood their kiss was something out of the ordinary, too. It made her seriously consider the future when she'd always been a live-for-today kind of person. When she'd never seriously thought about settling down. But mostly, it made her feel all warm and fuzzy inside—maybe even in *love*.

Are you crazy? the little voice inside her head screamed.

Okay, okay, maybe she could say—just a *little* bit in love.

How about that?

Her psyche calmed down to match her overall really serene mood after three orgasms, and the world righted itself on its axis.

Jake did say on the way home, though, his expression and voice sober and wholly sincere, "I haven't felt this good *ever*."

"Me, too. Nice, hey?" she said with the unruffled calm of someone who had satisfactorily reconciled reality and fantasy.

It was even nicer that night on the porch outside his bedroom with the fireflies flitting by the screens and the moon big and silver in the sky and the night air gently wafting in the windows. It was magical in every way, their lovemaking leisured, their kisses sweeter, a sense of having come together beyond the seething drama of orgasmic release conjuring up altogether new emotions.

Perhaps even perilous emotions.

Or maybe just inexplicable ones for two people traveling into the unknown.

Thirty-one

Two hours after the wiseguys had driven away from Liv's, a man entered Ben's office asking to speak to Leo. He was from Greeley Transport, he told Ben.

Leo smiled when the man from Greeley Transport was announced. "Show him in," he promptly ordered, his gleeful tone unmistakable. Punching the Off button on his phone, Leo double-checked that all the lines were shut down before coming to his feet. Moving from behind his desk, he strode toward the door with the swagger of a victor.

He even shook the messenger's hand as he entered his office.

Knowing Leo's aversion to germs, Ben did a shocked double take before closing the door behind him. Racing to his desk, he delicately pushed down on the intercom button.

Dead air. Shit. This was top secret stuff.

He leaped for the door, pressed his ear to the burled pear wood, and strained to hear what was being said. The man from Greeley Transport might have been wearing a custom suit and handmade shoes, but he was no businessman unless killing people counted as a business.

"Your package is on the way," the man said, reticent on the nature of the package.

"When can I expect delivery?"

"Tomorrow morning, first FedEx delivery. You can pick it up at the office."

"You're sure?" For a moment, Leo had doubts. Everything had been accomplished so swiftly.

"I'm not here for the hell of it."

"No, of course not. Tell your employer I appreciate the excellent service."

"The office—anytime after nine."

The man in the custom suit turned, walked away, and opened the office door so quickly, Ben barely had time to jerk open the supply cabinet door and grab the first thing he saw.

"If you overheard anything, chump, I suggest you forget it," Carmine's messenger growled, his gaze flicking briefly to Ben's white-knuckled grip on a printer cartridge. "I know where you work, and I can find out where you live. *Capisce?*"

"Yes, sir." No way was he going to even attempt a lie. But whatever the man had told Leo—and he had a good idea—had made Leo real cheerful. He could hear him whistling from here.

In fact, Leo's good cheer was so pronounced that when he called Ben into his office, he actually smiled and said, "You're doing a good job. I just wanted you to know."

Ben's jaw literally dropped at both Leo's smile and his astonishing praise. Recovering quickly, he said, "Thank you, sir. It's a pleasure to work for you."

"I'll be out tomorrow morning. Cancel my appointments. And take the morning off yourself. All work and no play, young man—you lose your edge," Leo jovially announced with a wave of his hand. "And make an appointment with Dan Wygren for late afternoon. I'll go to his place. Make it five o'clock." Reaching over, Leo flicked his phone on, leaned back in his chair and, quietly humming under his breath, looked up at Ben as though he'd suddenly become a stranger.

Ben knew that cold, blank look; he backed out of Leo's office.

Leo hardly noticed. He was busy calculating the money he'd saved by having Carmine appropriate the flash drive. As if he'd even consider giving that bitch fifty million dollars, he resentfully thought. Or think of giving up his son. Janie Tabor, soap opera diva, didn't have a clue who she was dealing with. He smiled evilly. She'd find out soon enough.

The minute he picked up his package with the flash drive, he'd let her know how a professional played the game. Take no prisoners. That's how a winner won. She wouldn't know what hit her by the time he was finished with her.

As for the information stored on the flash drive, he and Dan would decide tomorrow afternoon how best to cover his tracks. This near disaster had forced him to contemplate some worst-case scenarios, and he didn't like the risk exposure. They would have to strategize on better options to screen or launder his financial assets. Safer alternatives that didn't pose the possibility of jail time.

But right now he felt like celebrating. Punching his direct line to Hannah, he exuberantly said, "Cancel your meetings, baby. I'm taking you out on my yacht."

His exhilaration was so out of character, Hannah experienced a thrill of excitement as she set down the phone. Would she have her engagement ring by the end of the day? Was all her planning and hard work finally going to pay off?

Dare she call him back and ask the reason for his good spirits?

Could she call Ben and ask him?

Would he answer her if she asked?

Nothing ventured, nothing gained. She hit the speed dial for Ben.

When he picked up, she purred, "Dear Ben, would you happen to know why Leo is in such high spirits?"

"I wouldn't tell you if I did." Hannah Reiss was the reason the word *unscrupulous* had been invented.

"You shit," she snapped. "Once I'm engaged to Leo, I'll have you fired!"

"I'll worry about that when the time comes."

"What the hell does that mean?"

"It means you're not engaged yet."

She slammed down the phone.

Ben didn't care. Right now, Hannah Reiss was the least of his problems. Should he rethink his sell order with Cal? Did he have to buy everything back? Was Leo going to come out of this on top again? Scowling, Ben began drumming his fingers on his desktop. Everything might still be in flux. Crap. What should he do?

Thirty-two

The next morning, Liv decided to ride with Jake when he drove into the cities. His restaurant crew's flight was scheduled to land at ten, but Jake wanted to meet with his contractors prior to their arrival.

"This could be a tedious day for you," he'd warned. "You might prefer staying at the lake."

"Am I not welcome?" Liv had teasingly inquired.

"You're always welcome. I was being polite." He no longer even questioned wanting her in his life, although he'd chosen not to scrutinize the reasons why.

While Jake was opting for his usual avoid and evade when it came to relationship issues, Liv was trying to deal with her equally novel feelings. She'd always prided herself on her independence and her ability to say, *It was nice; don't call me, I'll call you*. And now, like some infatuated young girl, all overwrought and adoring, she found herself wanting Jake to stay. It was unnerving, bewildering, messing with her mind big time, because if Mr. Wonderful had just walked into her life, there wasn't much chance he'd be staying.

Damn.

She stole a quick glance at Jake as he drove, and the adoration factor kicked in with a vengeance. My Lord, he was gorgeous. How shallow was she to think about falling in love just because he was beautiful? Worse, how stupid, when she'd been around megahandsome men for years in the modeling business. Then Jake turned to her, smiled a luscious, sweet-as-sugar smile, said, "Thanks for coming along," and she decided maybe it wasn't his good looks alone that was making her melt with longing. Maybe he was nicer than nice in *so* many ways.

"My pleasure." But her utterance was half-breathless, for a wild, leaping desire had fluttered through her senses and settled exactly where she'd rather it didn't settle, seeing as how they were on the freeway in the middle of rush hour.

"We should try out Chaz's bed later on."

He knew. He could always tell. "I'd like that," she said, trying to breathe normally when her body was already gearing up for action. Urgent lust bathed her vaginal tissue in fluid heat, an equally reckless ache of arousal throbbed deep inside her, and normal breathing was suddenly at issue. "I don't suppose we could stop," she whispered.

He glanced at her, then at the traffic. "Everyone's going eighty, babe. I'd say come sit on me, but this time of day, we'd have a helluva lot of company." The traffic was three lanes, bumper to bumper, high speed. You could practically reach out and touch the car on either side.

"I know, I know." She took a deep breath. "Forget it. I'll be fine."

He gave her a sympathetic look. She didn't sound fine; she sounded really hard up. "Look, scoot over. I'll drive with one hand."

"Would you really? I mean, thanks—*jeez*—keep your eyes on the road. Look, no sense in killing ourselves. I'll survive. I'm not some horny adolescent. I can control myself."

He grinned. She didn't look like an under-control kind of woman right now. He patted the console between them. "Come on, babe. It's almost an hour into town. Lean back against the door, bring your tush closer, and I'll give you a ride you'll remember."

She'd be stupid to refuse. Then again, maybe he was just being ultracourteous. "Are you just being polite?"

"Fuck no. I wouldn't offer if I didn't mean it. Here, babe, bring that sweet sugar within reach."

She shouldn't. She should have enough self-discipline to last for an hour or so. In fact, it was ridiculous that they were even having this conversation.

"I don't know how busy I'll be once I get there," he said in warning.

Oh, jeez, why did he have to say that? She'd probably have to spend the whole day looking at him from afar, with tons of people around and no way to have time alone with him.

He shot her a grin. "Hey, this isn't a moral issue. I'm just being practical."

"Then, if you don't mind," she said, smiling back, "one pragmatic orgasm sounds pretty good." She was already hitching up her dress and kicking off her sandals. "Lucky I wore a sundress today," she cheerfully said, slipping off her panties and shifting in her seat so she was leaning against the door.

He winked. "Lucky I can do two things at once."

Her smile was pure sunshine. "For which I thank you in advance."

"Damn," he muttered, taking in the provocative sight of his number one turn-on zone unclothed, available, and obviously ready for action, if her glistening pink labia was any indication. "You can get me hard in under a second, babe."

"We could exit at the next town."

He glanced at the clock on the dash. "I wish." He drew in a deep breath, reminded himself he actually had a restaurant to open, and he stoically yielded to present circumstances. Shifting slightly in his seat in order to position his arm properly—or more particularly his hand—he slid two fingers inside her soft, clamoring flesh, found the little rough patch on the roof of her vagina, and gently rubbed back and forth in a slow, come-hither, zigzag motion.

Liv uttered a long, blissful sigh, stirred in her seat to rise into the glorious sensations, and a moment later whispered, "I owe you big time for this."

"I intend to collect." He slid his fingers deeper into her pulsing, swelling passage. "Just as soon as I can."

She didn't seem to be listening any longer; her eyes were shut, her hips were lifting and swirling around his hand, and when she urgently gasped, "More . . . more," he shoved a third finger inside her slick warmth and pushed.

It was a matter of staying in his lane, stroking her quivering tissue, forcing his fingers in and out of her melting flesh, and seriously trying to ignore her wild little cries in order to hold it together and not pull off onto the side of the freeway. When she began panting and her vaginal muscles tightened around his fingers, he willed himself to concentrate on the road and separate himself from his own needing-to-get-laid cravings.

When she climaxed, it was even harder for him. She was so steaming hot and wet, so frantic to get screwed, she'd been begging him to pull over. "I can't," he'd grunted tersely, his fingers white-knuckled on the wheel.

She must have discerned the tension in his voice, for the second after she came, she instantly tried to make amends. Coming to her knees, she threw her arms around his neck and between passionate kisses, whispered, "Thank you, thank you . . . you're the most darling man on the face of the earth. I'll pay you back, see if I don't."

He smiled and kissed her back and politely said they'd work something out.

"Don't be mad," she breathed, nibbling on his ear.

"I'm not mad. I'm horny." He shot her a grin. "You can take care of that later."

"I will, I will—whatever you want."

He chuckled at her enthusiasm. "Sounds good. Now, cover up, babe, so I can stop thinking about jumping you."

"Yes, sir." Smiling brightly, she reached for her panties. "Whatever you say, sir, Mr. Chambers, my lord and master," she teasingly added.

"I'll let you know what I say," he noted with a wolfish smile. "Just as soon as I deal with everyone at the restaurant, you're gonna be first on my list to get orders."

• • •

By the time they drove into the parking lot at Jake's restaurant, they'd both achieved a level of calm. Liv, particularly, who had had the opportunity to relax more than Jake, was in a relatively serene mood and willing to wait any amount of time for Jake to finish his business.

Walking into the restaurant a few moments later, they entered a major construction site, electricians tripping over plumbers tripping over HV guys tripping over carpenters. Jake politely introduced Liv to one and all, explained to her what was going on, and took her on a guided tour of the entire lower level. When the tour was finished, he discussed the orders of the day with his project manager.

The L.A. people arrived as expected shortly after, and another round of introductions ensued.

Four people had come out from L.A. to help Jake: three men, Eduardo, Sam, and Gunther, and one stunning woman named Elena.

The moment Liv met the sleek woman's cheeky gaze, she knew without a doubt that Elena and Jake were or had been more than employer, employee. She was Peruvian it' was explained, her speciality naturally, her native cuisine. No mac and cheese then, Liv thought churlishly. That left her pretty much out-chefed. It didn't help either that Elena's exotic beauty was a perfect foil to Jake's dark good looks. Nor that she had a habit of leaning in real close when she talked to him and whispering in Spanish.

Get a grip, Liv cautioned herself as a wave of jealously gripped her. She'd never deluded herself that Jake was a monk. She'd always known there was a long list of women in his past. And it wasn't as though *she'd* spent her leisure time home alone, knitting.

Keep it real, she reminded herself. Their relationship was about sex—no hearts and flowers, no Hallmark card sentimentality.

It was temporary fun and games.

And she'd better not forget it.

"If you don't mind, Liv, Eduardo and I are going to check out the kitchen. It might take a while. Why don't you go upstairs. I'll be up when I'm finished here."

Leaning over, he kissed Liv gently on the cheek, giving out the message loud and clear that she was special.

How could she refuse such politesse? Or argue? She couldn't say, *I don't want to leave you with her*, without sounding juvenile or—horror of horrors—possessive. "Not a problem," Liv murmured. "I'll wait upstairs."

But waiting turned out to be torture. She kept imagining that Jake and his sexpot lover were flirting, teasing, touching each other, maybe even making plans to meet later. Jake had never said he intended to stay at Deer Lake for any length of time. Now that his L.A. people were here, perhaps he'd stay at his restaurant.

She found herself watching the clock.

She paced.

She tried watching TV.

She flipped through magazines. Chaz apparently didn't read books.

Fidgety and restless, climbing the walls, faced with a serious jealousy problem for the first time in her life, she managed to talk herself out of going downstairs for more than half an hour.

Okay, thirty-two minutes, ten seconds.

But only because she'd curbed her impulses by hanging onto the railing at the top of the stairs for a promised count of two hundred before she let go.

Racing down the stairs, she recalled how she'd walked up these same stairs one evening not too long ago and had experienced a major seismic event. There was no other word for Jake Chambers in her life. He'd shaken her placid, predictable world to the core. Case in point: she was frantic with jealousy.

She heard the men's voices before she reached the bottom of the stairs. Jake's and possibly Eduardo's. The accent sounded like his.

"Tell me about this babe with the great body and bad wines. This is the Liv you were talking about. Right?"

"She's the one."

"So only words of glowing praise will do, I assume, when it comes to any discussion of local wines."

"I'd appreciate it. Although it's not as though her wines are absolutely terrible, it's just that—"

"They're not up to your superior standards. Is that it?" Liv rapped out, her voice hot with rage as she walked out from behind the cooler. Her wines *were not* terrible. What a hypocritical prick! He hadn't had the nerve to say that to her face, had he? He'd just lied through his teeth every time they'd drunk her wines! "For your information," she snapped, bristling with fury, "you can take your fucking taste in wines and go fuck yourself!"

"I'll catch you later," Jake murmured, dismissing his manager with a nod before turning to Liv. "It's not like that," he gently said as Eduardo beat it out of the kitchen. "Eduardo misunderstood me."

"It didn't sound like he misunderstood," Liv shot back, her face flushed with anger. "It sounded to me like you were agreeing with him. Who the hell do you think you are, saying my wines are terrible?"

"I'm sorry. I'm really sorry. I'll make it up to you, I swear."

"You mean, make it up to me by screwing me and making me forget all about being angry? You think I'll just forget the fact that you can't stand my wines because you'll make me feel so-o-o fucking good. Is that it, you lying prick?" Cranked up, boiling hot, she clenched her fists to keep from slapping his sanctimonious, double-dealing face. "Here's a news flash for you," she said, her voice terse and bitter, "getting sex isn't a problem for me. There's lots of men who can make me feel good. So do me a favor. Stay the fuck away from me." She jerked her hands up as he moved toward her. "I mean it. Do. Not. Touch. Me."

Each word was cold as ice. He stopped, took a step back, let his hands drop to his sides. "Let's talk about this," he said very, very softly.

"No thank you." Each word was pissy, her gaze gelid. Then, turning, she walked away.

"You don't have a ride home. I'll drive you."

"I have friends who'll give me a ride home. You stay here and drink some of those French wines you ordered. You know, the really good ones," she said with withering contempt.

"In case you forgot, you're staying at my place." A definite Hail Mary pass.

"Fuck if I am."

The kitchen door slammed behind her.

Jake swore under his breath. Although it wasn't as though he could make her damned wines better by waving some god-damn magic wand, he wished he could if it would get him back into her bed. He swore again, the thought of her having sex with other men messing with his head. She knew plenty of men, she'd said, and he didn't doubt it. He couldn't think of a man with a heartbeat who would refuse her.

So now what? She wasn't exactly in the mood to listen to reason at the moment, and if push really came to shove, he didn't know if he was willing to grovel.

Not if it meant having to pretend her plonk was world-class. Okay, it wasn't precisely plonk, but it wasn't grand cru either.

And seriously—he wasn't that good at duplicity. Not over the long haul.

Also, come to think of it—reality check time—he wasn't in this for the long haul.

He softly sighed. Maybe this blowup was for the best. He should have been staying here at the restaurant anyway, working every day, not fucking his brains out like some hot-to-trot, randy teenager. Maybe fate had stepped in at the right time.

He had his best players here with him.

Everyone knew the drill when it came to getting an operation off the ground.

Maybe it was time he started acting like a man with a restaurant to open.

If they kicked ass—with luck—they could have opening night at the River Joint in four or five weeks.

Thirty-three

Who the hell did he think he was, Liv fumed, walking fast toward downtown. Robert fucking Parker? Screw Jake Chambers. She didn't need his insults. She'd gotten along just fine before she met the almighty, know-it-all, fancy-smancy restaurateur. She'd always hated wine snobs anyway. Most weren't willing to give their benediction to American regional wines unless they were already vetted by some celebrity connoisseur. They couldn't think outside the box. Even many of the now-famous California wines had struggled to be taken seriously in the early years.

So to hell with Jake Chambers.

Diss my wines, diss me; that was her motto.

Although it wasn't as though she was unrealistic about her wines. She understood all the unknowns: the incompatibilities with accepted norms, the rough provincial edges, the variables of weather. Still, she considered her wines promising; in some cases, fairly seamless examples of earthy, down-home, delicate to voluptuous wines. They were not and maybe never would be grand cru quality. But her vineyard was blessed with good terrain and serious slope, often prerequisites for distinctive wines, and in that instance, luck was definitely on her side.

At base though, luck aside, it was simply pure pleasure to produce her own wines.

And she wasn't going to allow *anyone* to get between her and her dream.

Squinting into the sun, Liv gauged the distance to Shelly's office. Another eight blocks or so. Good. It would give her time to cool down—or partially cool down—and disengage from the tumult in her brain. She kept thinking of clever insults and slurs she could have served up to Jake. Wasn't that always the way, though? You think of the good stuff when it's too late.

But as the politicians say: we don't want to talk about the past; we're interested in the future. In her case, her immediate future required a ride home. She'd ask Shelly. It wasn't as though the wiseguys were interested in her anyway. She didn't have anything they wanted, unless they were into Minnesota wines. And with luck, Janie might have hashed out her settlement deal with Leo by now and everyone could—la-dee-da—go their merry ways. Hopefully.

Of one thing she was certain, however.

She wasn't going back to Deer Lake.

Pulling her phone from her purse, she called Janie to clue her in. Their conversation was short. Liv didn't mention any

Peruvian beauties. She only mentioned Jake's disparaging re-marks about her wine. "So I'm not coming back to Deer Lake. I hope you understand."

"Of course, darling," Janie replied. "What a terrible thing to say when you've worked so hard on your vineyard. He's a jerk. Don't give him a second thought."

Then Janie had begun talking about something Roman had said that was so utterly sweet she was giddy with joy, and Liv's problem was sidelined.

Not that Liv had expected more, well-acquainted as she was with Janie's self-centered views on life. Actually, it made the con-versation easier. She hadn't been required to angst over anything or explain her feelings. That was the beauty of dealing with Janie. Everything was always about her.

Shelly was quick to shut her door behind Liv after she walked into her office. Waving her to a chair, Shelly said sympathetically, "You look angry. Need some help?"

"Yes and yes," Liv muttered, dropping into the chair in front of Shelly's desk.

"Seeing how you've been largely incommunicado of late, I'd venture it's man trouble."

"Definitely man trouble." Liv scowled. "He doesn't like my wines, the prick. Can you imagine the gall?"

"He said that to you?"

"No. He's not that stupid. I overheard him talking to someone."

"How did he respond when you confronted him. Knowing you, I assume you did."

"Damn right I did. He said he was sorry; it was a misunder-standing. If it was a misunderstanding, why did he have to say he was sorry?" Liv spread her arms wide. "I rest my case."

"I understand you're angry, but let me play devil's advocate for a second. Are you sure his not liking your wine is reason enough to toss away a darling like—I presume you're talking about the handsome Jake Chambers?"

Liv gave her friend a jaundiced look. "That's like me asking you if you'd put up with some guy who told you you weren't capable of making money in the stock market."

Shelly dipped her head. "Touché. So what can I do for you other than listen to your whining—and I mean that in the nicest way. You heard your share from me about Darren." Compared to Shelly's divorce battles, *Star Wars* intergalactic struggles would qualify as a day at the beach.

"If you could drive me home after work, I'd appreciate it. I rode into town with *him*," Liv said with disgust, "so I'm without transportation."

"Will do. I may not be able to leave very early though."

"I don't care. My place is supposedly in a combat zone any-way. Another day to let things cool off won't hurt."

Shelly's brows rose. "The phrase *combat zone* requires some explanation, if you please."

Liv rolled her eyes. "This is so far out, I'm not sure you're going to believe it, but here goes. Think of it as *Law and Order* meets the mean streets of New York." Liv went on to explain Janie's divorce issues that had necessitated Leo sending out wise-guys, which in turn caused their flight to Deer Lake.

"Wow. That's not business as usual, is it? Everyone's safe?"

"Yep. And Janie et al. are enjoying their stay at the lake."

"So your chef has a place on Deer Lake? That's a pretty nice lake."

"Don't say that like I should reconsider my feelings because he has some high-priced property. It's not his, anyway. It's his aunt's. I'm not looking for a man because he has money. Unlike you, I might add," Liv said with a grin. "And I say that in the most respectful way."

Shelly laughed. "So we're looking for different things in men."

Liv smiled. "Haven't we always? And it's not as though your choice of a husband was jim-dandy. Darren might have been a rich, brilliant lawyer, but he couldn't keep it in his pants."

"Maybe I'll have the next one vetted first; you know, have a detective check out his amusements."

"Whatever. Look, I'm not questioning your life goals. Finding the right man's a crapshoot however you look at it."

"You really liked him didn't you?"

"Yeah, I liked him. Too much."

"But you just fought over your wines—right? That was it?"

"Hey—that's enough. It's not as though I make wines between my duties on the Supreme Court and taking care of homeless cats. This is my life."

"I know, I know. I was just wondering if maybe there was some other reason you two had a falling out. Like, in my case, other women—lots of other women."

Liv grimaced.

"I knew it," Shelly rapped out. "I knew there had to be more."

Liv put up a restraining hand. "Don't get all excited. It wasn't about a woman per se, although, I admit, the reason I even heard him trash my wines was . . . . I suppose . . . Okay, who am I kidding?

I wouldn't have heard him criticize my wines if I hadn't gone downstairs because I was worried about this woman who had just come in from L.A. She's from Peru, absolutely stunning, and is his—I don't know—personal something or other. Everyone apparently has some speciality in the kitchen. Anyway, she's the kind of woman who can literally silence a room when she walks in—"

"As if *you* can't," Shelly interposed.

"Believe me, this woman radiates give-it-to-me hot sex. And Jake hasn't turned it down. I'd bet the farm on that."

"You *could* call him, you know."

"And say what? I forgive you for thinking I make shit wines? Come over and screw me?" Liv snorted. "I'm not that hard up."

"If you like him, you should at least *consider* discussing this misunderstanding."

"Jeez, Louise, since when did you turn therapist? You threw all of Darren's clothes out the window and set them on fire when you found out about his extracurricular activities. Then, while his designer duds lit up the neighborhood, you called a divorce lawyer."

"That was one great fire, wasn't it?" Shelly murmured, her smile one of satisfaction. "And with that memory in mind," she said a tad more briskly, back on track, "I understand you being pissed. Your wines are really good. And he's an ass. Maybe we should go out tonight and see what's out there? You know, get right back on that horse—"

"No way. Right now, the entire male gender is on my shit list," Liv muttered. "Give me a few days to decompress and reconsider my feelings on the opposite sex. In fact"—Liv glanced at the clock—"I think I'll do what I like best. I'll go window shopping at those two new wine shops on Seventh and Eighth and get in a better mood. A little wine tasting, a little wine talk, and life will be good again." Liv smiled and came to her feet. "What time should I be back?"

"I'll quit early. Say four."

"Why don't I buy you dinner on the way home? Considering the balmy weather, how about somewhere on a lake?"

"That place that makes those fabulous French martinis on White Bear Lake."

"You got it. See you at four."

Thirty-four

Roman received a call from Vinnie at noon. "Rolf's on the line. Wanna talk to him?"

"Give me a minute." Everyone was at the kitchen table eating the lunch Amy had made. "Janie and I have a phone call," Roman said with a glance for Amy and Chris. "It shouldn't take long, okay?"

Amy looked at her husband. "We'll watch Matt."

"Sure will," Chris said, giving Roman and Janie a thumbs-up. "Take your call." The next phase of dealing with Leo had been discussed before everyone pulled up stakes for Deer Lake.

Roman escorted Janie outside and well away from the house before getting back to Vinnie. "We're ready," he said. "Put him on." He handed the phone to Janie. She wanted the satisfaction of personally settling the score with Leo. Even more so since they'd been terrorized by Leo's hired guns.

"Hello, Leo," Janie said, cool and calm. "Do you have the custody papers and my money ready?"

"Are you some kind of nutcase?" Leo roared. *"You're gettin' nuthin!"* His voice racheted up higher. *"And I'll have Matt back just as soon as I serve you papers! Nobody fucks with me, bitch! Understand?"*

"Are you finished, Leo? Because I have something to say," Janie said, her voice smooth as silk. "FYI, I still have several copies of that flash drive. So, send the papers giving me sole custody of Matt to Roman's office no later than Tuesday. Then wire the fifty million to my personal account on Wednesday at two o'clock. Did you get all that? Would you like me to repeat it so you can write it down? Leo? Are you still there?"

"You mother-fucking cunt."

Ignoring her husband's murderous growl, Janie smiled. "You didn't really think you could outsmart me, did you, Leo?" she murmured. "I mean, consider what it takes to get from a trailer, as you mentioned in our last conversation, to my current position. If any fool could do that, Leo, don't you see—every trailer park in America would have to close. Now, then." Her voice shifted from soap opera diva to ice queen. "The papers on Tuesday, my money on Wednesday, or I'll start sending this flash drive to interested parties in the government. Are you still there, Leo?"

"You goddamn, son of a bitching, no-good—"

"Don't waste your breath. Just send the papers and the money ASAP or plan on spending your retirement years in jail. It's your choice. If I get what I want, you get all my copies of the flash drive."

"I'll see you go to hell for this!" Leo shrieked.

Janie held the phone away from her ear for a second, then said, "I'm hanging up now. If you have any questions, talk to Roman's office."

Flipping the phone shut, she handed it back to Roman.

"I'll give Vinnie a heads-up," Roman said, punching his speed dial. "You were awesome, baby." He grinned. "Remind me never to get on your bad side. Hey, Vinnie, listen closely. Here's the deal."

Thirty-five

While Janie's party was enjoying a summer day at the lake, Liv was wine-tasting downtown, and Jake was busy with construction, Leo was strategizing with his personal accountant.

The custody papers were in the works. He'd given orders to his attorneys shortly after talking to Janie.

But Leo didn't lose gracefully.

He planned on suing for custody just as soon as the flash drives were in his hands. If she said she'd give them all back, he was pretty sure she'd do it, because she wanted Matt and the money. Even if she held on to a copy for insurance, it wouldn't matter, since she was going to be in jail so fast her head was gonna swim. This wire transfer deal Dan had figured out was *his* insurance against Janie. Stupid bitch. As if she thought she could put one over on him.

In fact, Leo and Dan were discussing the means by which to accomplish two objectives in regard to the money. First, Leo didn't want Janie to actually get her hands on his fifty million. Second, she was going to be implicated in an illegal activity when the fifty million was wired to her account.

"Now, one of your black box accounts will source the money," the accountant explained once again. The discussion had been going over the same ground for some time, Leo's manic state doing a number on his concentration. "The account is registered in the name of a Panamanian company. It's perfectly clean."

"You're *positive* my name's nowhere on this account?" Leo queried. Again.

"Each account is just designated by number, Leo," Dan explained with the patience of a saint—or a man who would profit nicely from this deal. "The bank doesn't divulge names. Not even to foreign governments who lean on them. We're talking about offshore banking on some minuscule, unheard-of island in the Pacific. Offshore banking and anonymous corporations are all that sustain the economy on the island since bat guano ran out, if you can believe it. Look, if the Russian mafia likes it, it's good enough for me."

"So once more for the record. You're telling me this scam is going to work, and not even a whiff of my name will be in the goddamn air—Pacific or otherwise."

"That's what I've been saying for the past hour. Relax. This is a simple transaction." And lucrative; Dan Wygren's cut was a mil. "One more time, Leo. The money goes into Janie's account in New York. As soon as it hits the account, we jerk out all but one mil—with Herbie Austen's help." Leo had an inside man at the bank. With all his offshore accounts requiring regular laundering, it was a necessity. "Then we call the feds. No names, a throwaway phone." Dan shrugged. "They're used to anonymous calls. The feds are told to look for some Colombian drug money sent via Moscow that's been wired to Janie's account. Then it's up to her to deal with the blowback."

Leo nodded. "Okay—okay. We'll go with it. You're good, Dan."

"Thanks, Leo, but it's all pretty routine. These wire transfers go on millions of times a day. The sheer number of transfers only adds to their anonymity."

Leo leaned back in his chair, steepled his fingers under his chin, and smiled for the first time that day. "It should work."

"Guaranteed, Leo. With Herbie on the inside cleaning things up, it's a sure thing."

"The bitch actually thought I'd hand over fifty million to her," Leo muttered. "Cold day in hell."

"Two days from now, she'll find out for herself." Dan wasn't a people person; he didn't empathize. He lived with two cats on the Upper West Side. The cats didn't care if he didn't talk or feel what they were feeling and his neighbors in the co-op appreciated a quiet resident.

Leo lifted the lid on his humidor. "I like when things go smoothly like this," Leo said, taking out a Cuban cigar.

"It's the only way. When you're dealing with money, you want everything to be a certainty."

Leo smiled. "A certainty. Excellent."

Thirty-six

In the interest of safety, everyone stayed at Deer Lake save for Chris, who came back to work with Liv.

"Apparently the next stage in divorce number four for Leo Rolf is about to take place momentarily," Chris explained the morning he returned to the vineyard. "Janie's waiting to pick up signed custody papers at a FedEx in White Bear, then the following day, she's supposed to get her big chunk of dough."

"We hope. Leo's not the kind who gives away either his kid or his money. Although I realize he's in a bind this time, but still, I don't trust him."

"Between Roman and Janie's husband, I'd be inclined to put my money on Roman. I get the impression with him anything's possible."

"Fingers crossed," Liv said, holding up her hands.

"If Leo has more money than God, he can afford to pay off his exes."

"The problem is, he doesn't want to. He'd rather spend his money in court trying to fuck them over. But, look, we're not going to change Leo Rolf nor impact this nasty situation. So, I'm all for wishing Janie the best and getting back to my life. How selfish does that sound?"

"Not so much. Roman's there for Janie. She doesn't need us worrying about her."

"Might Amy be back in a few days then?"

"That's what it sounded like. Apparently all this divorce stuff is on some fast track—so Leo can get his flash drive back, I suppose. After that, Janie's talking about going to Europe."

"With Roman?"

"I couldn't tell. He doesn't give anything away; talk about a sphinx. And when Janie lapses into her wheedling sweet talk routine, he really shuts down. But, hey, with her fifty million, she can find lots of friends besides him." Chris jerked his head toward the fields. "A matchmaker I'm not. Let's go back to work. I've missed these killer grapes we're growing. Should we call back the crews or wait until we know Leo isn't going to send out any more goons?"

"I walked through the vineyards yesterday when I came home. We'll be good for another few days. I prefer being cautious."

Chris didn't ask about Jake. He'd been warned not to by his wife. But Liv didn't look as though she'd slept much.

An hour later, Janie walked into a FedEx office, gave her name, and walked out with an envelope. Ripping it open the second she got back into the car, she quickly scanned the pages of legalese.

"Here it is: 'Full and complete custody of Matthew Tabor Carter Nicholas Rolf to Janie Jewell Tabor Rolf,' she read. "You look," she added, a note of apprehension in her voice as she handed the document to Roman. "Tell me it's real."

"First, let's see if it's signed." He flipped through the pages and nodded. "Leo's signature." Then he scanned the appropriate passages and looked up. "You've got it, baby."

Janie slumped back in her seat and drew in a deep breath. Slowly exhaling, she turned to Roman and smiled. "We're halfway home. Now it's up to you, darling, to pull off the next stage."

"Two o'clock tomorrow we'll know for sure."

"Hey—hey." Janie sat up. "What's not to be sure of? You told me this was a slam dunk."

"Nothing's for sure until it's over, baby. That's all I meant. But I have a good feeling about this one. My man's in place. Leo's lawyer, I expect, will be where he's supposed to be. The second the first keystroke lights up my screen tomorrow, it's a go.

"The hand-off of the flash drives should take forty seconds or so. Longer, hopefully; Rudy has orders to stall. But Leo's stooge is going to want to check out the drive and get back to Leo ASAP. Once Leo knows he's in the clear, Rudy will give us a call. The wire transfer should begin shortly after, and once it does, we'll only have thirty, forty seconds tops to shift the transaction. You know what to do now?"

"When Rudy calls, I wait for him to say, 'Go.' If he does, you start looking for the codes you want."

"There, you see? It's gonna be simple. I'll do the rest."

What the rest entailed was using Roman's considerable expertise hacking into secure Web sites. Not to mention, he had the advantage of having all Leo's bank account numbers and passwords already coded into his program.

"I don't suppose we can celebrate yet," Janie said wistfully.

Roman squeezed her hand. "After two tomorrow, baby, we'll have a real celebration."

"Somewhere far away, I hope. I know you're not afraid of Leo, but I am. Fifty million is more than he gave all three of his former wives. Way, way more."

"Don't worry. I have a charter jet standing by. We'll fly anywhere you want." Roman also had plans to tell Leo that if he valued his life, he'd forget he ever knew Janie. He was pretty sure he could be convincing.

Janie grinned. "Lucky Matt and I have our fake passports."

"It's not such a bad idea." Roman had several, including a Canadian one like Janie and Matt.

"I'm not going to sleep a wink tonight," Janie grumbled. "I don't know how you can be so calm."

Roman had meditated on a Japanese mountain for six months once. He knew how to block out the world. An asset in his business—maybe even a necessity. "I'll stay awake tonight and watch over you and Matt. Will that help you sleep?"

"Maybe you could do something else for me to help me relax," Janie murmured, gazing at Roman from under her lashes.

Roman grinned. "You got it, babe."

Thirty-seven

Janie had been staring at the clock on the car dash so long, her eyes were hurting. "God, I'm seeing stars," she groaned.

"Five more minutes," Roman murmured, not looking up, his gaze trained on the screen of his laptop balanced on his knees. "It's almost over, baby. Almost over," he said under his breath, his fingers poised over the keys. "Get ready. Rudy should be calling soon. Four minutes, twenty seconds and counting."

Amy was watching Matt at the lake, and Janic and Roman were parked outside Coffee Talk using their Wi-Fi connection, waiting for their two o'clock Wednesday deadline.

"Here we go! He's early!" Roman rapped out. "Where the hell's Rudy?"

Just then the phone in Janie's hand rang, and she put it to her ear.

"Him?" Roman snapped.

"Yes." Her heart was beating like a drum. Rudy had said, "Go," and hung up.

"This is it, babe." Roman's voice was calm now, his fingers were flying over the keys, keeping time with the string of numbers dancing across his screen. "Come on, come on," he whispered, as though urging on the person keying in the bank routing numbers on the other side of his computer screen. "Come on, asshole, I'm in a hurry. There, there—*yes*! A few more digits now, dude, and it's hel-lo Switzerland," he muttered, keystroking like a fiend. "Now . . . now . . . almost finally . . . finally . . . yes, it's in!" he crowed, hitting the power button hard and snapping the lid shut on his laptop.

He didn't want anyone to have even an extra nanosecond to pick up their trail.

"Buckle up." His voice was all business. "We'll pick up Matt and your luggage and head for the airport," he added, tossing the laptop into the backseat.

"Is it over? Did it go *through*?" Janie clamored, dropping the phone. "Tell me this *instant*!"

"You're a very rich woman, baby," Roman said, pulling out onto Main Street. "You have fifty million in your Swiss bank account."

"I didn't even *have* a Swiss bank account before I met you."

"I'm a man of many talents," he said with his usual restraint. Then he turned and gave her a playful smile. "Happy?"

"Have you ever lived in a trailer?"

"Close—an apartment in a bad part of town."

"Then you'll understand when I say I'm over the moon in every possible way! I adore you, absolutely, positively, forever and ever. And I'm taking you on a long vacation to Europe right this very minute!"

"We'll see."

She punched him hard. "Don't you *dare* say that!"

"Okay, I can be away for a couple weeks anyway."

"Puur-fect." Janie had every confidence she could keep him interested longer than two weeks. "Two weeks is *just* perfect."

Thirty-eight

Two other people were monitoring the wire transfer. Dan Wygren and Leo's inside man at the bank. They both saw the routing number for the New York bank being keyed in and waited for the confirmation that the money had reached Janie's account.

And waited.

And waited.

And . . . waited.

Herbie Austen murmured, "Crap," real softly when he realized what had happened.

Dan Wygren sat openmouthed and ashen.

Herbie didn't really care one way or another. He didn't have a piece of this major blunder. He was just the pickup man.

Dan immediately went into survival mode. Not that he hadn't made previous arrangements for fleeing the country. Working for Leo was not for the faint of heart. Picking up the phone, he rang Leo. "We're good," he said cryptically, offering the prearranged signal for a successful transfer. "I'm heading downtown to check on Herbie." A few moments later, Dan opened the door of his wall safe and swept its contents into a duffel bag. Zipping the bag, he replaced the curio cabinet displaying his accounting diplomas that hid his safe and, walking past his assistant in the outer office, said, "I'll be gone for the afternoon."

An hour later Leo had begun pacing, the further confirmation he'd been expecting to receive from Dan not forthcoming. When he called his accountant's office, Dan's assistant could only tell him that Mr. Wygren was out for the afternoon.

A call to Dan's personal cell phone number informed him that the number was no longer in operation.

At that point Leo began to panic.

He called Herbie at the bank, when he knew never to call Herbie at the bank. But fifty million dollars made one break the rules.

Herbie said curtly, "I'm sorry, he's not here," and hung up. Not that he didn't understand why Leo had been so rash as to call. But that didn't mean *he* wanted to risk his future.

After Herbie's brusque dismissal, unable to breathe, Leo collapsed in a chair and struggled to draw air into his lungs. Christ almighty, was he dying? Was he having a heart attack? Gasping for air, he yelped for Ben.

"A shot—of—whiskey," he panted when Ben appeared.

"Should I call a doctor? You look"—Ben didn't want to say *like you're dying*—"a little pale."

"Whiskey," Leo choked out.

Maybe this was the big one, Ben thought, as he walked to Leo's wet bar. Maybe Leo Rolf was going to pack it in. Fortunately, he wasn't required to make life-or-death decisions—only take orders. Sliding aside the frosted glass door that concealed the bar, Ben reached for Leo's favorite single malt, poured half a glass, carried it back, and placed it in Leo's shaking hand.

"Fifty million!" Leo muttered, trying to get the glass to his mouth without spilling it all over. Fucking fifty million, and he didn't even know where it had gone.

Ben wasn't sure he wanted to know anything about fifty million dollars that had damned near iced Leo, but in the end, curiosity overcame him. "Pardon me?" he said, trying to look caring and concerned.

Leo's steely gaze locked on Ben. "Don't you have something to do?" he growled.

Ben swiftly exited the office, knowing Leo was on the mend. No one could deliver evil-eyed malevolence like Leo.

He was back in fighting form.

The banker on the island of Nauru had done a quick double take when the fifty million he was wiring seemed to flicker for a split second in midtransfer. But the visual flutter was gone before he could seriously question it. Some brief electrical malfunction, he decided. Or maybe a momentary glitch at the bank on the other end.

Little did he know that it was Roman's software program being triggered at the first indication of Leo's password. Once inside the transmission, Roman's programed worm monitored the keystrokes coming out of the bank in Nauru. Immediately it recognized Janie's bank routing number, and the worm simply substituted her previously coded-in Swiss bank account routing number for the New York bank number. The fifty million shifted direction. Seconds later, the money was in Switzerland, the transaction was executed, and the worm deleted itself.

Thirty-nine

Due to a certain urgency surrounding their departure, Janie didn't come to personally say good-bye to Liv, but she called from the plane.

That evening, when Liv finally came in from the fields, she listened to Janie's breathless, convoluted, and apologetic message. She smiled as Janie talked excitedly of their trip to Europe and all the sights they were planning to see, telling Liv that the Hockney was going to be picked up by one of Roman's employees, that she was having Brad serve Leo with divorce papers. And best of all, Roman was going to have a little *talk* with Leo in a few days. "To make sure that Leo will never give me any grief," she'd added with a giggle. "Ciao, darling," she'd said at the end in her best soap opera voice. "I'll keep in touch."

Good for her, Liv thought, hanging up the phone. It sounded as though Janie had actually trumped the king of mean.

Not that Roman hadn't contributed mightily.

But having Roman's help was really nice for Janie.

And for Matt. Roman was kindness itself to the boy.

With all the unreserved happiness exploding from Liv's message machine—Janie's triumphant coup, the fifty mil, Roman and Matt at her side—Liv was left feeling slightly melancholy. Okay, maybe more than slightly. More like whiny and grumbly and uncharitably envious.

Why didn't improbably good things like that happen to her?

Janie had fifty million dollars, a darling little boy, and Roman for a friend and lover. *She*, on the other hand, had two horses, three cats, and a grape crop that may or may not turn out well.

Why did her life suddenly seem to suffer in comparison?

Fortunately, she was not melancholy by nature, so it only took her a few minutes of deductive reasoning to talk herself out of being stupid. She was still living the life she'd always wanted, and she had plenty of personal and business interests to keep her both grounded and content. If Jake Chambers and Janie's marital whirlwind hadn't blown into her secluded, happy-as-a-clam universe, she wouldn't have given a moment's thought to fifty million dollars or anything else of Janie's.

There. It was just a matter of putting things into perspective.

She could feel herself mellowing out.

For one thing, she had her peace and quiet back—no small thing for someone who was a hermit at heart.

And she didn't have to answer to anyone; her schedule was her own.

She liked to have the house to herself once again. Really.

Bringing up a bottle of wine from her cellar, she went out on her porch and sat in her favorite lavender rocker. Pouring herself a glass of Frontenac red, she took a sip and surveyed her vineyards, bathed now in the magenta glow of sunset.

Was this nice or what?

Seriously, she wished Janie the best. If anyone would enjoy the lifestyle fifty million would buy, it was Janie Tabor from West Texas. She loved the jet-setting life; she'd married Leo for his money, after all. And now she had the financial security she'd always wanted.

Liv knew she would never be happy in the jet set. In fact, she'd deliberately left it behind. *So count your blessings.*

Lifting her glass to the setting sun, she did just that.

To old friends like Janie.

May the wind always be at her back.

And to her own life, newly becalmed and restored to normal.

Now, it was all well and good to rationally assess her feelings, and by and large, Liv was successful in locking away any confusing emotions during the daytime. In the bustle and activity of the vineyard, she successfully kept thoughts of Jake Chambers at bay. Her crews were back, and she and Chris were occupied with myriad tasks. They'd just purchased a new stainless steel vat that had to be squeezed into the limited space in their winery and incorporated into their production line. They were propagating new grapevines, monitoring new hybrids they'd developed, and adding new plantings to the fields. Deliveries had to be made, along with the ordering and invoicing that never went away. Life was hectic, and for that Liv was grateful.

The night hours were the problem.

She decided a week or so after her blowup with Jake that the reason she was still thinking about him was probably just a matter of physical withdrawal. She'd never spent so much time with any one man. Or, more pertinently, spent so much time having sex with any one man. As a remedy for what she perceived as these withdrawal symptoms, she'd seriously considered accepting one of the many invitations for dates that constantly came her way. Hadn't she always enjoyed her social life? But when she should have said yes to a date or hanging out, she didn't.

She'd make some excuse; generally she'd blame her heavy schedule. "Maybe later," she'd politely say, "when the grape harvest is in."

As if her work had ever stopped her from dating before.

But there was no point in going there. Opening that can of worms would require she admit to something she didn't want to—that she missed Jake. Or needed him. Or worse, was infatuated with him more than she wished. And since he hadn't called *once* since she'd walked out of his restaurant. *And* since he was probably *real* busy with his drop-dead good-looking Miss Peru assistant chef or whatever, it looked as though she was missing him a helluva lot more than he was missing her.

Damn.

It was like seriously bizarre. She didn't in the least feel like going on a date—having to be nice and chat up some guy she couldn't care less about. For sure, she wasn't in the mood for sex. This from a woman who had always viewed sex as part of a healthy lifestyle.

Correction. She was in the mood for sex all right, but the list of candidates was extremely short—and therein lay the rub. Jake wasn't looking to have sex with her; he was busy screwing his sexpot chef.

One day, Shelly called and said in a voice that one would use to upbraid an employee who was a perennial fuck-up, "I'm only going to say this once. I have been extremely patient with your moodiness and, quite frankly, full-blown denial the past three weeks. But if you don't come into town tonight, I'm going to drive up there, forcibly throw you into my car, and bring you back to the cities for a girls' night out."

"First, you can't throw me anywhere," Liv replied, clearly unafraid of a woman she'd known since grade school. "I outweigh you. And secondly, I really *do* have a tremendously busy schedule, so thanks, but no thanks."

"Like hell you have a busy schedule. You don't work at night. I know, 'cause I talk to you almost every night, and you're moping around, drinking wine and eating ice cream and pizza. We can throw one of your bottles of wine in the car, and I'll get you a pizza down here, if that's what it takes. You're never going to get over him if you don't even look at another man."

"I don't know what you're talking about. There's no one to get over."

Shelly snorted. "When was the last time you had sex? Let me answer that question for you. It was twenty-two days ago. That's a record for you."

"It is not."

"Whatever—the point is, you're in the dumps. Amy called me. Okay? So it's not just me who's noticed. We'll go out on the town tonight. Betsy said the new bartender at Quantum is so-o-o hot, he's worth fighting your way through the crowd to the bar. His name's Sonny, he's ripped, and has the longest lashes anyone's ever seen. So get dressed. I'm not taking no for an answer. Wear something sexy. I'll be there in an hour."

"It's Thursday. Let's at least wait until the weekend."

"Nope. You'll have some other excuse then. I'm coming up."

"Don't, don't—okay, okay. I'll drive down."

"If you're not here in one hour fifteen, I'm on my way north. No more excuses. I've heard them all the last three weeks. There's plenty of other fish in the sea, and I'm taking you fishin' tonight."

Liv laughed. "You're a pain, but you're probably right."

"*Probably?* It's either this or a therapist, and they cost more than they're worth. At least this way, you get to drink one of Sonny's famous libations in the bargain. Wear your Issey Miyake—that chartreuse number with the halter top. I'm hanging up. You're on the clock."

Forty

Jake hadn't been moping around, but he'd not been exactly his old self either. Unlike Liv, who'd been playing the hermit, Jake and his colleagues had been out every night. They'd eaten at every restaurant of note in the cities, they'd gone to all the hip bars and night spots. They'd even availed themselves of the various invitations to sleep over they'd received.

Or three of them had.

Jake had turned monkish.

Elena didn't believe it and was still in hot pursuit, even though he'd turned her down.

"I don't want to be rude," he'd said when she'd climbed into his bed the night of her arrival, "but maybe we should leave things where they were when I left L.A."

Shrugging faintly, she'd moved away. But only to the edge of his bed, where she'd surveyed him with a lazy smile. "Is it about that blonde who left in a huff?"

"Nah. It's a Zen thing."

"So this Zen thing requires celibacy?"

"Let's just say it does right now."

Her brows rose. "You *are* burned out."

"Something like that." He must be burned out. He'd never been selective about his fucking. It had always been anyone, anywhere, anytime.

"Would you mind terribly if I just slept here tonight?" She nodded at his crotch. "If I promise not to attack your spiritually converted cock?"

"Be my guest." He could be tactful; he wasn't completely off his nut. Other than not wanting to fuck Elena, who had always been eminently fuckable. But he wasn't joking about the Zen thing. He just wasn't in the mood.

Had he been less secure in himself, he might have been shaken by his sudden volte-face. But self-confidence had never been an issue, and right now he didn't feel like fucking anyone.

Oh really, a damnable voice inside his head had snidely intoned.

"I need a drink. How about you?" Swinging his feet over the side of the bed, he'd quickly risen. No way was he going to lie in bed and obsess over *her*.

In the following days, the frantic construction schedule aside, they all spent hours in the kitchen working on menu choices for the River Joint. They cooked old favorites and far-out fusion dishes, they experimented with drinks and desserts, baked a variety of artisan breads, constantly tasting and discarding, agreeing and disagreeing, choosing finally the bare-bones items that would be regulars on the menu. To those would be added seasonal dishes, creative whims, and frequently asked-for foods from customers.

Each day brought Jake's dream of a neighborhood joint closer to fruition.

Each day he tactfully evaded Elena's advances. He even understood her persistence. They'd known each other a long time.

Each day he put up with kidding about his new virtue from his male colleagues.

And each day he had to force himself not to make the call he wanted to make.

He actually drove all the way up to Liv's place twice in the wee hours of the morning and then just parked out on the road. Both times he couldn't quite bring himself to drive in. That reluctance was either testament to his self-control or lack thereof.

A therapist would have to figure out which.

Thursday night or not, the club was crowded. For most people, the evening started at one of the bars with couches, easy chairs, and quiet jazz, but later on, everyone was at one of the bars like Quantum, where the music rocked, the vibe was hot, and getting it on was the name of the game.

When Liv and Shelly entered Quantum and moved toward the roped-off section, one of the slowly rotating spotlights caught Liv in its tinseled blaze. Her beaded chartreuse silk dress shimmered under the brilliant luminescence, her pale hair glowed, her long, shapely legs under her short skirt lured every male eye as did her barely there halter top that left little to the imagination.

Maybe Jake inadvertently moved when he saw her, or maybe his banquette in the VIP section was directly in her line of vision.

Who saw whom first was uncertain.

But their eyes met through the flashing lights and raucous din.

Liv came to such a sudden stop Shelly walked into her.

Jake went rigid, his conversation left off midsentence.

Elena took note of his intent gaze.

Then the drummer's solo riff came to an abrupt end with an ear-shattering frenzy, and the room went silent. A second later, the crowd erupted in clamorous applause.

And Jake and Liv recovered.

Jake finished what he'd been saying, as though nothing had happened.

Liv quickly turned and detoured to the bar. She wouldn't be sitting in the VIP section tonight.

"Did you see him?" Shelly hissed loudly enough to be heard through the din.

"Yes, I did. It's no big deal."

"Is that the Peruvian beauty sitting next to him?"

"In the flesh." They'd reached the bar, where a crowd of men had made room for them. "Could we please talk about something else?" Liv said, lifting her hand to gain the bartender's attention.

Not that her gesture was necessary; Sonny himself appeared as though from nowhere.

"What can I do for you ladies?"

My Lord, Shelly was right, Liv thought. His long, dark lashes were amazing, his upper body visible above the bar, the glorious consequence of months and years in the gym. "I hear you make some special drinks," Liv said, liking his warm, open smile and direct gaze.

"For you ladies," Sonny said, his blue eyes focused on Liv, "we'll do something extra special. Tequila or vodka base?"

"Tequila, Patron Silver," Liv said. She almost said, *Straight up*, but didn't want to be uncivil when he was noted for his creativity.

"Vodka," Shelly said. "Something healthy for mix," she added with a grin. Shelly came from the same Nordic ethnic background as Liv, and while Liv may have been a cover model, Shelly was tall, blonde, and beautiful as well. A veritable swarm of men immediately surrounded them.

In contrast to Liv's glittering chartreuse dress, Shelly's club finery was a jewel-tone magenta organza that showed off her long legs and toned body. Shelly was not only consumed with work, she pumped iron with equal zeal.

Over her second drink, Shelly caught Liv's eye in the midst of flirting with their admirers and grinned.

Liv grinned back. She didn't have to say, *You're right*. Shelly knew it.

And really, for up to ten minutes at a time, Liv was able to forget that Jake was sitting across the room with his newest bed partner. Okay, honestly, maybe it was more like five minutes. And she wouldn't actually swear on a Bible about the accuracy of that five-minute thing.

As a result of her stubbornly irksome resentment, Liv drank a little more than usual trying to dismiss the image of Jake looking sexy and gorgeous—and even more so, the picture of Miss Peru looking totally smug.

She swore the bitch had smirked.

The only sensible recourse was for her to decide which of these really great men she'd prefer to have serve as surrogate for Jake Chambers tonight. Shelly was right, of course. She really *did* have to move on, get back in the game.

Maybe she'd just have to shut her eyes and point.

Or maybe Sonny was available?

If he was as good in bed as he was at concocting fabulous drinks, she could look forward to a potentially gratifying diversion.

Speaking of drinks, she'd had so many, she had to pee. Tapping Shelly on the shoulder, she nodded her head toward Quantum's famous powder room. "I'll be right back," she semishouted to be heard above the din.

Every new club in town was competing to have the most innovative, glamorous, or bizarre restroom. These fabrications ran the gamut from mirrored Art Deco splendor to rustic facsimiles of cabin outhouses. Quantum's fell somewhere in between. It was arty, colorful, semiretro, and had the added advantage of soft, comfy chairs for those who needed a five-minute nap. Right now, one of those chairs was luring her tush. She'd rest for a few moments, try to come to some decision in terms of getting back into the dating game, then return to the bar and do the deed.

Jake saw Liv walk toward the restrooms.

As did Elena. Quickly coming to her feet, she murmured, "Order me another drink."

Jake grabbed her hand. "Don't."

"What? I have to go to the bathroom." Shaking off his hand, she slid from behind the table and followed Liv.

Eduardo gave Jake a resigned look. "There's trouble on the move."

He could have stopped her, Jake thought. Then again, what for? "Maybe Elena will let it go."

Sam snorted. "Yeah, right. And world peace is right around the corner."

Jake shrugged. "It's not my problem. They're old enough to take care of themselves."

"You're throwing that blonde to the wolves," Gunther murmured in warning. "If Elena's not back in ten minutes, someone better go and stanch the bloodshed. Don't look at me like that. Remember Carla?"

"I thought that was an accident," Eduardo noted.

Gunther rubbed his bleached buzz cut, slouched lower in his chair, and looked at his companions with a jaundiced gaze. "Maybe it was, and maybe it wasn't."

"Elena doesn't have a knife this time," Jake pointed out. "Consider that a plus, but okay—maybe you're right." He glanced at his watch. "I'll give her ten minutes."

Forty-one

Quantum's powder room was extra large, so there weren't the usual long lines outside. But it was busy *inside*. Definitely too busy, Liv decided, when she walked out of a restroom stall and saw Elena stationed like a sentry near the door into the lounge. Damn, she'd been thinking longingly about resting in one of those comfy chairs. Not likely now.

Liv was hoping to brush by with just a quick nod.

No such luck; Elena grabbed her arm.

"We have to talk."

No we don't, Liv felt like saying. But she was pretty sure she wouldn't get her way with Elena's steely grip on her arm. "Look, I don't have anything going with Jake. I'm not in your way, if that's what you want to talk about."

"If that were true, I wouldn't be here now, would I? You *are* in my way."

"We're holding up traffic for sure," Liv said, even as a little voice inside her head was screaming, *What did she mean, "You're in my way?"*

As Elena pulled her toward the lounge, Liv debated making a scene. She could break away if she wished. Farm work built muscles, too. On the other hand, in a few moments she could just explain to this woman as simply as possible that she wasn't interested in Jake. A few succinct words would clear the air, Miss Peru's issues would be resolved, and they could get on their way. More or less politely.

Elena came to a stop in a quiet corner, and Liv pulled free. Figuring the sooner she made her case, the sooner this embarrassing situation would be over, she immediately spoke up. "Seriously, I have no interest in Jake. I'm not in your way—or anyone's way. I don't know how to make it any clearer." She turned to go.

Elena quickly stepped in front of her, the large red stones on her necklace and earrings sparkling like fireworks as she moved. "You must have done *something* to him," she said, bitterly. "He's into some Zen celibacy kick. And, that's not Jake."

Here's where it was *real* tempting to say something bitchy like, *Maybe you don't turn him on.* But a "Hallelujah Chorus" had just started up inside Liv's head, because Jake was about the last person in the world she would have pictured celibate. In fact, the idea was so preposterous, Liv blurted out, "You're kidding!"

Crap—she should have said something mature and noncommittal instead—like *Maybe you should find him a therapist.* And she might have, if the choir in her head had stopped singing so she could concentrate.

"I'm *not* kidding." Elena leaned in, the brilliant scarlet of her mouth set in a sullen pout. "And *you're* pissing me off, because it's your fault."

Liv didn't back up an inch, even with Elena's breath on her face. "Don't blame me," she muttered. "I haven't seen him or thought of him in weeks." So part of it was a lie. But she'd never get this woman out of her face if she said she was missing him— like twenty-four/seven.

"Then tell him it's over."

"I already did." Even her perfume was fabulous. Did she have any defects at all? Outside her bitchiness, of course, which was pretty much out there.

"I don't believe you." Elena's black brows came together in a scowl. "Obviously, you didn't make it clear enough."

"Believe me, I did. This *is not* my problem." How many ways could she say this? More importantly, how could she get the hell out of this worthless conversation? "Look," Liv said, speaking very slowly and carefully, "whatever you two have going has nothing to do with me. Nada. Zip. Diddly. Okay?"

"You fucked him up *some* way. You must have cast a spell over him," she hissed.

The look in Elena's dark eyes was a little alarming. But Liv calmed herself by noting that a crowd of women was within earshot. "Listen, I wouldn't know a spell if it wrapped itself in gold lamé and knocked on my door," Liv firmly noted. "Maybe Jake has a virus or something. Maybe he's overworked getting his restaurant open. Maybe some bad karma dropped in." Oops, that bitchiness slipped out. "I gotta go," she quickly added and walked away before she said something rude.

Liv was halfway to the outside door when she began to think she might have actually gotten through to the resentful, in-your-face Miss Peru. A couple more steps, and she was home free.

Just as she opened the door, a hand on her shoulder pulled her to a stop.

"Just a damned minute."

Why me? Liv thought. She started counting to ten, figuring she could hold it together and act like an adult if she really tried.

"Just a word of warning," Elena said, sulky and peremptory. "Stay away from Jake."

Liv didn't take orders well; she spun around. "Listen, bitch. It's not up to me who he screws. Okay?"

"Maybe it is," a deep, familiar voice asserted.

Liv turned back, and there was Jake leaning against the corridor wall—male centerfold material in jeans and a black T-shirt—looking even hotter and sexier than she remembered. Drawing in a sharp breath, she struggled to withstand her body's instant response to his sexually explicit gaze: the tiny flutter in her vagina, the warmth flushing her cheeks, the libidinous craving streaking through her senses.

With supreme effort, she managed to speak calmly, even as her heart was pumping wildly. "Don't involve me in this."

"There, you see?" Elena interposed, her smile assured. "You're wasting your time."

"Get the fuck out, Elena," Jake softly said.

The explosive cursing was in Spanish, but Liv got the general idea. "If you two will excuse me," she murmured, "I have friends waiting." She'd worked at forgetting Jake too long to even think about returning to square one. And bottom line, with her vagina pulsing at warp speed, escape was essential.

"About those friends of yours," Jake growled, pushing away from the wall.

Liv jerked her hand up to stop him. "Don't you dare," she said, heated and low, then turned and walked away as fast as spiky heels would allow.

"Can't you see she doesn't want you?" A high-pitched staccato rush of words, half-English, half-Spanish—and had she known, wholly in error.

"This doesn't concern you." Jake's voice was so cold, Elena took a step backward. "I want you on a plane to L.A. in the morning." Spinning away, he strode toward the music and bright lights, not entirely sure what he was going to do. Correction. He knew what he was going to do, but he wasn't certain he could accomplish it without the bouncers getting involved.

Catching up with Liv just short of the bar, he grabbed her hand and pulled her around. "I have something serious to say, and I'd rather say it outside."

"Jesus, Jake, stop. I'm not up to it." Mostly because she didn't want her too-susceptible emotions all shook up again. "Go get it on with Elena. She wants you, and she's hot. What are you waiting for?"

"Maybe she's not as hot as you." He could be rude, too.

"Is that a compliment? I can't tell." Snide, arch words.

"Give me a minute, and I'll make it real clear," he brusquely replied.

"*No, no, no, no!* I don't know how much plainer I can *be*!"

"Is this dude bothering you?"

A guy who looked like he could lift a Mack truck was in Jake's face.

"Fuck off," Jake snarled.

Liv glanced at the towering man, then at Jake, who was clearly out of his weight class, and her survival instincts kicked in. "Are you crazy?" she said, jerking on Jake's hand. Turning to her world wrestling knight errant, she said with a supercordial smile, "I'm really fine. We were just having a little disagreement."

Jake could have ignored Liv's conciliatory overture and said, *Bring it on*, to the guy on steroids. He could break a cement block with his hand and any number of other black belt maneuvers. But given this incredible opportunity, he said instead, "It was entirely my fault we were arguing. Sometimes I just can't keep it together." Turning back to Liv, he murmured, "I'm sorry, babe. What d'you say we kiss and make up?"

He knew better than to wait for an answer.

He also knew what that flush on her cheeks meant, and it had nothing to do with anger. Bending low, he kissed her—no hands and gently, gently, until she swayed forward the merest distance. As the warm softness of her breasts brushed his chest, he drew her into his arms, understanding what her tacit acquiescence implied.

She hadn't meant what she'd said.

She wanted what he wanted as badly as he.

Oblivious to their audience, they gave in to their long-deprived desires, to weeks of privation, to necessitous appetites, their kiss prolonged, protracted, and in due time sweetly conciliatory. When they finally came up for air, the crowd around them broke into applause and cries of "Get a room!" rang out.

"Can we leave now?" Jake murmured.

"Will your girlfriend let you?" She couldn't resist.

"Smart-ass. I might ask the same of you." He nodded toward the bar. "There's a helluva lot of guys over there."

"I was going to draw straws tonight."

"You wouldn't have made it to the door."

She smiled up at him. "I love it when you go all cave man on me."

He grinned. "I know what you love, babe. Believe me, I've been thinking about it nonstop for three weeks. Want me to drag you outta here?"

"Tempting, but under the circumstances"—she glanced around—"we should probably be discreet."

He laughed. "I didn't know you did discreet."

Her brows flickered. "I have my moments. Let me say good-bye to Shelly, and then we'll go."

"Your place or mine?"

"You're not alone—right?"

"I'll kick them out."

She just loved how he casually offered her the world. He didn't equivocate; he did as he pleased. Or in this case, how she pleased. "If you don't mind the drive, let's go to my place."

"I'm not the one who usually can't wait. You sure you can make it? We could check into a hotel."

"I like waking up in my own bed."

"Done deal, babe. You talk to Shelly, I'll give Eduardo a heads-up."

"She might put a hex on you."

"She would have already if she could. Don't sweat it. I can handle Elena."

Liv almost said, *I'll go over there with you*, but restrained herself. It was a rare totally adult moment apropos her out-of-control passions for Jake Chambers. She'd been pretty much in the grip of demon desire since she'd met him, and now, look, she was acting all grown-up. "See you in five," she said with a smile.

He gave her a quick, assessing look as though trying to gauge her bland expression. "You sure? Come with me if you want."

"I really don't want to." She liked that she meant it. No jealousy, no paranoia, no doubt he'd be back.

"Gotcha." Bending low, he dropped a light kiss on her cheek and walked away.

Forty-two

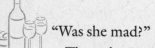 "Was she mad?"

The valet was bringing up the car. Jake looked at Liv blankly for a moment before the identity of *she* registered. "I didn't notice," he casually said. "Elena's going back to L.A. in the morning anyway. Eduardo's taking over for me for a while."

Sweet, sweet, sweet, Liv thought, trying not to openly gloat. "For a while, how nice," she said, politely, when she was really thinking she finally understood the true meaning of the phrases, *on top of the world, on cloud nine, happy as a lark,* et al.

He smiled at her bland reply. "You bet your ass, it's nice. The way I'm feeling right now, I may not let you out of bed for a month."

She blushed, his look so scorching it sent shock waves through her body. "Except for work; I have to work," she murmured, trying to keep some perspective on her life, trying to keep her voice from shaking. "I don't have time for a holiday right now unless you help me out."

"No problem. I'll help you do all kinds of things, babe," he said, husky and low.

"You two have yourselves a good time," the valet said with a wink, having overheard Jake's remark.

Jake grinned. "Thanks, man."

The men exchanged keys and money, Jake helped Liv into the car, and minutes later they were on the freeway north.

Jake was holding Liv's hand, their arms resting on the console between them. A song about love lost and found was quietly playing in the background, and if it was possible to measure happiness, the aggregate sum in the car would have been off the charts.

"I've never felt this good in my whole life," Liv murmured, smiling at Jake.

"Ditto here, babe," Jake said with a smile so sweet it could have been packaged by Hershey.

"One sure can't plan, can one? I mean, fate sometimes takes a hand, doesn't it?" She squeezed his hand. "Who knew you'd be at Quantum tonight?"

Since he'd been there almost every night lately, he did. But he understood what she meant. "We should probably send Shelly a thank-you gift."

Liv smiled. "She'll be happy enough saying *I told you so*. She'll rub it in forever."

"She won't get any complaints from me. Or from Eduardo either. He's been giving me worried looks for a long time."

"Wow," she softly exclaimed. "I absolutely adore being this happy!" One person apparently could turn on that switch.

"And we're staying that way, baby. From now on." But even as he spoke, he knew he'd have to take a chance on wrecking that blissful state. He had to apologize for his remarks about her wine. Or did he? Could he just let it go? Could he pretend it never happened?

At some fundamental level, he knew he couldn't. For the first time in his life, he wanted to be open and aboveboard with a woman—a shocking admission from a man who had preferred obtuseness in all his previous female relationships.

But Liv was different—better in every conceivable way—important to his damned peace of mind, not to mention his sex life and general happiness.

"I want to apologize for what I said about your wines," he said bluntly, going for broke. "It was rude of me and wrong and insulting. And I couldn't be more sorry."

"Thanks. I suppose I didn't have to get all bent out of shape either. Everyone has different tastes." She smiled. "And selfishly, I like my wines, so what other people think doesn't matter." She'd had plenty of time in the last three weeks to assess the comparative value in holding a grudge or getting what she wanted—in her case, orgasm-wise, contentment-wise, maybe even love-wise. And seriously, she knew wines pretty damned well, and hers weren't all that bad.

"Still, I could have been—"

"Less of a liar?" she said, her brows raised.

"Yeah, sorry. I didn't want to piss you off. That's my only excuse. It's not a good one, I know, but I'm more than willing to do penance. And as far as your wines go, teach me about them. I'd like to learn."

"Ummm . . . penance: what a nice idea," she said with a grin. "I'll have to start my list."

Jake laughed. "Christ, you're making it sound pretty damned good. I wish we'd had this talk sooner. I could have saved myself three weeks of feeling like shit."

"Why didn't you call?"

Her directness caught him off guard. "I suppose," he said, debating how best to answer, weighing tact and honesty against her possible response, "I was trying to tell myself that I could live without you. I figured I'd gut it out, my craving for you would go away, and everything would be as it was."

"Would you have *ever* called?"

He didn't answer for such a long time, she tried to pull her hand away. But he held on tightly, and when he spoke, it was clear he was trying to find the right words. "I've never before . . . felt the way I do about you. It's like waking up on another planet and trying to get your bearings in a whole new landscape. But I would have figured things out eventually. I sat at the end of your driveway a couple times at three in the morning, wanting you so badly I could taste it. So, sure, I would have called. For one thing"—he grinned—"I couldn't be celibate forever, and no other woman appealed to me. That's one powerful incentive."

"So this is about sex?"

He gave her a narrowed look. "You trying to start a fight?"

"So it's not just about sex."

"Is it for you?"

This time she didn't answer for a lengthy interval. "No," she finally said.

He half-smiled. "It's not so easy, is it?"

"No." She nibbled on her lip for a moment. "It's not just fun and games this time. It's not even close."

"Exactly. We're mapping uncharted territory—right?"

She finally smiled, a real smile, not one that you could have offered to just anyone. A warm, for-you-alone, loving smile. "We'll have to make sure we don't fall off the end of the earth. But despite all the unknowns, I'm happy I walked into Quantum tonight."

"Not as happy as me. I think my heart stopped for a second when I saw you. It sure as hell felt like it. I realized then that this—you and me—wasn't business as usual, no matter how much I might want it to be."

"I kept telling myself I could pick any of the guys Shelly and I were flirting with and have as much fun with him as I did with you. In fact—"

"Don't say another word. I'm getting pissed just thinking about it."

She gave him a considering look. "Are you jealous?"

"No shit."

She smiled, liking that they were in accord. "Me, too. Your old girlfriend was making me see green."

"She was never a girlfriend."

"She apparently didn't agree with you."

"Whatever."

The indifference in his voice was a gift—really like something from Cartier or Tiffany. But she wallowed in her smug happiness for only the amount of time it took her to begin to wonder whether he would be speaking of her in that same tone before long.

That was the huge problem with wanting someone too much, she decided. It screwed up your independence big time. "We have to keep this relationship—and I use the word loosely—in perspective," she said. "For instance, I don't want to get all rankled and bitter if you look at another woman."

"You're kidding, right?"

"I don't think so."

"You'd better be, 'cause if you look at another man I'm gonna get cranky. Forget this perspective, shit."

"Be reasonable, Jake. You won't even be here a few months from now."

"Who says?"

"I do. You have two restaurants on the West Coast and a house or an apartment there, I presume. You aren't seriously thinking about settling down in Minnesota are you?"

"Maybe I am."

"Hey—you don't have to say that."

"The thing is, I'm thinking about it. Or," he said, holding her gaze for a moment, "I was also thinking that you might not be too busy in the winter, and we could, like, split our time between here and the West Coast."

She smiled. "There's no need to sweet-talk me. I understand all the practicalities. Okay?"

"Just for the record, I'm not sweet talking you. And also for the record, I've had three weeks to deal with missing you, so I'm *mucho* serious about making some plans."

"Could we talk about it in the morning?" The last thing she wanted to do was fight right now, and any talk about leaving her vineyard was bound to be a contentious conversation.

"Good idea." First things first, his libido cautioned, highly in favor of conviviality at the moment. Plenty of time for complexities after a few orgasms. "Tell me what you've been doing since I saw you last."

"Whining and sulking and pretending I didn't miss you."

Jake laughed. "Funny, I was doing the same thing. Only difference was you were farming, and I was cooking."

"How long can you stay?"

"As long as you can stand to have me around."

"Yum . . . what a pleasant thought. Like you'll be around—"

"To give you whatever you want, whenever you want it."

"Oh my God," she whispered, every nerve in her body revving up on hearing his promise of sexual pleasure. "Do you think you could drive just a little faster? I mean, if you think it's safe enough this time of night."

At the tremor in her voice, he shot her a look, quickly debating her bed against his backseat. "We'll be there in twenty minutes." He checked his rearview mirror and the road ahead. "Are you gonna make it?"

"If I waited three weeks, I can wait another twenty minutes."

He floored it but noted her restlessness as she shifted in her seat. "Think about what you might want for breakfast," he suggested, trying to get her mind on other things. "In the morning, I'll bring you breakfast in bed."

"Jeez, you know . . . I *am* hungry."

He was pleased to hear a degree less impatience in her voice. "I'll make you something tonight then—afterward."

She turned to him and grinned. "You said that the first night I met you."

"That's right. We ate tapas."

"You say that like you didn't remember."

"No, no, I remember." *Now.* "I just don't ordinarily cook for women, that's all," he added. "You must bring out the Boy Scout in me."

"Lucky me."

"Lucky us. What do you think about Tarte Tatin for breakfast?" He figured if he kept talking food, they'd make it to her
bed. That small backseat was murder for a man his size. Not that
there hadn't been a time when he'd been perfectly willing to
make the adjustment.

But not now—if he didn't have to. "You eat eggs, right?"

Forty-three

She'd smelled the peaches cooking in her dream, so when the bed dipped and Jake said, "Breakfast for my baby," she didn't know if she was asleep or awake.

But his kiss was real; she could taste sugary peaches on his lips.

"Hmmm . . . I must be in heaven," she whispered, levering her eyes open.

"Damn close. Or after last night, I'd say it's a toss-up. What do you think about this love stuff? It's pretty damned great from where I'm sitting."

"Oh, yeah . . . definitely fine." She smiled.

"I don't even feel like running away. Could this mean we're all grown-up?"

"Or maybe we were just slow learners."

"Or maybe we were just waiting for the right person to come along."

"Such a rarity seems to have transpired," she said with a delectable smile. "Speaking of the right person, would that person happen to have some peachy stuff handy? I'm starved."

"At your service, babe. Tarte Tatin with a slight variation; you didn't have any apples. Also scrambled eggs with herbs, fried green tomatoes, espresso mocha or mimosas or both."

Reaching over, he removed a tray from the bedside table, said, "Move over," and when she did, deposited the tray in the center of the bed.

As he eased into a sprawl on the other side of the tray, Liv came up on one elbow and murmured, "Déjà vu."

"Get used to it. I'm not going away."

"Promises, promises," she purred.

"You can take that promise to the bank, baby. Peaches first?" he added, casually scooping up a spoonful of peach tart.

Her heart did a little flip-flop; he was promising a future even in the cold light of day. But before she had a chance to reply, the most scrumptious, buttery, sugary peach tart was deposited in her mouth, and she was suddenly debating the relative merits of fabulous sex versus fabulous cooking.

As if he could read minds, he said with a grin, "One thing at a time. I'm saving sex for dessert."

"I happened to be thinking about today's vineyard schedule," she said through her chewing.

"Liar."

His knowing smile inspired her to say somewhat huffily, "You don't know everything."

"I'm not saying I know *everything*. But when it comes to you and sex, I'm pretty well clued in. And don't get sulky, baby; the fact that I know when you want it just makes it easier to please you. Open up, here's some more."

How sweet was that? she thought, opening her mouth for another delicious spoonful of peach tart with whipped cream and crème anglais and then another and another. Really, it was impossible to be miffed at someone who only wanted to please you sexually and could cook as well.

"Janie sent a postcard," he noted, picking up a card from the tray and handing it to her when she'd had her fill of tart. "She sounds happy."

While Liv studied the picture, then read the card, Jake ate.

"Do you really think they're in Monaco?"

"God knows, with Roman's rerouting abilities. They could be next door. I didn't get that part about her shoes though." Janie had mentioned green beach sandals.

"Oh! I know where they are then! We both had sandals made for us in Florence years ago. They're in Florence!"

"There you go. We're gonna have to read her cards for clues. Like the Hardy Boys."

"Do you think it's serious with them?"

Jake shrugged. "Hard to tell. You know Janie; she's not exactly trustworthy over the long haul. Although Roman's seen it all; he can take care of himself."

"It would be nice though, wouldn't it?"

"Not as nice as it is for us to be in it for the long haul. And I mean that in the most romantic sense," he said, his gaze over the rim of his espresso cup, amused.

"I may prefer a smidgen more sentiment."

"I'll go online to one of those poetry sites. They write anything you want."

She snorted. "Now, there's the personal touch."

"If you want personal, babe, just let me know when you're done eating, and we'll get as personal as you want."

"Maybe I want poetry."

"You'll have to settle for food and sex. I don't do poetry."

"Okay," she said. Really, there was no contest.

He grinned. "No equivocation?"

"Do I look stupid?"

"No. You look sexy as hell, and I'd really be happy if you'd finish your breakfast pronto so we could get on with my schedule for the day."

"Schedule?"

He smiled. "It's a euphemism."

"Ah."

"Damn right." He nodded toward the tray. "You *could* finish later."

"Okay."

"You're easy."

"You make it easy to be easy. I'm not about to turn down a couple dozen orgasms."

"Wow. I've got my work cut out for me."

"There's no doubt in my mind you can do it."

His smile was wolfish. "You got that right."

And she was.